Dear Reader,

We're in Phoenix, Arizona. Young men are being brutalized. A judge is receiving death threats. And a woman and her young son are missing. Several baby boys have died, apparently of SIDS—but some people are beginning to wonder if that's really the cause and they point to a pediatrician as the prime suspect. A larger-than-life scenario? Sure.

But come a little closer. At close range, things can look very different.

You trust the folks you've known and associated with for twenty years. You trust your most valued employee, your right-hand man. They've always been there for you. Or have they?

At close range, religion isn't always spiritual. Cops aren't always good.

And at close range, the person in the bed next to you might not love you at all.

What people say isn't always the truth—when you get close enough.

And up close, what you see is only one perspective.

At close range, you're mostly alone. Nothing is clear. And fear awaits.

Come a little closer....

I love to hear from my readers. You can reach me at www.tarataylor.com or P.O. Box 13584, Mesa, AZ 85216. Let me know what you think—and how you feel— about this book.

Tara Taylor Quinn

TARA TAYLOR QUINN

AT CLOSE RANGE

MIRA®

ISBN-13: 978-0-7783-2552-9
ISBN-10:   0-7783-2552-0

AT CLOSE RANGE

www.MIRABooks.com

Printed in U.S.A.

To Mindy Barney, whose intelligence, dedication and heart bring promise to a world that needs them, help to children who might otherwise be lost and cohesion to a family that loves you very much.

1

Members of the Phoenix press filled her court-room. Tension filled her gut. Maricopa County Superior Court Judge Hannah Montgomery leaned forward.

"We are back on the record with case number CR2008-000351. Would those present please identify themselves?"

Hannah heard the attorneys state their names for the record. She knew both lawyers well. Had been listening to them drone on for six days now in this trial that seemed as though it would never end.

But she wasn't looking at them.

Her eyes locked on the dark-suited man who'd just slipped quietly into the back of the room. There wasn't anything particularly remarkable about him. He was twenty-nine years old. Average height. Average weight. His straight brown hair was thick and short. Wholesome. Businesslike.

Hannah couldn't seem to pull her focus away from him. Because she'd been dreading this moment for the entire nine months she'd been administering this hideous case? If so, the nondescript man would have been a disappointment.

Surely an icon, a godlike figure to his followers, should stand out more.

He met her gaze and nodded, his expression properly respectful. Taking a seat in the second row, arms at his sides, he glanced around with an air more curious—more childlike—than controlling.

Jaime, Hannah's bailiff, cleared her throat, catching Hannah's attention.

Robert Keith, attorney for the defense, had reintroduced the young man at his side, Kenny Hill. Mr. Hill, wearing a navy suit today, made eye contact with the jury.

Just as he did every time he was introduced.

The eighteen-year-old had more bravado than years and sense combined. As had his Ivory Nation compatriot who'd sat in that very seat twelve months earlier, in a trial almost as long as this one. That kid, another young "brother" in Arizona's most influential white supremacist organization, had cried in the end, though, when Hannah had sentenced him to twenty years for breaking and entering, kidnapping and weapons theft.

Her judgment had been overturned on appeal while Hannah was taking family leave, mourning for the adopted son she'd lost to Sudden Infant Death Syndrome. A mistrial had been declared and that young man was free.

Sweating beneath the black folds of her robe,

Hannah glanced at Keith. "You may call your next witness."

"The defense calls Bobby Donahue, Your Honor."

"Mr. Donahue." She forced herself to look at him again. And to look away. "Please step forward and be sworn in." She indicated Jaime, who'd risen from her seat to Hannah's left.

"Please raise your right hand and state your name." Jaime's voice didn't falter, and Hannah made a mental note to congratulate her youngest employee. Jaime had been nervous at the prospect of facing this dangerous leader.

"Bobby Donahue."

Bobby. Not Robert. Not Robert G. Just Bobby.

Bobby, who couldn't appear that morning, in spite of the subpoena, due to a Wednesday church service he'd officiated without absence for more than five years. Bobby, who'd offered to appear in her court at 1:30 that afternoon instead.

In the interests of justice and saving the state the money it would cost to enforce the original subpoena, Hannah had approved the request.

"Do you swear to tell the truth, the whole truth…"

Jaime's voice faded as Hannah watched the witness, getting too clear a glimpse of the man's eyes. Ghost. God. Infallible. Unstoppable. All words she'd heard applied to Bobby Donahue over the years.

"I do." Donahue regarded Jaime with apparent respect.

He's vindictive. That was the warning Hannah and her staff had been given by other court employees, the press, even the honorable William Horne, Hannah's social companion and fellow judge who'd officiated far more Ivory Nation trials than Hannah.

While he had yet to get caught at any offense, Bobby Donahue never allowed a wrong to go unpunished, a disloyalty to go unavenged.

Or so they said.

And Hannah, having fought her way off the streets and into college, didn't compromise the law for anyone.

Dr. Brian Hampton was not in the mood to cooperate. Especially with a reporter. And dammit, why wasn't Hannah answering her phone? She'd said she was staying in her chambers for lunch, preparing for the afternoon session of a trial that was taking far too much out of her.

That last was his assessment. Not hers.

Not that he'd told her so. As a friend he'd earned the right to speak frankly with the beautiful, blond, too-smart-for-her-own-good woman. But he'd also learned when it was best for him to keep his mouth shut.

Hannah Montgomery had mastered the art of independence.

Right now, he needed her to answer the private line that rang at her massive cherrywood desk.

When his call went to voice mail a second time, Brian shoved up the sleeve of his blue dress shirt with barely controlled impatience, glancing at his watch. And stopped. Hell.

Where had that hour and a half gone? Last he'd looked, it had been barely noon. And now it was quarter to two?

He'd only seen...

Brian paused. Counted.

Okay, he'd seen seven patients in the past hour. Seven patients under four. Which explained the missing hour.

The explanation didn't help him at all.

He'd had a message that morning from a polite *Sun News* reporter who wanted to talk to him "at his earliest convenience." As long as Brian's convenience happened sometime that day—otherwise he was going to print his story with a "no comment" from Dr. Hampton.

His story. That was all. No hint about the content. Or even the topic.

For Brian, a man who spent his days with people under the age of twelve and his nights largely alone, a meeting with the local rag was not a comfortable proposition.

And what could they have on him anyway? His biggest offense was an inability to keep track of time, arriving either very early or very late—no prejudice either way—to just about every appointment he'd ever had.

As much as he tried to come up with even a parking infraction—or an unpaid speeding ticket—there were none.

He hadn't had his stereo on in weeks, didn't have anyone around to yell at, hadn't thrown a party since graduating from med school. And the only woman he'd slept with in the past year was his steady girlfriend, Cynthia, a twenty-seven-year-old single mother, so an exposé of his wild lifestyle was out.

Of course it was possible, probable even, that they wanted him to corroborate a juicy story about someone or something else.

The only juice he could think of was the glass of cranberry he'd gulped that morning.

Still, the thought of the four o'clock appointment he'd scheduled unsettled him. Brian did enough public speaking on behalf of his newest passion—the fight against SIDS—and he'd been misquoted enough to be wary of talking to the publication known for making mountains out of molehills that didn't exist.

This was a time when a man called on the help of his friends.

Friend.

The woman who was well connected enough to know, firsthand, practically every *Sun News* reporter in the city.

Where was his judge when he needed her?

"Do you know this man?"

"I do." Bobby Donahue identified the defendant.

Robert Keith's next questions were rote, but necessary to establish a fair trial. And a fair judgment from a jury who'd been sending Hannah pleading glances since the first day of testimony. That was when prosecutors described the sodomy and three-hour beating death the nineteen-year-old victim had suffered, allegedly at the hands of kind-looking Kenny Hill, whose affluent parents were sitting on the bench directly behind him. Right where they'd been every time their son's case had been on the docket over the past many months.

The victim, Camargo Cortes, was an illegal immigrant and, had he lived, would have stood trial for statutory rape of the seventeen-year-old daughter of the newly elected Arizona senator, George Moss.

When pictures of Cortes's body had been shown, Hannah had had to excuse two jurors to the restroom to be sick. At the request of the defense, she'd later dismissed both of them.

She wasn't taking any unnecessary chances that might result in a motion for mistrial. With luck, no one would have to repeat the past six days, to see the things that those present in the courtroom had seen.

With luck, Kenny Hill would be put to death.

Brian worked through the half hour he'd allowed himself for lunch. Three-year-old Felicia Summers had had a sore throat on and off for more than a month. He wouldn't be overly concerned except that the child was underweight. And had already had her tonsils removed.

He didn't even want to think about leukemia. Or any other serious condition. Certainly didn't intend to alarm her parents at this stage. But he'd ordered blood work, just to be sure, and went down before his two-thirty appointment to get the results.

A day that had been diving rapidly now sank completely.

"Mr. Donahue, where did you and Mr. Hill meet?"

"At church."

"How long have you known each other?"

"Most of his life. His parents and I have attended the same church for more than ten years."

With a short nod, Donahue acknowledged the older couple sitting, hands clasped, on the front bench. The corners of Mrs. Hill's trembling lips turned slightly up, before she lowered her gaze. Her husband, a bit more successful at hiding intense emotions, nodded back.

Both of them spent most of their courtroom time staring at the back of their only son's head.

Character reference questions continued for the next forty-five minutes. Hannah attempted to show no reaction to the jurors who continued to look to her for guidance. If she believed this witness, they would, too.

And if she didn't…

This was a jury trial for a reason. It was not her job to decide this particular verdict. She was here to officiate the process. To allow or disallow testimony. To apply the law when attorneys, in the name of winning, veered away from it. Or challenged it.

She was here to ensure that the defendant's rights were upheld.

They were talking about possibly taking a man's life here. A young man. Who deserved to die if, indeed, he'd committed the horrendous acts that had ultimately left another young man dying an atrocious death.

"Where were you on the night of March 9th of this year?"

"That was a Sunday," Bobby Donahue said.

Robert Keith nodded, his shoulders squared in front of the witness box. "That's right."

The chief prosecutor, Julie Gilbert, narrowed her eyes.

"I was in church."

"Are you sure?"

"I am."

"Can you tell the court why you remember this so specifically?"

"Once a year we have a joint Sunday-evening meeting, combining the usual men's Sunday-night gathering with the women's Wednesday-morning assembly. It's always the second Sunday in March."

"What hours were you in church?"

"The service started at five and ran until almost midnight."

"With a meeting that long I'm assuming people come and go?"

"No. The doors are locked the entire time. Not to keep people in, but to prevent interruption. Our services, particularly that once-a-year meeting, are sacred to us. That's why I remember the date. These special gatherings are very emotional and interruption breaks the spirit."

"But the doors could be unlocked. Someone could become ill. People would need to access the facilities. Surely, if a person was careful, he could leave without disturbing you."

Donahue shook his head. "The sanctuary is self-contained. There are bathrooms at one end. And a small kitchen, too, with an attached nursery. I'm the only one with a key."

Horrified, Hannah kept her eyes on the file in front of her. She'd heard stories about the infamous white supremacist "church," but never in this much detail.

"So if someone comes late, say, maybe they have a flat tire, they miss this once-a-year, spiritually enriching meeting?"

"Of course not," Donahue said. "One of the brethren always volunteers to keep his phone on vibrate for just such emergencies. Members are notified of the number the week before."

"Then you'd interrupt the meeting to unlock the door?"

The witness remained straight-faced and serious. "Hymns are strategically placed throughout the meeting to allow for any interruptions."

"Do you remember whose cell phone was on vibrate that night?"

"Matthew Whitaker."

Hannah recognized the name from the defense's witness list. The man was slated to be called to the stand next.

"And did Mr. Whitaker notify you of any such calls?"

"Yes."

"Who called?"

"Kenny Hill." Of course.

"At what time?"

"Five forty-five."

The time of the attack, which had been announced during opening arguments, and ad nauseam since, had been established at between seven and ten on the evening of March 9th.

"Did he say why he was late?"

"There'd been an accident on the freeway."

Glancing at Julie Gilbert, assuming the prosecutor would be writing a note to verify that there was record of a crash on I-17 on the date and at the time indicated, Hannah was disheartened once again. The woman's pen was still.

There was no guarantee that the accident had been reported to the police, but even a mention of no record could significantly weaken Donahue's testimony.

Face impassive, Hannah continued to preside objectively.

"What time did you let Mr. Hill inside the sanctuary?"

"At five-fifty-four."

"At what time did you next unlock the door that night?"

"Just before midnight."

"And you're absolutely certain that no one, specifically Mr. Hill, left the sanctuary before then?"

"I'm positive."

Keith, expensively dressed from his silk tie to the tips of his shiny black wing tips, requested that an order of service be admitted as evidence.

It was recorded. And then the attorney approached his witness.

"Do you recognize this?"

"I do."

"Please tell the court what it is."

"The program for this year's combined service."

"And what is the date printed at the top?"

Bobby Donahue leaned forward to read it, as though he didn't already know the answer.

"March 9, 2008."

Slowly approaching the jury, Keith gave each of them a chance to read more than just the date on the program he held out for them to see. There followed a listing of well-known Christian songs that were slotted to be sung. Scriptures to be read.

A sermon to be heard.

"Tell me, Mr. Donahue, do you log the attendance at these church gatherings?"

"Yes, we do."

"And did you that day?"

"Of course."

Keith pulled out another exhibit. Had it admitted. When asked, Ms. Gilbert didn't object, but she looked as though she wished she could.

"Is this that log?" Keith held a black, leather-bound book open to a page halfway through.

"Yes."

"And what is the last name on the entry?"

Again Donahue leaned forward. "Kenny Hill."

"Were you present when Mr. Hill signed this register?"

"Yes."

"How can you be certain?"

"Because I offer it personally to every member to sign."

"Doesn't that take a long time?"

"Not really. I stand at the door and the brethren sign in before entering the sanctuary. I greet each and every member upon arrival. I make it a point to be accessible to everyone."

Or did he make it a point to keep everyone firmly under his domination?

Donahue lifted one shoulder slightly. And Hannah shivered. "In Kenny's case, I remember distinctly because he came late. He signed in alone. On a break."

Another piece of evidence was admitted. A small envelope. The kind many churches distributed to their members for offerings. This one was signed and dated by Kenny Hill. And then a cancelled check, dated the same day with the same signature was produced.

It had a Monday, March 10th bank stamp on it. All the evidence was circumstantial. When Julie crossed, she'd be able to point out the possibilities of forgery, money dropped off before or after the church service. But if she left the shadow of a doubt in the mind of even one juror, Hill would go free. That was the risk she took when she slapped a capital charge on the case. It was the only charge that required the jury to be convinced beyond the shadow of doubt.

Any other charge would have carried only reasonable doubt stipulations.

The prosecutor knew that. She'd been confident. Hannah wasn't as confident. And maybe Julie wasn't either, now, judging by the look on her face. Hill was going to walk. He'd brutally murdered a young man who'd done nothing more than make love with a girl who loved him back. Cortes had spent the last six hours of his life being tortured in ways a human being shouldn't even know about.

And Hill was going to walk free, out into the streets to act again.

"Mr. Donahue, did you see the defendant speaking with anyone that night?"

"Yes."

"Who?"

Donahue mentioned a couple of other names from the witness list Keith had submitted at the pretrial conference.

"I have no further questions, Your Honor."

Julie Gilbert did her job well—the car accident notwithstanding. But then maybe she'd remember to confim the accident without a written reminder. She could bring the information up later if it helped her case. Or maybe she'd already heard this part of the testimony during her own interview with the witness. Maybe she'd already confirmed it.

And maybe Hannah needed to quit worrying and stick to doing her job. She was no longer a prosecutor.

No longer charged with bringing the bad guys down, but rather, with protecting the rights of everyone who entered her courtroom—victims and defendants alike.

Bobby Donahue didn't leave the stand for another hour and a half. And not until after it was established that the church registry could have been forged. The check dropped off anytime that day. But Bobby Donahue was absolutely positive he wasn't mistaken about Hill's presence in church at the time of the murder. He assured the court that he could produce more than 200 other witnesses to the same.

Before the afternoon was over, Hannah could pretty much read her jury.

The defense had managed to establish a shadow of doubt. The state was going to lose.

Society was going to lose. And there wasn't a damn thing Hannah could do about it.

Kenny Hill gave her a barely discernible smile. Hannah felt it clear to the bone. And shuddered.

Was her name already on a retribution list?

2

Brian missed the *Sun News* interview. In fact, he forgot all about it until he saw Hannah's number flash on the screen of his cell phone at six o'clock that evening. As always when he was at work, the phone was on silent. Glancing at the blinking light on the corner of his desk, wishing he could answer the call and escape into friendships and gentler topics, he focused, instead, on the middle-aged couple across from him.

"As far as I can tell from this preliminary test, it's in the early stages," he told Felicia Summers's parents, sliding a box of tissues toward the petite, slightly graying woman sitting there clasping her husband's hand.

Lou Summers, a technician at a local helicopter manufacturer, didn't make the kind of money that would support the care his toddler was going to need, but he had insurance benefits that would cover it just fine—unlike many of the guardians of Brian's young patients.

"Is she going to die?" Lou asked.

It was the question he'd been dreading. A question no one was ever prepared for.

"Possibly," he said, his gaze direct as he met first Lou's and then Mary's worried scrutiny. "But maybe not," he added, speaking with a calm that hid the churning in his stomach. "We caught it early. If we can get her into remission, she has a good chance. So, next week I'm sending you to the best pediatric oncologist in the state, Jim Freeman. He'll take excellent care of Felicia. She's going to love him. And so will you…."

Contrary to his usual practice, Brian didn't return any calls on the drive home. The world could wait until morning. So could the thoughts trying to worm their way into his consciousness. Losing himself in the noise blaring from his car stereo, the old Eagles hit "Take It Easy," Brian sped along the freeway. The music reminded him of earlier days, easier times. He made it through the first song on the greatest hits CD without allowing his thoughts to take over. Soared through the next one, swerving his sleek, high-performance car in and out of traffic as though he was eighteen instead of thirty-eight. And then the speakers screamed, *He was a hardheaded man…*

Brian slowed down. He'd been there. Done that. *She was terminally pretty.*

Terminal. There was that word again.

Back in college, he'd figured life in the fast lane meant having the money to travel to exotic places, to eat out several times a week, frequenting all the finest restaurants. Having season tickets to Broadway Across America at Gammage Auditorium and the Phoenix Symphony and being recognized in all of Phoenix's and some of Vegas's and L.A.'s most elite clubs.

He'd figured the fast lane was about money. And, like his father before him, he'd intended to have a lot of it.

Tonight, the fast lane meant a way to get home more quickly. It meant knowing that a little girl might have to cram a whole life into five or six years.

It meant living every moment because it might be your last.

It meant drinking to escape the sounds of shrieking metal, of Cara's voice crying out. Of sirens. And his own wail of pain.

When "Lyin' Eyes" came on he thought of all the women he'd known in the ten years since Cara's death—experienced women like the one in the song escaping her rich old husband with hands as cold as ice to visit the cheatin' side of town and the lover with fiery eyes. He hadn't sought out married women, though he hadn't paid that much attention to marital status, either. He'd gone strictly for mutual pleasure, mutual escape. No strings attached.

He used to imagine it was Cara's body he was sinking into. Never once, since his beautiful wife had died in his arms at the side of the road, due to the recklessness of a teenage illegal immigrant, had he made love to a woman with only that woman on his mind. The woman, as soon as he undressed her, became nameless. A fact that didn't endear him to anyone—particularly himself.

And as his surround-sound system crooned about coming to his senses, Brian grabbed his cell phone and dialed. There might not be a lifetime to get on with it.

"Cynthia?" he asked as his call was answered on the first ring.

"Hey! What's up?" Cynthia's enthusiasm took away some of the chill he felt even in the hundred-degree September heat.

"Not much," he said, then added, "How about bringing the little guy over for a dip in the pool?"

"Sure! I'd love to. Joseph? It's Brian! You want to go swimming?"

The polite "yes, please" he heard in the background brought a smile to his face. There'd been a tinge of excitement in the four-year-old's tone. What a difference from the solemn, completely silent child Brian had first met at the free clinic almost a year before.

That first day, when he'd seen Cynthia there at the free clinic, chewing the nails on one hand while she rubbed her sick son's back with the other, Brian had just wanted to help ease the burden of worry. But it wasn't long before he'd had to pass Joseph's professional care on to one of his trusted associates because he was seeing Cynthia as much more than his patient's mother.

She'd been struggling financially since losing her

uninsured ex-husband in a car accident the previous year and even before he'd started dating her Brian had hired her to replace the bookkeeper who'd just quit. He suggested that she go into his office in the evenings so he could watch Joseph for her and save her the cost of a sitter.

She'd readily agreed and had been keeping his books balanced to the penny ever since. Cynthia was smart. Caring. And vulnerable. She was the first woman he'd dated more than twice since Cara's death.

"Cyn? Bring nightclothes, too." Brian's voice softened on that last request.

"You got it." The response was more eager than he deserved, and just what he needed.

It was time to move on.

Hannah was not having a good day. Though she'd parked in her reserved, covered spot, right next to another judges-only covered spot, her two-year-old gold Lexus GS—originally bought for child safety but now appreciated for the luxury it afforded after a stressful day on the bench—had a key scratch marring its perfect paint job. Running from the driver's-side mirror to the back bumper, it wasn't a little scratch. And it wasn't superficial. She could see down to the metal.

It happened. Everyone knew where the judges parked. And in spite of security, every once in a while one of their cars was egged. Or had its tires deflated. Two of her peers had found threatening notes during Hannah's years on the bench. A half-dozen or so times there'd been reports of cards left on windshields by zealous reporters. Once she'd heard about a letter taped to a door; it was from a relative of a young woman about to be sentenced. She should have expected her turn to come.

Just not today.

Not when she'd had Kenny Hill and Bobby Donahue in her courtroom. Of course, she'd also spent the morning with more than fifty family members and friends of other alleged lawbreakers as well, on pretrial motions, pleas and arraignments. Any number of them could have been pissed at her.

Or maybe some local high school gang had made keying a judge's car a requirement of new-member initiation. Hannah didn't automatically assume that Kenny Hill or any of his "church" brethren was behind the vandalism. But she couldn't assure herself that they weren't.

After fifteen minutes with security, waiting while pictures were taken and listening to the older sheriff's deputy drone on, Hannah felt a little better. She still had the ugly scratch that meant a day in the shop, a loaner that would probably smell and the loss of her insurance deductible, but apparently there'd been several other keyings in the area that were thought to be gang related. It was going to cost her. But she hadn't been specifically targeted.

A fitting ending to the day.

Too bad she'd already agreed to meet William for dinner. As fond as she was of her former law-school classmate and fellow judge, she'd rather go straight home, turn up the air-conditioning, run a hot bath in her Whirlpool tub, then have a good soak and a cry.

He knew her name. As he felt the pressure building, felt his climax coming, Brian kept his eyes open, focusing on the woman lying next to him, moving her hips in tandem with his. Eyes closed, her mouth slightly open as she moaned, Cynthia Applegate was a beautiful woman.

"Ah, Cynthia," he said, emptying himself into her. "Yes." He felt her answering tremors as she came, pulses of release that contracted around him, completing an intense moment.

She sighed. And smiled. Opening her eyes.

"I love you," she said. It wasn't the first time.

Pressure built again—less pleasurable this time.

"It's okay," she continued, lifting a finger to his lips as he tried to speak. "You don't have to say anything. I don't expect anything from you. I just wanted you to know."

He should speak anyway. She deserved more than the long kiss he gave her, so Brian caressed her in the way he knew she liked, bringing her to a second orgasm. It wasn't enough. But it was a start. More than he'd been able to give any other woman.

And during the aftermath, as he lay with her, there was none of the usual letdown, and not as much of the guilt. As always, an image of Cara's face after they'd made love appeared in his mind. Her features were hazy. Quickly replaced by another sight. His wife's face smeared with blood. His and her own.

And then the sounds replayed themselves. Her cries as she tried to free herself from the wreckage.

And the young man's words as he stood outside their smashed vehicle. "Won't do no good for them to deport me. I'll come back."

The words were in his native tongue. But Brian had spoken Spanish fluently since college.

"Let me out!" It took him a second to realize it wasn't his panicked, dying wife he was hearing.

Cynthia was already out of bed.

"Let me out!" Panic filled the childish voice. "Let me out!"

By that third call Brian was halfway down the hall to the spare bedroom where Joseph Applegate slept when he and his mother spent the night—something that had only happened on weekends. Occasionally.

"He's at it again." Cynthia's voice also held a bit of panic as Brian caught up to her. She stood back as Brian raced to the boy, grabbing him off the chair by the window where Joseph was pulling at the blinds and pounding on the glass.

"No!" he screamed, kicking and punching, as Brian wrapped his hands around the youngster's waist, removing him from immediate danger. "No!"

"You're all right now, Joseph." Brian spoke in quiet, reassuring tones, holding on to him until, spent, the boy fell limp in his arms. He handed Joseph to Cynthia.

"Shh, baby, it's okay." Cynthia's voice was calmer now that she was with her son, holding him. Now that he was safely away from the window. Clothed in the robe she'd pulled on as she'd run from Brian's room, she held Joseph to her, speaking softly but firmly.

Joseph snuggled his face into his mother's chest, breathed a ragged sigh and settled back to sleep.

"He's soaked," Cynthia whispered, rocking the boy as though he weighed nothing. Once his breathing was even, she quickly laid him on the bed, changing his soiled disposable undergarment with the ease of practice. She'd been handling the boy's sleep-walking episodes far longer than Brian had.

Brian gave the small head a professional caress. The toddler was cool to the touch. "He'll probably sleep fine now until morning."

"And as usual he won't remember anything, so we still won't have any idea what's causing this." She sounded tired, resigned, but worried. At Brian's recommendation she'd taken Joseph to Dr. Roberta Browning, one of Arizona's best pediatric psychiatrists; Brian had already run every medical test he could think of, and found nothing to explain Joseph's symptoms.

There was no sign of internal organ illness. No sign of physical or sexual abuse.

If the lack of answers frustrated Brian, it had to be excruciating for his mother.

"Something must have happened when he was with his father." He repeated what he'd told her before—the same thing Roberta had said. It wasn't much of an explanation.

It was all they had. "It's odd that he doesn't

mention the father he saw regularly," Roberta had told Brian. Though Joseph's parents had been divorced since he was a baby, Donald Applegate had had regular visitations until his death.

Brian had asked Cynthia about it. Other than the fact that her ex-husband had had another lover while married to her, she'd said nothing negative about her son's father. It was obvious, at least to Brian, that she still carried feelings for the man whose life had been cut short.

That was something they had in common. Unexpectedly losing someone they loved.

Brian took one last look at the window, wondering what would have happened if it had been open— what could happen in the future, if they didn't get things under control.

"Let's bring him in with us just in case," he said now, an arm around Cynthia's shoulders as he led her back down the hall.

The boy needed security. Whatever was causing the sleepwalking, whatever was causing the bedwetting, might never be known to them, but the symptoms could still be treated. The cure, Brian was certain, especially in one so young, was a stable, two-parent home environment. An environment like the Summerses had to offer Felicia.

An environment he could offer to Joseph and his mother.

"Have you seen the *Sun News?*" Hannah didn't bother with a hello when Brian finally answered his phone at four forty-five the next afternoon. She'd just come off the bench to be handed a copy of the weekly paper by her judicial assistant. Brian's picture took up half the front page. Hannah's name was in the second paragraph.

"Hannah? No, I've had back-to-back patients since I got in this morning. To be honest, I'm not even sure what time it is. What's up?"

Relieved that he hadn't been broadsided, that she could break the news to him gently, Hannah silently reread parts of the article. Her protective instincts reared all over again.

"They've gone too far this time," she said, pissed off and ready to take someone on. "It says here that you refused to comment."

"Only by default. I had some bad news to deliver to the parents of a three-year-old. The reporter completely slipped my mind."

Immediately taken back to her own experience as the parent of one of Brian's patients, remembering the strength he'd given her when she didn't have enough of her own, Hannah glanced away from the paper.

Kids were supposed to be free from worry, from stress and pain. Childhood was for naiveté and laughter. Playing. No responsibility.

Or so they said.

"Is the three-year-old going to be okay?"

"It doesn't look good."

Holding back the tears that would fall if she'd let them, tears that she'd grown adept at fighting over the past year, she looked again at the article while questions she couldn't ask raged through her mind.

How long had the little girl been sick? What were her symptoms? How old were the parents? Were they a close family? Were there other kids? Did they have the resources for treatment? Was there any hope?

"So how bad is the article?" Brian's question brought her out of a nightmare and into a mess.

"Bad," she told him, because that's how they were. Always honest. Always there for each other. Loving but never lovers. "Someone's done a lot of talking out of turn followed up by incompetent research."

"Okay." His tone told her to get on with it.

"They say that there've been an unusual number of SIDS deaths in the valley over the past year...."

"That's not true. Our educational seminars have had an impact already. The statistics are changing."

"Yeah, they mention that." Hannah's voice dropped. Since shortly after her son's death, she and Brian, a mother and a doctor, had been traveling around the state speaking to groups of expectant parents, offering two different perspectives but delivering the same message. There were ways to lessen the chances of SIDS. Easy ways. "Which is why it's a concern to this reporter that there's one doctor who's seen an upswing in sudden infant deaths among his patients."

"Me."

"Right."

His silence was difficult to take.

"He doesn't name his source but he claims that he's gone through public records to verify his facts."

"Which are?"

"You have three-hundred percent more cases of SIDS than any other doctor in the city."

Again, he said nothing.

"Is that true?"

"If every other doctor in the city averages one death a year, yes."

"You've had four."

"And you knew about all four of them."

Yeah. She had. She just hadn't realized...

"He says that all four of your patients were Hispanic babies." Hannah could hardly hear the words she was speaking for the undertones in this conversation. If Brian...

But that was impossible. She'd known him since college. Had loved him like a brother. He'd been a great friend. And a great husband to her best friend, Cara. More, he'd helped Hannah adopt Carlos, had been her son's doctor and watched over Carlos as diligently as if the baby was his own. His and Cara's.

Cara. He'd taken her death hard.

Hard enough to quietly, gradually, unhinge him as the article implied?

"You know better than anyone how much time I dedicate to SIDS awareness, education, research and fund-raising." Brian's voice, lacking any hint of his usual charm, fell flat.

"Yeah," she said, also remembering the months

after the accident. The bitterness that had poured out of Brian in his darkest moments, usually after imbibing more alcohol than he'd had during even the most raucous college parties. His wife, the only really close female friend Hannah had ever had, was killed by an illegal immigrant—a young man who'd crossed the Arizona/Mexico border with his parents as a child, without paperwork and, therefore, without the means to take drivers' training or get a license.

"The fund-raising is part of the problem."

"How so?"

"Without some SIDS deaths, there'd be no funding."

"Without SIDS, we wouldn't *need* the funding."

"The implication is that some of the funds we raise line your pockets." Hannah didn't believe it for a second. If for no other reason than because Brian didn't need the money. That wasn't the implication that bothered her.

"You know me better than that," he said when she didn't continue.

"I think he only put in that part to explain away the volunteer time you spend on behalf of SIDS victims. They can't write an ugly exposé and have you coming off looking good."

"So why write one at all?"

And here was the real problem.

"It talks about Cara and the accident."

Hannah could tell by his silence that he was hurting. And she hurt with him. Even while looking for reassurance that he was as sane as anyone. As incapable of killing another human being as she was.

"There's a picture of the car, a line about you screaming at the other driver while they tried to cut Cara free from the wreckage."

"Which I don't remember at all," he said softly.

Brian had hit his head in the accident. His memories were select. The doctors had warned that he might never remember everything.

"And they talk about the trial…."

"And the fact that the kid wasn't tested for drugs at the scene? That he got away with some misdemeanors and a few months in jail?" Even while she understood his anger, shared it, it scared her for a second.

Because she was stressed. Worn out. Not at her best.

"What's this got to do with SIDS?"

"They imply that you're trying to rid the state of immigrants because of Cara. They printed a picture of you, taken ten years ago, at that rally downtown…."

"For stricter enforcement of immigration laws, I remember. But this guy can't actually think that because I support immigration patrols, I'd resort to murdering innocent children. I'm a pediatrician, for God's sake!" Brian's incredulity struck a chord in Hannah. Her momentary doubts dwindled into nothing—the result of a long day, a long week. A trial that still hadn't ended.

"Crazy, huh?" she asked her dear friend. Cara's death had changed Brian forever. Changed them both. But he wasn't unstable. He wasn't disturbed enough to take the law into his own hands, as the article implied.

"I'd say someone has way too much spare time. Does it say how I supposedly bring about these deaths? Or how rich I'm getting with the supposed kickback I'm getting from the SIDS fund-raising?"

"Of course not."

"Did they mention Carlos?"

She blinked. And blinked again. She'd only had her sweet boy for eight short weeks, but what an impact he'd made on her heart. On her life. For eight weeks out of forty years she'd been what she'd always dreamed of being—a mother.

"No," she said when she could speak. She'd accepted that her grief was going to be a permanent part of her. And had learned to live with it. "None of the children were named."

"So the only mention of you was regarding the seminars?"

"Yes."

"I should sue them."

"All they did was state facts and then imply. You can't stop that."

"There aren't enough sick and twisted people in the world, doing ungodly things, that they have to drum up something like this?"

"Sick and twisted is too commonplace. The *Sun News* is always looking for the big angle. The story no one else has."

It was going to be okay. The story was just that. A story. She'd overreacted.

"I wouldn't hurt a child for anything. Not even the son of the man who killed my wife."

"I know that."

"I loved Carlos."

"I know."

"I'm sorry this came up now. You didn't need it. I should've remembered the damned call. I probably could've prevented the whole thing."

"Or not. You know how these people are. They had some interesting coincidental facts and that's all they need to sell papers."

"I don't understand why anyone reads that crap."

"Makes their lives seem better, I guess," Hannah said, not wanting to hang up. On days like this she longed to be back in college when she and Cara and a few others had all lived in the same block, sharing life's ups and downs. "You know, they see someone worse off than they are and think they have it good."

"I hate seeing you hurt."

"The feeling's mutual."

"I've had negative press before," he said, sounding as tired as she felt.

So had she. Most recently the previous week when a certain unnamed reporter thought she'd been too lenient in sentencing a girl convicted of vehicular manslaughter in a hit-and-run.

"If there's a drop-off in your patient load you can claim damages..."

"That would have to be a drop-off in my waiting list," he said with more weariness than pride. "The accusations are ludicrous and while some people will believe anything, I have to hope this article's going to generate more awareness of SIDS. It might actually help save a few lives."

Trust Brian to come up with a positive spin. A fix. He was the ultimate fixer. Bodies. Minds. Hearts.

He spent his entire life fixing—as a means of escaping the things that couldn't be fixed?

No matter how many lives he saved, he'd never be able to bring back the wife who'd died in a car he'd been driving.

"How's the trial going?" he asked and Hannah was glad he wasn't ready to hang up, either. It had been a couple of weeks since they'd talked and she'd missed him.

"Not great." Glancing at the file in front of her, the one that was thicker and far more bothersome than the rest of the stack her JA had left on her desk, she said, "Based on statements made by the defense, the state, who'd already rested, moved to admit testimony from the victim of a crime the defendant was convicted of as a juvenile."

"I thought they couldn't bring in prior convictions because it's prejudicial."

She smiled, loving the fact that Brian paid enough attention when she talked about her job to pick up on the basics.

"Generally that's correct." Opening the file, she stared at Kenny Hill's mug shot. And then let the folder drop shut. "But in this case, the victim of the previous crime can give information relevant to a claim the defense has made on this charge. Had the defense not made the claim, this door wouldn't have been opened."

"So what'd you do?"

"I took it under advisement." Which meant she wouldn't be getting any sleep tonight. "I told the attorneys I'd have a ruling for them by ten in the morning."

"Do you know what you're going to do?"

"I think so." Still, she couldn't act rashly. She needed to mull over all the angles. To research. To make sure. "I don't want this case losing on appeal."

"It's a capital case, right? If he's convicted isn't it pretty much a given that it'll be appealed?"

"Yep."

"I don't envy you."

Thinking about his young patient who didn't have much hope of a future, about the ones he lost and the grief he suffered for each of them, Hannah shook her head. "Some days, I don't envy you your career, either."

"I'd suggest dinner or a stiff drink, but I've got…to get home."

His hesitation, accompanied by a strange tone in his voice, piqued her interest. "Why's that?"

"Cynthia's moving in. Tonight."

What? "The young woman with the four-year-old?"

He'd seen her more than twice, but… "She's moving in as in *with* you, or as in renting a couple of rooms?"

"With me."

"In a relationship. With you."

"Yeah."

"I'm...I don't know what to say."

"I don't either, really. But it seems like the right thing to do."

"Is she still doing your bookkeeping?" Hannah asked.

"Yes."

"At night so you can watch her son?"

"Yes." Consciously fighting a twinge of jealousy that he had what she'd lost—a little boy to care for and love—Hannah refused to give in to the depression that had buried her for the long months after Carlos died.

She could look at other families now, other mothers with babies and toddlers, and not fall apart.

"I didn't know you were still seeing her."

"Yeah."

"And it's that serious?"

"Yep."

"Needless to say, I'm shocked, but if you're sure this is what you want, I'm happy for you." Brian's happiness was as important to her as her own. "It's about time you joined the ranks of the living."

"That's what I thought."

Though she was worried he might get hurt, Hannah wished him well. Told him to tell Cynthia hello. To give Joseph, whom she'd met only once at a SIDS fund-raiser, a hug. And then she hung up, staring at the wall of bookcases across from her.

Something about Brian's news didn't feel right; she just couldn't pinpoint what that would be.

She wasn't jealous, was she? She and Brian were close friends, nothing more.

So why wasn't she as happy for him as she should've been?

Sliding the pile of folders in front of her, Hannah grabbed a pen. She was tired; that was all. The week had already been too long and wasn't over yet. She'd feel better after she got some rest.

She'd feel better after Kenny Hill was convicted.

3

Lights welcomed Brian as he pulled through the entrance of the gated community and up to his home on Thursday night. The landscapers had been there earlier in the day and his half acre of colorful desert plants, squeezed into an entire street of similarly coiffed properties, provided a much-needed sanctuary from another long and trying day. The three-thousand-square-foot house was too much for him—he'd known that for a couple of years. But on nights like tonight, Brian couldn't bear the idea of giving it up. He'd had to admit a six-year-old with an extremely high fever to the hospital this afternoon. With any luck, he wouldn't be called out again that night.

The room-to-room stereo system was blaring the "Itsy Bitsy Spider" as he came through the garage door into the laundry room. A far cry from the peace and quiet he was used to. But it wasn't wholly unwelcome.

With a smile, Brian entered the adjoining kitchen.

Joseph, busy with crayons and paper at the table, didn't notice him. Neither did the beautiful brunette standing at the granite counter, reading a newspaper. A few unopened moving boxes lined one wall. Cynthia had told him she didn't have much as she'd rented her apartment furnished. If those boxes were the extent of her goods, he'd say her comment had been an understatement. How did one raise a child with only four moving boxes' worth of belongings? Where were the toys? The picture albums and booster seats?

"Hey, doesn't a guy get a hello after a hard day's work?" He raised his voice to be heard over the childish chorus.

Joseph's quickly indrawn breath, the speed with which the boy jumped down from the adult-size seat he'd been kneeling on, almost completely distracted Brian from the sight of Cynthia quickly folding and trashing the paper she'd been poring over so intently she'd missed his entrance.

"I made this for you, Brian," Joseph said, holding out a wrinkled and slightly ripped piece of drawing paper.

Squatting, Brian had to consciously restrain himself from pulling the boy into his embrace, a sign of affection that Joseph could not yet accept, as he studied the artwork. A wobbly circle dominated the page. Several colors rimmed what Brian assumed was a ball. Rays of sun came out of the edges of the ball and ran off the sides of the page. The center of the ball had been left blank.

"This is great, son," Brian said. "Is it mine to keep?"

Wordlessly, eyes wide as though fearing the reaction to his offering, Joseph nodded.

"Well, thank you. This is the nicest present I've had in a long time." His ear-to-ear grin wasn't the least bit forced. "I'm going to put this in my briefcase right now. I'll take it to work with me tomorrow and hang it on the bulletin board by my desk so I can think of you every day."

Joseph stared at him, leaving Brian to wonder what the child was thinking. Eventually the boy nodded and moved slowly back to his chair where he returned his focus to his latest creation.

Brian examined the picture he'd been given, certain there was a message for him if only he could decipher it. Looking to Cynthia for help, Brian was surprised to see her busy at the stove, her back to him.

Without a greeting.

And he remembered the paper. There'd been no mistaking the *Sun News* logo.

She'd read the article. Knew that someone thought he might be responsible for the deaths of four infants. Not sure whether to discuss the article with her or ignore it, Brian thought again of how quickly she'd disposed of the paper when she'd known he was there.

Sparing him?

Not wanting to insult him with doubts?

Maybe she needed some time to figure out what

she wanted to do about what she'd read. Some time to determine how much she trusted the man she'd just moved in with.

Maybe it was best to wait. To let her mention it when she was ready.

He had nothing to hide. Something that was perhaps, right now, better shown than told.

"Hi," he said, placing an arm around her waist as he leaned in for a kiss. Her lips, warm and full as always, clung to his, her tongue darting into his mouth with the ease of familiarity—and pleasure.

"Mmm. I can see I'm going to like getting back to the business of fully living," he murmured, his body stirring at the unmistakable darkening of her eyes.

The sound of Joseph's crayon dropping in his box, little fingers rummaging for a different color, reminded Brian that he was not alone with his beautiful housemate. His lover.

"More later," he whispered, leaning down to kiss her behind her ear. Cynthia tilted her head back and emitted a soft moan that would keep his blood boiling, he was sure, until bedtime.

The woman was very, very good for him. And to him.

As good as he wanted to be for her. And her troubled son.

"Did you see this?" He held out the drawing.

Tending to her rice, she nodded, her expression not quite steady. She was obviously no more immune to him than he was to her. "He has a fascination with circles," she said.

"It's not a circle, Mommy, it's the earth," Joseph said from the table.

So much for the boy tuning out their world.

Note to self, Brian thought, chuckling as he went upstairs to change. *Little pitchers have big ears. Save coming on to the mama until the child is in bed.*

Much later that night, Brian stared at the ceiling. He had a woman in his arms, her head on his chest. In his bedroom. At home. A woman whose scant collection of clothes hung in the closet next to his. Whose toothbrush was in the ensuite bathroom.

He didn't regret having her there. He'd made the right decision. Moments like these, moments of discomfort, when he didn't feel like himself, were to be expected. Living with a woman again was a huge change. There were bound to be adjustments.

"The hospital didn't phone." Cynthia's voice broke into his thoughts.

"I know," he said, holding her closer. "Which should be good news."

Her palm rested, unmoving, on his chest. "Did you hear from the parents of the little leukemia girl today?"

"No. I'm planning to do a follow-up call tomorrow. Sometimes when people hear bad news like this, especially about a small child, they go into denial. Their defense mechanisms don't allow them to believe it and they fail to get the proper treatment. In Felicia's case, immediate treatment is critical."

As she did many times, she asked about his caseload that day. And the next. She asked about a couple of kids, cases she knew from doing his accounts, who'd been in for tests, about a ten-year-old who'd been burned, a twelve-year-old future professional baseball player who'd broken his collarbone.

And, telling himself that he was lucky to have a woman who listened, one who cared enough to remember what he did with his days and wanted to share them with him, Brian answered her.

But shouldn't they be making love instead of talking about work? This was their first official night of living together and he was staring at the ceiling.

When silence fell, her lips planted gentle kisses around his nipple, but she didn't push him for more—almost as though her heart wasn't into love-making, either. He settled her more deeply into the crook of his arm, liking her weight against him.

And tried to drift off to sleep.

Eventually, when her breathing didn't deepen and he could feel her eyelashes blinking against his skin, he gave up.

"Why'd you hide the paper?" It wasn't what he'd meant to say. They needed to discuss the ludicrous-ness of the reporter's comments; he needed to assure her of his innocence. She'd just moved her son into his home. She deserved at least that. But he'd wanted her to bring up the article.

She needed to know that if she had concerns, she could come to him. She *had* to come to him. Or they would never work. Never be a real couple.

"I… What paper?"

Disappointed, Brian took a deep breath. Tried to put himself in her shoes. She was a young woman with few resources and a troubled four-year-old to raise. She'd just taken one of the biggest risks of her life, moving the two of them into his home. And he'd sort of, been accused of murder.

She deserved his patience, if nothing else.

"I saw you reading the article in the *Sun News* when I came in," he told her, resolving to take care of her, instead of holding her up to unspoken expectations.

"Oh." That was all. No questions. No accusations. No rambling fears. As if she was unaware, half dead, although he knew her to be a multidimensional, occasionally intense human being.

"It's okay, Cyn," he said softly. "You don't have to take me at face value. You can have doubts. You can ask questions."

He wasn't sure she was going to respond even then, she lay so still against him. But then, lifting her head to rest her chin on his chest, she stared up at him in the dim light coming in from the window. "I want to take you at face value." Her voice was sweet, tender—and also laced with conviction. "I just can't seem to do it. Every single time I've trusted someone, I've been hurt. And my son has been hurt. I can't let that happen again."

He wanted to interrupt, to reassure her. But knew he had to hear her out. No matter where she was going with this.

If she left before they'd really begun, he'd survive. He didn't want her to go, but he'd survive.

And he'd watch out for her, too. He'd show her, one way or another, that she wasn't alone anymore. He'd committed himself to this small family. For good or bad.

"I'm all he's got," she said with that hint of intensity that always drew him to her. "He has to come first."

"Of course he does."

Shaking her head, Cynthia sat up, adjusting her nightgown and hugging her knees to her chest. "It's more than that," she said now, her eyes wide as she met his gaze. "He doesn't just come first, he comes *only.* I will do anything for Joseph. Sacrifice anything for him."

"As would most mothers for their children," Brian said. He heard the doctor tone enter his voice, but couldn't seem to stop it. "Where do you think the saying 'mother bear with her cubs' came from? It's true. Mothers are infused with a need to give up their own lives, to kill if necessary—in a symbolic sense—to protect their young. You don't have to apologize for that."

"I just…" He could see in her eyes that she was trying to tell him something vital. But he couldn't quite figure it out.

"I love you, Brian."

There were those words again. And the timing was critical.

He couldn't keep running and expect her to stay.

"I love you, too." There. Offering the proclamation hadn't been as hard as he'd expected. There were many ways to love a person. Many ways to love a woman.

"I mean it. I really, really love you."

Brian stroked her hair, caressed her cheek with the back of his hand. "Okay."

He was a lucky man.

"I realize now that I've never really loved a man before."

God, she was lovely. He was going to do everything in his power to be worthy of her. To give her everything he had left to give.

Lord knew he wanted to. Brian just wasn't sure it would be enough.

Because he didn't have more words, Brian kissed her. Once. Softly. And then again. His hand at the back of her neck, he guided her lips against his, opening to her, coaxing her to open to him.

And, as always, she was instantly responsive, as though she knew what he needed before he did. When it came to sex, this woman was a natural. Or maybe it was the loving that she was getting right.

"I…" Cynthia broke the kiss, her lips parted as she again met his gaze. "Please, no matter what choices I make in Joseph's best interests, don't ever, ever forget that I honestly and truly love you."

That article again. She was struggling to trust him. Considering her past, her marriage to a man who swore to protect her and their son forever and then was unfaithful, he could certainly understand.

"I want you to remember something, too," he said, his forehead resting against hers.

"What?"

"No matter what choices you have to make, I'll

be there for you. I won't desert you. Whether you live here or elsewhere, whether you stay with me or not, you have a friend for life. You got that?"

For the first time in the many months he'd known her, Cynthia's eyes filled with tears.

"The insinuations in that article are lies, babe." Some words wouldn't come. These would. "The reporter took a few facts and put a heinous spin on them. I did fight for stronger border laws after Cara's death. The kid who hit us was an illegal immigrant, had come across the border with his parents when he was a toddler. But I have never received a dime from any of the volunteer work I do, not from SIDS seminars and certainly not from the free clinic. Nor would I ever knowingly harm a child—whether that child was in my care or not."

"Do you hate Mexicans?" Her voice was uneven, and there were still tears in her eyes as she clutched at his hand.

"Of course not. I didn't hate illegals, as people, even then. I hated the system that allowed them to live among us without following our laws." He talked about statistics, real ones, about health-care rights. About school-system dollars spent teaching kids who couldn't speak English. About below minimum-wage work being offered that took jobs away from those who weren't allowed to work for less. And about the Emergency Medial Treatment and Active Labor Act that requires all U.S. emergency treatment facilities to treat anyone needing care, including illegals. Which meant that in highly illegally populated areas, centers closed down because they had to treat too many who didn't pay for services, leaving Americans without care. Or those where American citizens waited in long lines for care—behind illegals. And about safeguards—such as the driver's test—that were denied to illegal's because, as far as the government was concerned, these people didn't exist. And he talked about the money spent every year by the state to prosecute and defend illegal immigrants.

And then, as she lay there silently—his lover who usually had lots to say about politics—Brian changed the subject, telling her about the SIDS program he and Hannah had developed.

If Cynthia needed time to digest the rest, she would have it. An accusation of murder wasn't a simple thing.

"They say that you shouldn't lay a baby on its stomach," Cynthia said. "They say that increases the risk of SIDS. At least, that's what they told me when I had Joseph."

"That's right."

Cynthia asked a couple more questions. He answered them. And then, when she appeared to be done for the night, repeated, "All of that aside, I want you to know I would never do anything to harm a child. Any child. For any reason." It was crucial that she understand that, if nothing else.

Her scrutiny wasn't light. Or easy. But he endured those moments without difficulty. And when she finally nodded, he believed she was satisfied.

4

Susan Campbell stuck her head in Hannah's door after lunch on Friday. "You ready, Judge?"

Sitting at her desk, wearing the black silk robe of her calling, Hannah nodded and accepted the compassionate smile on the face of her twenty-six-year-old judicial assistant.

She wasn't ready. How could you ever be ready to do something that was going to anger a large powerful group of thugs—a group known for getting away with unconscionable acts of violence?

Moving with purpose, she left her chambers and looked both ways as she walked into the secure hallway outside her door and stepped toward the back entrance of the courtroom.

Her job was to administer justice. Kenny Hill might be convicted by a jury of vetted American citizens. If that happened, she'd sentence him to prison—and society would be safer.

But he had brothers. Ivory Nation brothers.

"All rise."

Hannah heard Jaime's spiel about the Honorable Hannah Montgomery, but barely waited for the bailiff to finish before she took her seat. Her deputy was there—standing at attention with his eyes firmly on the defendant who was seated at the table directly in front of her bench.

Other deputies were there, too, called by the sheriff's office to oversee this trial.

Only members of the press and the jury were absent—the jury sequestered in another room. They couldn't be privy to this particular motion lest their judgment be impaired. The press would line the back of the room again as soon as she gave the okay to let them in from the hall.

"Be seated," Hannah said clearly. Loudly.

She could do her job. She had no doubt about that. She would do it well.

And she would deal with the ensuing exhaustion, the emotional panic that sometimes resulted from days like today.

"We are back on the record with case number CR2008-000351. The *State v. Kenneth Hill*. Before we bring in the jury, we have a matter before the court concerning new evidence received by the state."

The benches in the back of her courtroom were filled to capacity. Whether the victim had as many supporters as the defendant did, Hannah couldn't be sure, but she didn't think so. She suspected the Ivory Nation ranks had been notified overnight. Was she supposed to consider herself warned? Intimidated?

The defendant's parents, sitting stiffly in the front

row, didn't seem to know any of the mostly young men around them.

Bobby Donahue, the group's leader, was not present.

Hannah noted every detail of her surroundings as she held the page she'd written the night before.

"The Court has reviewed the motion to suppress testimony filed by Robert Keith on behalf of the defendant, Kenny Hill, the argument presented by the prosecution, as well as case law pertinent to the matter before us…"

She continued to read, citing case law brought before her during the motion, reminding the defense that it wasn't within the jurisdiction of trial court to find existing laws unconstitutional. She discussed the Arizona statute about allowing prejudicial evidence, specifically pertaining to cases where evidence pertaining to a previous case is also pertinent to the current one.

In other words, the victim of Kenny Hill's earlier assault would not be appearing as a victim, but as a witness to the possibility that a certain weapon used in that crime, had caused injuries in this one.

And then, sticking to the plan she'd devised the night before—not to look up from her notes, even once, not to give them anything, any hint that she was human or afraid—she delivered her findings.

"The court has prepared the following rulings," she said, gaining confidence in herself as her voice remained steady. "It is ordered that the motion to suppress be denied."

Funny how a room could be filled with negative energy, with savage anger, that emitted not a sound.

The only thing Hannah could hear was the rapid tapping of her court recorder, fifty-year-old Tammy Rhodes. Jaime, the other human being within Hannah's peripheral vision, was staring down at her desk.

"The state is warned that any mention of a previous conviction for this defendant will result in a mistrial."

That was it. She'd reached the end of her ruling. Of her notes. There was nothing else to do but look up.

The trial that had already run two days over its time allotment was continued until Monday—the earliest the state's newly approved witness could be brought in. Which meant that the weight hanging over Hannah would be there all weekend.

She and William had tickets to a concert at Symphony Hall the next night. His son, a student at a private school for the arts, was a guest violinist in one piece and, as William rarely saw the boy, he'd been thrilled to get the invitation. Hannah hoped, as she drove home on Friday, that she'd be able to stay awake. Put her in a comfortable seat, in a dark room with soft music and—

What was that? She saw a pile in the road by her driveway. Driving slowly, Hannah tried to identify the curious shape. Her heart was pounding, but she told herself there was no reason for that.

Some trash had fallen from a dispenser during that morning's pickup, that was all.

But there was something too familiar about the tan and beige with that streak of black. What had she put in her trash that week? Some kind of packaging maybe.

What had she purchased? Opened? Had she even bought anything new?

As she drew closer, her pulse quickened yet again. The blob didn't look like packaging. It looked… furry. Like an animal.

The exact size of Callie Bodacious.

Hannah's beloved eleven-year-old cat. The direct offspring of a gift from Jason, the man she'd married—the man who, at seventeen, had been diagnosed with leukemia and, at twenty-three, had died in the bed she'd shared with him.

"No!" Throwing the car in Park in the middle of her quiet street, Hannah got out, the door of the Lexus wide-open behind her as she sped to the shape in the road.

Callie wasn't a purebred. Wasn't worth much in a monetary sense. She was basically an alley cat. One who wasn't particularly fond of people—other than Hannah.

And she was all the family Hannah had left.

Dropping down on her knees, reaching out to the animal, Hannah blinked back tears so she could see clearly. The black between the eyes told her it was definitely Callie.

And she was still breathing. Sobbing now, Hannah

glanced up, around, looking for help. And then grabbed the cell phone out of the case hooked to her waistband.

Addled, frustrated that there was no ambulance she could call for cats, no feline 911, scared out of her wits, she hit the first number programmed into her speed dial.

He answered. Thank God.

"Brian? Where are you?"

"On my way home. What's wrong?"

"It's Callie! She's hurt. Oh, God, Brian, what am I going to do? She needs help and I'm afraid to move her. Her head's at a bad angle."

"What happened?"

"I don't know," Hannah wailed, growing more panicked with every second that passed. "She's in the road so she must have been hit by a car, but I don't see a lot of blood."

Brian asked her to check a couple of things, including lifting the cat's eyelids. And then he told her to sit tight and wait for him.

Brian wished he could say he'd never seen Hannah Montgomery in such a state. Wished it so hard the tension made his head throb. Watching his good friend grieve was not a new thing to him.

And not a distant memory either. It had been less than a year since he'd sat on this very same sofa, in this very same house, sick at heart, holding this vibrant, beautiful, intelligent woman while she sobbed uncontrollably.

Less than a year since another little body was carried out of this home.

"I...I...she...I...she must've slipped out this morning. And..."

She couldn't finish as another bout of sobs overcame her, the sound harsh, discordant in the peaceful room.

"I was just...so...pre...pre...preoccupied...."

He held her, resting his chin lightly on her head. He wanted to let her know that he was there. She wasn't alone.

"...the trial..."

His mind froze at her words, at the reminder of the dangerous case she was handling, his attention completely, singly focused now as a suspicion occured to him. And he remembered something else.

"You said you were sure you saw her on her cat tree when you left."

"I...must've...been mistaken...."

Or not.

Looking around the room, all senses on alert, Brian wondered if Hannah's windows and doors were secure. He wondered if they should be calling the police.

Or if he was overreacting.

Surely, anyone who meant to do Hannah harm would have done so while she was driving home. Running her off the road. Making it look like an accident.

Instead, they'd done...this. But they wouldn't be so bold as to attack a judge in her own home. That would make them too easy to find. Detectives would know who to question and fingerprint and…

"We need to call the police."

A sheriff's deputy came to the house. Callie's body was being taken in as evidence.

"I'm sure you're right and there is nothing criminal here, Judge," the thirtysomething, well-weaponed man said, his beige uniform not helping him blend in with the desert landscaping at all. It would be hard to overlook the big, burly man.

Completely calm, completely professional, Hannah nodded.

"There's no sign of forced entry, no unlocked windows or doors, no threatening note. But we can't be too sure. We have to follow up on every call."

"The Ivory Nation generally leaves warnings of some kind," Hannah said. She'd been dry-eyed since Brian had called the police. Withdrawn into herself.

Brian would have preferred the crying. It was healthier.

"Putting a signature on their job feeds their sense of power," she continued, outlining a profile the deputy probably already had. Giving Brian one he'd rather not have had.

Brian stayed one step behind Hannah, silently supportive, as she spoke with the deputy. He'd like to prescribe some sleeping pills, but knew she'd refuse to fill the perscription. She wouldn't want them around. Wouldn't want to be tempted to use them. He knew she feared getting addicted. She'd told him so when Carlos died. Hannah might be strong, but there was a limit to everyone's capacity.

"I'd heard you had an Ivory Nation member on trial this week. You might want to consider recusing yourself."

Hannah's frown put an end to that idea. "Is that an official suggestion, Deputy?"

"No, ma'am." The deputy looked down, and Brian almost pitied the guy.

Deputy Charles closed his book and picked up the satchel containing Hannah's dead cat. "Keep your doors and windows locked, Judge," he said, on his way to stop at the door. "We'll be doing extra drive-bys and keeping a watch on the neighborhood just in case." His words were appropriately reassuring but Brian worried anyway.

Hannah knew she really should let Brian go home. He'd called Cynthia before arriving so she wouldn't be expecting him, but that didn't mean that his new live-in lover would want him spending the evening at the home of another woman.

"Can I get you something to eat?" she asked, while Deputy Charles reversed down the drive.

"I thought maybe we could call for Chinese."

Her stomach rumbling at the thought of food, Hannah nodded. That would give her another hour or so before Brian had to go.

An hour to get herself under control, to beat the panic that was turning her into a scared, weak woman.

Something Hannah hadn't been in a very long time. At least not admittedly.

Brian found the menus while Hannah took her morning's coffee cup from the sink and put it in the dishwasher. And then he rechecked the windows and doors, even though Deputy Charles had already done so.

Brian was a sweet man. A very sweet man. She was lucky to have had him as such a close friend all these years.

Forgoing her usual single glass of wine, Hannah reached for the bottle of scotch she kept at the back of a cupboard over the stove. Her last foster parents—the ones who'd helped her get into college—had had a fondness for scotch.

Taking the long way around to the refrigerator—avoiding the monogrammed plastic mat where Callie's bowls still sat—she filled two glasses with ice. Added a small splash of scotch into both, filled hers with 7-Up and Brian's with water and handed him his glass as he came back into the kitchen.

He attempted to meet her eyes as he held the glass, but she couldn't look at him.

"Cheers," she said, offering her glass for the traditional clink—a throwback to their college days when they'd all thought it bad luck to drink without toasting first.

The theory, as far as she could remember was along the lines of "you can't toast without someone there and if there's someone there, you won't ever drink alone."

Drinking alone had been their definition of a drinking problem.

Brian's glass still hadn't touched hers.

Hannah could feel him watching her. And the look in his eyes, when she finally met it, told her he wasn't letting her get away with running. Or hiding. Or shutting him out.

"Here's to friends," he said, his voice warm as he held out his glass. "And knowing that they're always there. No matter what."

She held her glass stiffly. There was safety in aloneness. And danger in believing in foolishness. You didn't need a toast to enjoy a shot of scotch. You didn't need a toast to keep safe.

Or a friend, either.

"Here's to friends," she said, dropping her gaze as she sipped.

Hannah's cell phone rang just as Brian was hanging up from ordering dinner. He reached for his wallet, getting the money to pay the delivery person, as he listened to her answer it, sounding more like herself than he'd heard that day.

"William. How are you?"

Her judge friend, Brian surmised. William Horne. He'd met the man more than once over the years.

"No. I'm fine. Just tired."

Brian froze with the money still in his hand, his eyes following Hannah as she moved to the sliding glass door to stare out into the backyard. She was just tired?

He wondered how many times he'd heard the same type of response when Hannah couldn't admit she needed something.

"Yes."

And then again, after a brief pause, "Yes.

"Judge Randolph? No, I didn't see her.

"That's right, I did decide to allow the witness.

Another, longer pause.

"Because it was the right thing to do.

"I know."

She nodded, apparently forgetting that William couldn't see her, then repeated, "I know."

And Brian felt a surge of impatience. The last thing Hannah needed just now was a lecture. Not that William had any way of knowing that.

"I came home to find Callie run over by a car."

Brian couldn't hear William's exact answer, but it was loud enough for him to know there was one.

"No." Hannah's voice broke. "She died." Her shoulders looked so fragile. Brian had to resist the urge to wrap an arm around them, to let her rest against him until she had the strength to stand alone.

"No, really, I'm fine," she said after another few words from William. "She was alive when I found her and I called Brian. He's still here.

"Yeah. We just ordered dinner."

Another several seconds passed as William spoke, though Brian could no longer hear him.

"I agree." Hannah briefly glanced up at Brian. "I know. I will." Not used to feeling so uncomfortable, Brian wondered if he should leave the room.

William spoke some more.

"The deputy didn't think so, either, and he went over the place thoroughly."

There followed a pause, long enough for Brian to grab their drinks from the living room and give Hannah hers. And then, with a bit more reassurance and a couple of "I wills" she rang off.

"William said to tell you hi."

Nodding, Brian tried to assess her expression. Which was never easy with Hannah. When he'd had money and she'd been a starving student, he'd played poker with her. And lost too often.

"He also said to tell you not to worry about the *Sun News* article."

"I'm not." Mostly.

One arm wrapped around her middle, she sipped her scotch. "He doesn't think Callie's death has anything to do with the trial."

Brian had hoped that was what her comment about Deputy Charles meant. "He would know, don't you think?" he asked.

Judge Horne had been on the bench twice as long as Hannah and had handled more capital cases than anyone in the state. More Ivory Nation cases, too.

"Yeah." She didn't look any less worried.

Brian probably would have pushed her a little further but the doorbell rang.

Dinner had arrived.

5

The Chinese food was gone. The first shot of scotch was long gone, too—having been followed by another and then, at some point, straight 7-Up. Too many hours were gone.

Brian was not. Nor did he appear to be in any hurry to leave.

"I'm all right," she said, rolling her head along the back of the couch, to peer down to the opposite end where he was lounging. "You don't have to babysit me."

Don't go, the little girl in her pleaded silently. *I'm afraid to be alone.*

"I've never, not once, seen you act like a baby. Or treated you as one."

"You suck at prevarication, Hampton."

"Well then," he said, staring her straight in the eye. "How's this? I'm not babysitting. I'm here because there's no place else I'd rather be."

"I'm guessing Cynthia wouldn't be too happy to hear that."

"Cynthia will understand. She knows how long we've been friends. She knows I love you like a sister. And…" he added, after a pause "…I don't think she'd throw a fit even if she didn't know. I almost wish she would."

"Why?"

"Because while we enjoy being together, I still don't quite feel as if we're really in love. It's like she doesn't entirely trust me to love her. Or rather, doesn't trust herself to be loved. She has no expectations. Counts on nothing. Including the fact that I'm going to come home to her every night."

Hannah didn't like the sound of that.

She'd been watching out for Brian—and he for her—more than half her life. She'd known him longer than anyone else. He was family.

That gave her the right to care, didn't it? Regardless of this new dimension in his life—a woman waiting for him at home. A woman who had first call on his loyalty.

His heart.

"You don't think Cynthia loves you?" she asked after a long pause.

Brian had suffered enough. Cara's death had held him captive for more than ten years. Hannah wasn't going to sit by and watch someone act carelessly with emotions that were only now coming out of storage.

"I think she does," Brian said.

"But you don't know it."

"Right."

"Does she say she does?"

"Yeah."

The scotch had relaxed her, possibly too much. Still watching him, Hannah wasn't sure what was happening—why these intimate feelings were coming out.

"Does she treat you well?"

"Yeah. It just always feels like she's holding back."

He'd loosened his tie—a Disney original dotted with Mickey Mouse figures—and unbuttoned the collar of his matching yellow shirt.

Mickey gave her courage. "Maybe *she's* not the one holding back," she said. "Maybe she's reacting," she added when he said nothing.

"To what?" he asked, but she thought he knew.

"To you. Maybe you're the one who can't give freely and that makes it less safe for her to do so."

"I'm ready," Brian said, a frown creasing his forehead. "I know I am."

"I'm sure you are," Hannah told him. "But being ready doesn't mean you're not out of practice. Don't be so hard on yourself, Brian. You don't have to be perfect at everything you do."

"So you think she's holding back because I am?"

"I'm saying it's a possibility. But hey, consider the source. I'm a careful observer, but it's not like I have any real experience at this."

"You had the best experience," Brian said quietly.

By unspoken agreement, they didn't refer to her life before law school. Her time with Jason.

"Yeah, well, maybe. That was a long time ago."

Too long ago. Another existence. A very brief idyllic period during which she'd dared to believe she'd finally found a real home.

"And yet, it's always right there, isn't it?" His dark eyes wouldn't let her hide her pain. Because he hurt, too?

"Yeah." She tried hard not to remember, even while images of Jason's smile lit her from the inside out.

"He was a great guy, Hannah. One of the best."

"I know." Which was partly why it was so hard to accept, even now, that he'd been given such a short time on earth.

"And he loved *you*."

Yeah. He had. As much as she'd loved him. A rare gift.

"Do you ever regret marrying him?"

"No." She didn't even need to think about that.

"I don't know if I could've done it. Being so young. And knowing he was sick."

"I was only seventeen," Hannah said. "But it felt like thirty-seven. I'd been in and out of six foster homes by then, living on the streets for weeks every time I ran away. I felt like I'd been on my own for years. It's not like I had any childhood left to cling to. Having a real home of my own—that was heaven."

"But you knew you were going to lose him."

"I knew it was a possibility, but I was still young enough to believe we'd fight his illness together.

That we'd win. I think, when you're in a situation like that, you have to believe in miracles. It's how you get through the day-to-day business of living.

"Besides, regardless of the threat of death, I had the honor of being his wife. I got to be with him every single day, in a life where they were all precious. I got to know every intimate detail about him. I was the one he talked to in the middle of the night. I got his wisdom, his laughter. I got to share his pain. And to ease it."

She had tears in her eyes, and didn't care. Jason deserved them.

"I wish I'd known him."

"I do, too," Hannah said now, knowing instinctively that Jason would've liked Brian. And although Brian already knew the story, she found comfort in telling it once more. "Cara met him a few times. He'd insisted he'd only marry me if I went to college, and I met up with Cara again that first year. We'd been best friends in junior high, two foster families before my last one. I only saw her during class at Arizona State for the first year or two because Jason and I spent all our time together, but she and I talked a lot. By the time Jason got really sick, Cara and I were close again. Jason wanted to meet her and she wanted to meet him. She started coming around on weekends. That was toward the end when he wasn't up and about much."

Brian settled back in the corner of the couch, his arm along the back with his fingers just inches from her head. His presence was a comfort, offering an odd kind of security—to a woman who'd never known much of that.

"She told me about him," he said now. "We were already dating by the time he died. I kind of assumed he was always pretty much bedridden."

"No." Hannah shook her head, smiling through her tears. "That was only the last couple of months. The first three years you wouldn't even have known he was sick except for all the medication in our bathroom. And the grocery shopping. We had to be careful about what he ate."

"With him being well, didn't that give you hope?"

"Sure it did."

"That must've made it even harder when he got worse."

She couldn't believe they were talking about this. Jason was a topic held very close to her heart, taken out only when she was alone. And yet, tonight, with Brian, sharing him felt right.

"Is it ever easy?" she asked. The question wasn't rhetorical and they both knew it.

"No, of course not."

"So which is better? To know beforehand, to be able to prepare, but to spend those last days in mourning? Or is it better to have your loved one there, perfectly normal and happy, enjoying what you think is a long life together, and then be left in shock when he's snatched away with no time to say goodbye?"

Brian shrugged. "They both suck."

It was her word. Her one leftover from the hardened teenager she'd left behind. She'd never heard him use it before.

"Yeah, but look at it this way, Brian. Most people are looking for that one great love, wishing for it, missing it if they've settled for less. Some of them will never know what it's like to find your soul mate. We had that. We know."

He studied her for several seconds, lips tight as emotion shone from his eyes. "You're right."

"I'd choose those three years with Jason over a lifetime of settling."

He nodded. "Me, too."

As a boy, Bobby Donahue had had trouble sleeping. Getting under his bed quickly enough to avoid a drunken attack from his father was impossible when he was unconscious.

Since taking control of his life, however, and later, control of the lives around him, the only nights he'd been up late involved a woman.

Usually the same woman.

Tonight was no different. The hours between Friday night and Saturday morning, he spent alone in the Flagstaff home he'd once shared with the two people he'd loved above all else. His wife and son.

He sat, dressed in nothing but his skin, and searched for his woman—Amanda Blake.

Stripped down he was completely raw, the man his Father in Heaven had crafted him to be.

Nudity kept him grounded when life was throwing him more challenges than he'd bargained for.

He was prepared for the hard work. Could handle anything he was given. He didn't doubt that. Not for a second.

He'd just found some things easier to conquer than others.

The trial had not gone well that day, but he had things in hand. One way or another, Kenny Hill, a zealous young man Bobby dearly loved, would be alive to continue his good works.

But Kenny wasn't the reason Bobby was up. Living without his son, knowing that a year had passed in Luke's life, a formative year, was slowly eroding Bobby's peace of mind.

He'd never loved anyone like he'd loved his son. Never.

Not even Amanda, the boy's mother. Luke's kidnapper.

The Internet was a wonderful tool. And his ability to hack into more sites than God didn't hurt—not that anyone else knew about that ability.

He stared at the screen.

"Father, I give it all to You," he said aloud. "Thy will be done. If Thou would have me search until my eyes go blind, I will do so." There was a clue here somewhere. He was certain of it. A newspaper article, a picture, a mention of a homeless woman's arrest, or better yet, some illegal activity for which he knew Amanda was well trained. Like breaking and entering.

With a twist.

Amanda would only go to homes that were empty.

She'd pick the lock. She'd take food, clothes and any cash she found. Nothing else.

Amanda was a class act.

And she'd only rob others if she was desperate.

Which she'd have to be, on the run, not only from the law, but from their church—the Ivory Nation.

No one escaped the brotherhood forever. Amanda had already set a record for length of time on the loose avoiding Ivory Nation capture.

With Bobby's son.

While he knew God would have him find the woman, bring her to penitence, Bobby also admired her. The only woman he'd ever loved. Amanda was good. The best. Which was why God had given her to him in the first place.

They'd had a great work to do together. Had done it well. And if she'd remained faithful, they would've done so much more.

Bobby reached for the hand gripper he kept close by and started to squeeze. When that didn't ease his tension he scrolled faster through the Web sites, reviewing incident after incident, detail after detail, looking for the telltale signs in police logs across the country.

And without his permission, visions of Amanda ran through his mind. Visions of her when she'd been a zealous follower of the Ivory Nation, proselyting on campus, while the brothers went about the seamier business of cleaning up God's world for His people.

He'd loved her.

And she'd loved him, too. For the first time ever,

he'd known what love felt like. Known what it meant to have it in his home.

In those first couple of years they'd never gone more than a night or two without making love. He, who'd had all the sex there was to have, wanted only one woman. He couldn't get enough of her. No matter how often Amanda spread her legs, no matter how long they were together, he always felt blessed by her beauty.

She'd been so much more than sex. She'd been his companion. A believer in his cause. A missionary.

She'd been a true daughter of God.

Bobby had seen the Lord's work in Amanda's ability to reach people, her soft voice and big eyes touching their hearts in a way Bobby couldn't. She could convince a crowd of undergrads at the college, or a roomful of executives at a business meeting, that giving money to support their work, to support certain political candidates, was something they wanted to do.

And she'd done so willingly. In the beginning, she'd begged him to let her help make a difference in this dirty, evil world.

And then she'd conceived a pure white child and he'd had to have her twice a day sometimes. When he looked at his woman pregnant with another of God's pure souls, his cock wouldn't be still.

He'd insisted on delivering Luke himself. Nothing would ever compare to the power and love he'd felt as he'd reached up and pulled out their perfect boy. He'd bawled like a baby.

In the months that had followed, he'd been there as his beautiful and loyal woman had suckled their infant, nourishing Luke through the miracle of her body. He'd held her breast while their son fed, and fed himself on the leftovers.

And he'd cried then, too, giving thanks for his changed life: from drinking tainted water to supping on God's nectar.

The blinking cursor brought Bobby back to the air-conditioned room. The house was far too quiet. Too dark and foreboding. This was no longer the house of love he'd built.

And he was no longer just lonely, worried and angry. He was also uncomfortably turned on. Bobby knew what he had to do.

The same thing he'd been doing since Amanda's defection two years before. He couldn't bed another woman. He couldn't be untrue to her memory.

God had made that clear to him when He'd told Bobby he'd have to give up Amanda. That He needed Bobby to make the supreme sacrifice.

He'd made Bobby promise that he'd never tarnish the memory of the love he and Amanda had shared by coupling with another woman.

And bedding a man would be a sin. God was very plain about that one.

With a couple of clicks, Bobby was in a private live chat, his Web camera aimed and ready.

And a minute later his screen revealed the naked body of an attractive woman named Jane, her glorious red hair and welcoming smile familiar as her voice filled the cold room with a warmth he was eager to enjoy.

He used the camera to show her that he was following her orders, while he watched her pleasure herself. The illusion they were creating washed over him, soothing him, giving him a few minutes of escape.

And hopefully enough of a release to be able to sleep.

6

Brian looked at his watch. Almost two in the morning. Once again, he'd had no concept of the time. "It's late."

"I know."

"I told Cynthia not to worry if I didn't make it home."

Hannah sat up and wrapped her arms around her middle. She'd never changed out of the navy skirt and jacket she'd worn to court that day. Suits were pretty much all he saw her in anymore. "No, Brian, go," she said. "I really appreciate you staying this long, but I'm a big girl who's been living alone for years. Most of my life, really. I'll be fine."

"I don't doubt that," he said, but still didn't intend to leave. "Just as I don't doubt that if the situation were reversed, there's no way you'd let me stay by myself."

"I…"

"My folks and Cara's were around after Cara died, but if they hadn't been, you'd have stayed, wouldn't you?"

"Of course, but…"

"And last year, with Carlos…" He'd avoided the name, mostly because he knew that her emotional reaction to Callie's death was worsened by the grief she'd already been fighting. "I never would have left that night if Joan, Maggie and Donna hadn't been here."

Joan had been a sorority sister from ASU, as well, though a year behind Hannah and Cara. Maggie and Donna were fellow judges Hannah had known for several years, though he'd only met them at Carlos's funeral.

"Cara and Carlos were people, Brian. Callie's a cat. People lose pets every day. You expect to lose them. Their lives are much shorter than ours."

"Hers shouldn't have ended yet. And expecting to lose them doesn't make it any easier when it happens, does it?" He threw her own words back at her.

He wasn't leaving. No matter what she said. Ever since her drug-addicted mother had lost her to the foster system sometime in Hannah's early youth, Hannah had been alone. He knew the story.

She'd taken care of herself. Survived.

But tonight, Hannah's eyes were communicating something else.

Tonight, Hannah Montgomery was afraid to be alone.

"Can I ask you something?" Hannah had no idea how late it was. A long time after their two o'clock check, but there was no hint of dawn through the window blinds. She'd taken off her sandals and jacket.

"Of course." Brian had stripped down, too. Sort of. He'd lost the tie. And taken off his shoes when he'd put his feet up on the couch. Though they sat close together, their legs weren't touching.

She and Brian rarely touched—except for the occasional supportive hug or hand squeeze.

"Do you think there's something wrong with me?" It was a leading question. She'd known that before she asked.

Even so, his answer mattered.

"What kind of wrong? Like do I think you should take a sleeping pill and get some rest—that kind of wrong? Or do you look like you're getting the flu kind of wrong?"

He knew what she meant. She could tell from the way he wasn't meeting her eyes.

She should just let it go. Soul searching wasn't a common practice with either of them. They both had too much baggage. To look was to hurt. Period.

But it was almost morning and she hadn't been to bed. Overwhelmed by exhaustion, both physical and emotional, she wasn't herself.

She studied him through eyes that burned with fatigue. Brian's features were strong, confident. But it was his mouth that drew her. It turned up just a hint at the corners, with full lips that smiled easily. They seemed to promise comfort. To promise that everything would be okay.

Must be what his patients' parents saw every day.

"I've been caregiver only three times in my entire life…" She broke off when she heard how far back into her thoughts she'd gone; she'd intended to leave most of the hell unvisited.

"Jason and Carlos. And Callie?"

"Right." God, how she hurt. How she'd always hurt. "And all three of them died younger than they should have."

Brian sat up on the couch. "If you think—"

Raising one hand, Hannah shook her head. She didn't need him to tell her the deaths weren't her fault. She'd already been over the facts a thousand times.

"I know they didn't die because of me." She wanted to make that quite clear. "I mean, I could hardly be responsible for Jason's cancer when he was diagnosed before we even met. But he was in remission when I met him. His prognosis was the best it had ever been. There was honest-to-goodness hope."

Brian stared at her. "And?"

For a second, she'd forgotten she was talking to a doctor. A pragmatist. When she'd first known Brian, he'd been an undergrad at Arizona State University slightly full of himself, and a little fonder of partying than she was.

"I wore him out," she said. "He wanted to make love all the time and I knew it wasn't good for him, that the doctor said he had to take it easy, give his body a chance to build the antibodies it needed…"

"I don't think he'd have put it quite like that," Brian said. "And while there's a lot to be said for rest, there's even more to be said for the power of the mind in combating some of these diseases. You being there with Jason—making him happy—probably gave him months he wouldn't otherwise have had."

Brian was a very sweet man. A good friend. The best.

"And I'm guessing, from everything you've told me about him, from everything Cara said, having you there in the end—an end that was inevitable—made those days priceless for him."

"I made it hard for him to go," she said now, remembering when Jason had lain in her arms, weak and in excruciating pain, in tears because he was going to die and she would have to face a life without him. In the end, the dream that he'd reiterated time and again, that he wanted her to fall in love, have a family, be happy, had fallen apart and he'd begged her to swear she wouldn't give another man what she'd given him.

Wanting to calm his panic, she'd made the promise they'd both known she wasn't likely to keep.

That had hurt him, too.

"And we both know that you took excellent care of Carlos."

"Jason and I tried to have a child," she said. Something she'd never told anyone before. "Our whole marriage. That's why he wanted to make love so often."

"You sure it didn't have anything to do with the

fact that he had a beautiful woman he adored in his bed?"

She might've been embarrassed if she hadn't felt exhausted. If this had been someone besides Brian.

"I wanted so badly to be able to have his child. I think it would've comforted him to know that whatever life I built would always include a part of him."

"It will anyway," Brian said, his face serious. "The best part. He taught you how to love fully."

Maybe. Probably. "Still, such a simple thing, getting pregnant, and I couldn't even do that."

"I'm sure the doctors told you that Jason's medication made him sterile."

"There was a slight chance he could still…"

"Very slight. Miraculously slight. Like a vasectomy reversing itself."

"It happens." Or maybe that was just an old wives' tale.

"Your lack of conception had nothing to do with you, Hannah." Brian's voice was firm. "And neither did Carlos's death."

"I laid him on his tummy."

Brian's sigh spoke volumes. They'd been through all this before. Carlos had been sick to his stomach and she hadn't wanted him to spit up and choke. That night, the risk of SIDS seemed far less than the risk of asphyxiation. That's what Brian had told her several times over the past months.

But she needed to say this.

"And look at Callie," she continued, her case

gaining strength as she presented it. "What kind of caregiver gets so involved in her own life, in a trial, that she doesn't notice her declawed and completely cowardly cat slipping out the door with her?"

"You're human, Hannah. And we don't know for sure that's how it happened."

"If we're going to believe there was no foul play, which everyone seems to, then we have to assume I let her out."

His sigh, this time, sounded more resigned. "Like I said, you're human. She's never slipped out before has she? From what I've seen, she ran and hid whenever you picked up your keys."

"She did. She hated riding in the car."

"And you had her eleven years."

She nodded.

"So having her slip out would be the last thing you'd expect. Or even watch for."

"Parents have to be on guard at all times. They have to expect the unexpected."

"And you did. I've never seen a more involved, conscientious and yet fun parent as you."

Being Carlos's mother had been fun. She'd managed to keep both promises she'd made to Jason—she had a family and was happy, but had fallen in love again, too—albeit differently.

And then one morning, it hadn't been fun at all. She'd gone in to check on her sleeping son before her shower and found him oddly still....

"I should've known."

How could she have been blissfully asleep when

her baby was dying across the hall? How could she have lain in bed for five minutes after she finally woke, stretching, anticipating the day ahead, with a dead baby in the next room?

"There's no way you could've known—"

"Instinct." She pounded on the one thing that no one could ever prove to her. Or disprove. "Motherly instinct," she clarified. "I don't think I have it. I don't know how to nurture."

"Bullshit."

Hannah blinked. The Brian she'd known in college might have said that. Not this one.

"Think about it, Brian. Think about where I came from. The first three months of my life I wasn't held, fed, changed on a regular basis. By the time Child Protective Services got me, I was suffering from malnutrition and God knows what kind of skin conditions. I knew my guardian ad litem better than some of my foster families. I missed a vital part of my emotional education."

"The learning to let others take care of you part, maybe." Brian's concession was dry. "Not the learning to care for others part."

"My lack of nurturing instinct is what makes me good at my job," she continued as though he hadn't spoken. "If I were a nurturer how could I possibly face an eighteen-year-old kid and make decisions that might help get him a death sentence?"

"Because what he did was heinous and to let him live would put other lives at risk."

"He's little more than a child."

"He brutally beat another kid to death, simply because that kid's skin wasn't white."

"And what about the mothers whose children I take away? Where's my compassion then?"

"With the children. Would you want them suffering from malnutrition and skin disease the way you did?"

"I don't know." Hannah shook her head, looking inward. "I examine the facts and make decisions. I don't think I feel anything at all."

When Brian's brows drew together, she figured she'd convinced him. And was disappointed that it hadn't been harder. She wasn't surprised, though.

"How well do you sleep at night?"

"Depends on the night."

"Any night after a trial." And when she didn't immediately answer, he added, "Or a sentencing. Which," he went on without letting her answer, "would be just about every Friday night, wouldn't it?"

The man remembered too much. Or else she talked too much.

"What do you usually do on Friday nights, Hannah?"

He knew what she did. She'd turned down enough invitations from him over the years.

"When I'm not at a SIDS conference, you mean?"

He nodded.

"I come home. Have a quiet dinner…"

"Usually a frozen dinner you microwave because you don't have the energy to cook. Though you love to cook."

Peering over at her with his head slightly bent, Brian reminded her of a teacher she'd once had who'd always seemed to think she wasn't giving him her best effort.

"I have dinner and then I either read a book or take a hot bath or both."

"And have a glass of wine."

"One. Sometimes."

"All to help you relax so that you can sleep."

Smart-ass.

"Am I right?"

He knew he was. There was no point in admitting the obvious.

"Just because my job takes a lot out of me doesn't mean I'm a nurturer."

Brian clasped his hands on his lap in front of him. "I'm prepared to argue this the rest of the night."

"So am I."

And they did.

In the end, Hannah felt a lot better. But she still wasn't convinced.

Watching the beautiful woman seated next to him in Symphony Hall Saturday night, William Horne couldn't help the frisson of worry in his gut. Hannah could hardly keep her eyes open, and while she'd said that she'd slept and was fine, he knew there were things she wasn't telling him.

His son, twelve-year-old Francis, had played his piece. William wouldn't be seeing him after the show. He wouldn't be seeing him at all until his mother had one more day in court. With a judge specially appointed from another county.

"You want to go?" He leaned over to whisper in her ear.

Frowning, she shook her head. "I'm enjoying this." And then, her expression suddenly compassionate, she added, "Unless you want to?"

He did. Kind of. But not if she was actually relaxing. Enjoying herself.

"No, I'm fine." He smiled. Covered her hand where it lay on the armrest between them—a rare show of the physical affection he fought so hard to hold in check.

She'd outdone herself that evening, dressed in a figure-hugging black dress that brushed her calves. Her hair was swept up in an array of curls, leaving her neck exposed. And the diamond hoops threaded through her earlobes had been driving him crazy.

Lately, everything about this woman drove him crazy. From her body to her intellect and personality, she was under his skin.

As the concert went on, shrouding him in a cocoon of darkness and classical music and Hannah's perfume, he let his mind dwell more intimately on the woman beside him.

He needed her with a hunger he hadn't felt even in his youth. Not an hour went by, it seemed, that he didn't have some fantasy about Hannah Montgomery naked. But it was more than that. He craved her smile when he woke up in the morning. Her voice on the phone at lunch. Her laugh made his insides jump. And when she took a firm stance, whether he agreed with her or not, he respected the hell out of her. Plain and simple, she made life worth living.

He'd never felt that way before.

Except when Francis was born. And right now, he couldn't think about that. He had to be patient. To let justice run its course. If Patsy wanted to try and prove that the threats against Francis's life, almost three years before, made him in any way an unsafe figure in the boy's life, let her try. He'd win this one.

He just wondered how much of his son's life he was going to lose in the meantime.

And when the acid started to burn his stomach, he quit thinking about Francis and concentrated on the music instead. The smell of perfume. And the woman who hadn't pulled her hand away from his.

7

"Mr. Ramirez, thank you for being here today. I know this isn't easy for you."

Butterflies swarmed in her stomach as Hannah sat on the bench after lunch on Monday, listening to Julie Gilbert begin the afternoon's session. She just hoped she hadn't made a terrible mistake in allowing these proceedings.

Robert Keith was going to regret ever alleging that the injuries suffered by the victim could not have come from the instrument found in Mr. Hill's car with only Mr. Hill's fingerprints on them.

And she might regret allowing the prosecutor to present the state's rebuttal. Not because she doubted for a second that she acted within the law, but because there might just be a time when one had to consider self before the job.

William certainly thought so. Had told her so, repeatedly, whenever the Ivory Nation or Hill's trial was mentioned. As recently as Saturday night.

According to William, she had a duty to the state,

a job to do, but it was only a job. When her life or safety was threatened, her duty was to herself first.

Of course, if that was the situation, if he was right, she should recuse herself.

And that would be wrong.

So here she sat, wishing she were snug on her couch in the middle of the night, with no one but an old friend to answer to.

The first questions were mostly innocuous, carefully worded questions that were meant to lead the jury to a mental picture, without giving away any information that might cause a mistrial.

Miguel Ramirez was nineteen. He'd been born and raised in southern Arizona, moving to Phoenix with his parents when he was fifteen. He still lived at home. He was a student at Arizona State University and worked full time as a cook in a Mexican restaurant.

What Hannah knew, and the jury wouldn't, was that his parents owned that restaurant. And that when Kenny Hill's older sister worked there, she'd fallen in love with the owner's handsome young son, Miguel.

They wouldn't know about the night a fifteen-year-old Kenny had lain in wait for the then-seventeen-year-old Miguel, taking him by surprise, torturing him.

"Mr. Ramirez, do you recognize this…tool?"

The prosecutor held up a homemade contraption that had already been submitted as evidence. It looked like a cross between a hand drill and a kitchen mixer, with a gunlike handle from which protruded a slim metal tube with an elongated beater on the end.

The weapon that had been used to kill Camargo Cortes.

Hannah could hardly watch as the witness looked at the weapon Ms. Gilbert held and then down at his hands. His chin trembled slightly, but he glanced back up almost immediately. "Yes, ma'am."

There was so much he could have said. But he'd been well coached. He knew how critical it was that his testimony remain within the boundaries of the law or this ordeal would be for naught.

"And without revealing how or why you are privy to this information, can you tell the court what kind of injuries this tool can cause?"

Very slick, Ms. Gilbert, Hannah silently applauded. A slight variation of that word, one letter different, and the whole trial could have gone up in smoke. If she'd said *caused* instead of *can cause,* she'd have been telling the jury for certain that the weapon had been used before. Which would reasonably implicate Kenny Hill for a previous offense and Keith would've been screaming for a mistrial.

Miguel Ramirez swallowed as though his throat was dry. He coughed. And then calmly and unemotionally, as if he was a stranger to the case, he said, "When used as a whip, it can break bones, inflict deep lacerations and bruises. Any of the normal injuries that would be sustained if you had, say, any heavy piece of metal swung at you. The...beater blade…at the end cuts unevenly, ripping the skin, making those lacerations harder to stitch."

Bravo, young man, Hannah thought, having to quell the emotion Miguel's demeanor inspired.

"Anything else?" Julie asked. Hannah noticed that the prosecutor didn't lead the young man to other injuries that had already been testified to during the trial.

"Yes." Again, Miguel swallowed. Started to speak and then stopped, apologizing.

"That's all right, Mr. Ramirez. Take your time. The court recognizes that this is a difficult situation. We've all had to endure some very distressing evidence over the past week."

Good again. The jury now had an explanation for the young man's discomfort, could understand that he probably felt as they had at various times this week—and none of them had been victims of a crime. So there was no reason to automatically assume that he had been.

And then Miguel Ramirez, his chin tight, his expression determined and resolute, looked straight at the prosecutor.

"The beater at the end, when inserted anally and turned on, destroys the colon."

The prosecutor asked a couple of other detailed questions for which Miguel had ready and confident answers, using laymen's terms to describe potential injuries.

"And how do you know this?"

"I've seen it used." He didn't say when. Which

meant it could have been during the committing of the current crime.

And then, looking not at Kenny Hill, but at his parents, sitting pale and rigid in the front row, Julie Gilbert said, "No further questions, Your Honor."

Heavy silence pervaded the room as those present absorbed the fact that earlier testimony from one of the state's expert witness physicians had just been validated.

Hannah called for a five-minute recess.

"We're back on the record...." Hannah repeated the words she'd said so many times she could quote the case number by heart. And then, after asking Miguel Ramirez to retake the stand and reminding him that he was still under oath, she invited Robert Keith to cross-examine the state's witness.

If she could have found a way to hold the young man's hand as he faced attack for having suffered a savage assault, she would have.

Robert Keith's confidence worried her.

"Mr. Ramirez, you say you've seen a tool like this before?"

"Yes."

All Keith had to do was trip Ramirez up once, get him to admit, without direct question, that he'd been a victim of Hill's previous crime and nine days of emotional turmoil and anguish, would be wasted.

"How many times?"

"Once."

"And were you completely sober at the time?"

"No."

Shit.

"In fact, you'd had at least three beers, hadn't you?"

"Yes."

Keith approached the witness stand. "How long ago was this?" he asked, as though speaking to a child.

"Three years." The defense brought it up. The defense alluded to the earlier crime. That meant no cause for mistrial.

"So three years ago you saw a tool that looked something like this while you were drunk and you're sure you know that this very tool could do the damage you describe."

"I wasn't drunk. And yes." Miguel's confidence didn't slip. At all. As a matter of fact, Hannah couldn't remember the last time she'd had a witness who'd spoken with so much authority. Still, Hannah wasn't sure that it would be enough. The prosecution had failed to disclose, or perhaps hadn't known, that Miguel Ramirez had been drinking at the time of his attack.

"How can you be sure?" Keith went on to divulge statistics that could be easily verified, stating margins of error for the human eye, the human brain, while under varying degrees of intoxication. "With all of that," he concluded, "how can you possibly expect us to believe that, from one sighting while under the influence three years ago, you're certain of a beater size?"

Miguel looked at the prosecutor, who nodded—and hung her head. It was up to him now. He could answer the direct question, but only the direct question.

"I am certain that is the exact tool that I saw."

Hannah's heart sank. Even a mediocre attorney could debate that—by simply bringing in an identical tool and having the two sit side by side. A better attorney would bring in two tools, one with a slightly larger beater and—

"Because of the acid mark."

Everyone, including Hannah, froze. They'd heard testimony the previous week, seen gruesome pictures of a young man's genitals having been doused with acid before he'd been tortured to death.

"Acid mark," Robert Keith repeated, all hint of congeniality gone. And Hannah could hear the attorney in her chambers already. The witness had been given details of the case.

"Yes, sir."

"What acid mark?"

"The one that washes out the brand name on the side of the drill."

Julie Gilbert slumped back in her chair, her head still bowed.

A mark that could've been sustained three years ago, or three minutes ago.

"Come on, Mr. Ramirez, you don't honestly expect the court to accept a mark you could've just seen today for the first time as proof that your testimony is valid, do you?"

"Yes, I do. I can prove that it's valid."

Julie's head came up. Robert Keith stood back.

He didn't want to ask the next question. But he'd led the witness here. If he didn't ask it, the jury would.

"How?" Keith asked, as though he didn't believe it for a second. But for once, Hannah saw more bravado than confidence in the man's posture.

"Because that mark is my thumbprint."

Brian was looking forward to getting home to Cynthia and Joseph Monday afternoon. He was far earlier than she'd be expecting and he hoped that would be a good thing. She'd been understanding about his night at Hannah's. But while she hadn't said anything, she'd also been agitated. A little short with him. Maybe even a little jealous. It was that display of ruffled feathers that had touched Brian more than anything about her thus far—it showed him she cared.

They'd had a good weekend together—he and Cynthia and Joseph. They were becoming a family.

Which reminded him, he had a phone call to make before he got home.

Hannah answered on the second ring. As though she'd been sitting at her desk next to the phone.

"I was all set to leave you a message. Figured you'd still be on the bench."

"Nope, I'm a free woman."

"Does that mean what I hope it means? The trial ended?"

"I just finished jury instructions." The lightness in

her voice was contagious. She was doing better. Or at least okay.

But then, he'd known she would be. Hannah Montgomery was a true survivor.

"They'll be back at nine tomorrow morning to begin deliberations."

He turned right then left, taking city streets home rather than the more direct expressway most commuters would choose. Brian didn't feel like being one of a crowd tonight.

Or like racing for his space.

"You expecting them to take a while?" he asked, enjoying the conversation. Enjoying just hearing her voice back to normal again.

"It's a capital case, so, yeah, I do. It depends on how many questions they send out, what kind of information they request."

"At least in the meantime you get to rest," he said, knowing that rest was a relative term.

"I'm actually picking a jury for another trial at ten-thirty in the morning, right after my calendar."

Which meant she and the attorneys and the defendant would meet in her courtroom, interview potential jurors, dismiss those unsuitable and hopefully end up with enough people left to fill the jury requirement. The attorneys each got a couple of strikes, but the final decisions were Hannah's. Brian had observed the process enough to know what kind of strain that put on her.

It was tough watching out for a judge. Hadn't been any easier when she'd been a prosecutor.

"Another murder?" he asked, when he'd have liked to suggest that she look into a career as a greeter at Wal-Mart. Good hours. Good pay. Good benefits. And safe.

"No," she said. She chuckled, still sounding far more tired than he'd have liked, but upbeat, too. "To be honest with you, I don't remember what it is, I just know it's not murder."

Murder, drugs, mayhem—they were all just things Hannah took in stride. A normal part of her day—reminding him of just how strong she really was.

She was going to be all right. She didn't need him.

"How are things with Cynthia?"

"Fine. Great. Better than ever."

"She wasn't put out by the other night?"

"Nope. She understood. Joseph, on the other hand, gave me a hard time for missing the pizza they had for dinner."

"Sounds like he's settling in well."

"He's improving." The child wouldn't let him or Cynthia out of his sight, but he talked more. Just not about anything that gave them any clue to—

"It's nice to hear your voice, friend." Hannah's words interrupted his thoughts. "What you did Friday night…I'm embarrassed…but…well, thank you."

"I was glad to do it," he told her with complete honesty. "And will be there for you anytime you call. Day or night. You got that?"

"Yeah, actually, I do." She sounded pleased.

And so was he.

The sun was shining. Phoenix's cerulean-blue sky was as vivid as ever. He had lifelong friends. And a new family at home. A woman to love. A boy to father. Life was good.

Another baby died Monday afternoon. Sammie Blanchard. One of Brian's patients. Three months old. A boy again.

He found out about it the next morning when he arrived at the office an hour before his first scheduled appointment and found a Mesa police detective waiting for him with a subpoena for the baby's records.

The Blanchards hadn't called him. Sammie was their fourth child. The fourth he'd cared for. And they hadn't called him.

"We understand from the mother that the infant was in your office about a week ago, with flulike symptoms."

"He was colicky," Brian corrected automatically, unlocking the door to his suite of offices in the centrally located medical plaza. "The first of her four children to suffer what is generally a very common ailment. Also the first she didn't breast-feed. We switched formulas and he's been fine."

Brian had called every day last week, just to be certain.

He hadn't called yesterday.

Sammie Blanchard was dead. He couldn't believe it.

Striding down the hall to his office, turning on lights automatically as he went, Brian tried to digest the newest tragedy, to make sense of yet another death. Had he missed something? Was there something he could have done? He'd been so certain they'd been looking at a classic case of colic. Sammie's temp had been slightly raised, but that wasn't uncommon. He'd given the baby a minimum dose of acetaminophen and Sammie had responded almost immediately. As he had to the changed formula. He'd had neither an elevated temperature, nor any signs of stomach upset the rest of the week.

"I'm assuming the medical examiner has the body?" he asked the detective waving the man to a seat in front of the massive desk as he opened his office door.

"The autopsy should be complete later today."

"Was there any sign of illness? Had he spit up?"

So many questions. And rarely any answers.

"His mother found him late in the afternoon. He'd been sleeping longer than usual and she went in to check on him. She called paramedics, tried CPR until they got there, but he'd already been dead long enough to develop blue patches."

Brian's heart ached as he tried to focus on the detective in front of him when all he could see was chubby cheeks, blue eyes, a round head covered in downy blond fuzz.

"I'll get his file," he said, sucking in as much air as he could as he retrieved what he needed from the file room. Everything was computerized, but Brian still insisted on keeping hard copy records of everything he did. Call him old-fashioned but he wasn't going to have a life at risk because a machine was on the fritz and he couldn't access the necessary information.

"I'd like to ask you a few questions if I may," Detective Angelo said as Brian returned to the office.

"Of course," Brian said, dropping into his chair as he met the police officer's direct gaze.

A gaze that was more suspicious than anything.

And that's when Brian remembered the *Sun News* article.

Surely they didn't think…

They *couldn't* think he had anything to do with this.

"Where were you yesterday afternoon, Dr. Hampton?"

Brian had answers for each of Detective Angelo's questions. With the exception of one.

"Do you have any explanation for Sammie's death?"

"No," Brian said, feeling as helpless as he had that day Cara died. "Unfortunately I don't."

"But if you had to guess, you'd say it sounded like SIDS?"

Brian's eyes narrowed and he realized he could no longer afford the luxury of emotions. This guy, as off base as he was, meant business. Apparently he had no more to do than the *Sun News* reporter.

Brian had patients to see in less than half an hour.

"Based on what I've heard so far, I wouldn't dismiss that theory," he said now, carefully.

Barbara Bailey, his receptionist, arrived. He heard her drop her keys in the drawer by her desk through his open door. And waited for the water to start running into the coffeepot—a job she insisted on doing no matter how often he assured her he could make his own coffee.

"You realize that Sammie's Hispanic, right?"

"I've been caring for his siblings for years. Of course I know their ethnicity," he said, again measuring every word.

This was crazy. Ludicrous.

"I understand that you first met them at the free clinic downtown."

"I volunteer there."

"And frequently take patients on full-time, sometimes even free of charge."

"I'm a doctor, Detective. My job is to save lives. Not just make money."

"Mmm-hmm." The detective wrote something down.

"I feel as though I'm on trial here all of a sudden, Detective," he said, leaning forward. "Do you have a warrant for my arrest?"

"No, Doctor, I do not."

Brian thought he detected an unspoken "yet" on the end of that statement. Or maybe his imagination was getting the better of him.

"Am I a suspect in anything?"

"No."

Did he hear another "yet"?

"If you think for one second that I had anything

to do with Sammie's death, or any child's death, you are completely, one-hundred-percent mistaken," he said, unable to keep the tremor out of his voice. "I love every single one of the kids who come through that door. And those that don't, as well. I've given my entire life to the health and safety of children. I would rather die myself than even inadvertently cause the death of a child in my care."

"I hear you, Doctor." Detective Angeles stood. "You'll be available if we have any further questions?"

"Of course."

"Thank you for your time. I'll see myself out."

The police officer turned, and with his footsteps muffled by the plush carpet, left—ignoring, or failing to see, the hand Brian had extended.

8

"Bobby? How are you?" Though the smile and tone of voice were upbeat, in deference to the other women milling about the sanctuary after Wednesday morning's service, her eyes held a different message.

And he knew Adele's eyes. He'd known her well, as he had all of the women in the Ivory Nation, until Amanda.

Blocking her from the view of the rest of the congregants, Bobby spoke softly. "You need a private moment?"

"I'm great, Bobby! Thanks for asking," she said with a smile, nodding an answer to his question.

"Well, that's good to hear," he said more loudly and turned away.

Moments later, as he stood at the door, hugging each of the sisters goodbye, he watched for Adele. And delivered his meeting instructions in her ear as he wished her a good week.

Adele was behind the small new-age shop in Flagstaff's historic downtown waiting for him when he arrived. As he'd known she would be. Loyalty was the backbone of the Ivory Nation. God's entire world was at stake and Satan was around every corner, trying to stifle God's people. Loyalty to the cause was a matter of eternal life and death. If God lived, Satan died.

And in the Ivory Nation, if loyalty died, so would hundreds of people.

"What's up?" Bobby asked the pretty blonde, squeezing her hand. "Don's not mistreating you, is he?"

He'd personally discipline any man who abused one of their women. There was a time and a place for violence. Using it on one of their own—especially a member of the weaker sex, was unforgivable.

"No." Adele shook her head. "Don's a good father and a good husband."

Bobby believed her.

"So, what is it?"

"I...was I anything to you, Bobby?"

The question surprised him. "Why do you ask?" He didn't play games with anyone. Especially not after being up all night monitoring the pay phone records that one of his Ivory Nation brothers on the Flagstaff police force had given him access to.

"I never told anyone about us, but Don said something once, that made me wonder if..."

Eyes narrowed, Bobby asked, "What did he say?" in a tone that let Adele know she'd be in more trouble if she didn't answer, than she would be if she broke her husband's confidence.

"Just that I shouldn't think too highly of myself because you and I…"

"Made love."

Her face relaxed into the smile he'd always been fond of. "Yeah. He said that you have sex with every woman who joins the Ivory Nation."

A total breach of the brotherhood code.

Shit.

If this was any other woman, Bobby would do what he abhorred within the nation. He'd lie.

But Adele was different: she'd been more to him than most. And now he knew she was tied to a weak man.

"I used to have sex with every woman who applied for membership, after she'd been otherwise approved," he explained. "Women give their hearts when they give their bodies. If they were willing to do this for me, I knew they'd be loyal in other ways."

Her face fell and Bobby reached out to lift her chin.

"I never slept with them, Adele," he said. "I never took them to my bed. I met them at a predetermined spot and had sex. One time only. There was no foreplay. No loving. Just physical penetration. Period."

Adele, who'd been single when they'd met, had shared his bed for weeks. She'd hooked up with Don almost a year after Bobby broke things off with her.

"So I was special," she said, half question, half confirmation.

"Of course you were."

"What about now? Do you still do that?"

Bobby shook his head. "I spent a weekend in communion with God when I asked Amanda to be my mate and He told me that I no longer had to carry the weight of determining the sisters' loyalty. He said that He'd take over."

"You do all you can do and God will do the rest, right?" She quoted one of Bobby's favorite sayings.

"Right."

"What about the guys who brought girlfriends into the cause," she asked.

"They showed their greater loyalty by allowing me to taste of their women's fruits. They knew I wouldn't do more than God required."

"And they were okay with that?"

"Every one of them was there, loving his woman while I did what I had to do."

She thought about that, and then nodded. Such was the trust Bobby demanded from the brothers and sisters in the Ivory Nation.

"If you hadn't met Amanda, do you think maybe we would've…you know…ever gotten back together?"

Every Ivory Nation member understood that Bobby would never marry. He couldn't. He was married to the cause. Just like Christ was married to the church. It was Bobby's promise to God and to the people he was there to save. The cause would always be at the top of his pyramid.

"Maybe," he said, seeing no reason to hurt her.

"Well…" She moved closer to him in the deserted alleyway, her hardened nipples brushing his arm. When Adele had been his woman, he'd insisted she lose her bras. As far as he knew, she'd never worn one since. "I've been thinking about you so much lately. Every time Don reaches for me...I can't stand the feel of his hands on my skin anymore, I can't stand knowing that it's him inside me. So I remember how it was with you. And I pretend..."

He was gratified. Not surprised, but gratified. And otherwise unmoved.

"I just thought that, with Amanda gone, maybe you'd need a little..."

"Adele, no," he said as gently, but firmly, as possible. "Don's a brother and—"

"He wouldn't have to know, Bobby," she said, her hand gripping his balls, massaging them the way he'd taught her to do. And for a second he was tempted.

But only for a second. He'd sworn celibacy as a way to honor Amanda and the love God had given them. He would die before he'd go back on that.

"We'd know, Adele, and more importantly, God would know."

The pained look on her face cleared, and she grimaced. "You're right," she said, sounding more like herself. "I'd have hated myself if you'd said yes."

"Because you'd have done it?" The question wasn't really fair. Or necessary.

"Yeah." Her honesty fed his ego and he was grateful to her for that.

"I have something else to tell you," she said when Bobby was considering how best to say goodbye.

He remembered Don's weakness—breaking code

by telling Adele that Bobby bedded others. Please, God, let that have been a simple slip of a man who was more human than godlike, a man who was a little insecure. A man who knew that Bobby had more to offer a woman than he did.

"What is it?" he asked when he was ready to respond to whatever he might hear.

"I overheard a conversation at the cafeteria yesterday." As part of her role in the Ivory Nation, Adele worked as a server at the Northern Arizona University in Flagstaff where Amanda had been employed—giving her access to young minds they could teach and convert. And keeping her pulse on the activities of enemies as well.

Flagstaff was Bobby's hometown.

"And?"

"A couple of girls were talking about David Jefferson."

The brother who'd betrayed him last year. Jefferson had taken Amanda to his bed instead of killing her as ordered. And then, while hiding Amanda away in his apartment in Tucson, he'd raped another woman in the name of the cause—a white woman married to a black man. Jefferson had put the cause at risk. Put the lives of his brothers at risk. And he was indirectly responsible for the death of a young man who'd become Bobby's protégé. Who'd shared Bobby's home after Amanda left.

Jefferson had been murdered.

And his crimes had made the news statewide for weeks.

"What about him?" Bobby said, his tone carefully neutral. He couldn't think about Jefferson's murderer now. About the other traitor—the young man who'd become family to the Donahues. Tony Littleton had failed not only the Ivory Nation, but Bobby and Luke, too.

It was a good thing Tony was dead. Bobby couldn't afford the distraction of torturing and killing him.

He couldn't afford the bitterness that such an act would instill within him.

God couldn't afford to have Bobby act in such a manner.

But if Tony were alive, God knew, Bobby would have had to do it.

Which was why God, in His infinite wisdom, had seen fit to have the boy killed with his own gun.

"These girls were talking about the rape," Adele was saying. "I guess that botanist who got raped and her black husband recently moved to Flagstaff. The guy's a history professor and he's teaching at NAU. One of the girls is in his class."

Interesting. But not earth shattering. He had no interest in the biracial couple, no lesson to teach them that they hadn't already learned. God would see them rot in hell.

"So?" He'd have heard about the move eventually.

"I was standing close to the girls because of their tattoos," Adele said, describing the mark of the Alliance, a gang that liked to call themselves supremacists, but who, in reality, didn't have a cause, except for beating up on people. Any people. They thrived on violence, not God.

And suddenly Bobby was interested.

"And?"

"One was saying that the woman who led the professor's wife back to her rapists last year was in touch with a friend of theirs in prison."

Amanda. She'd given the white woman back to Jefferson as a means to get to Bobby, to get Luke.

"It sounded like Amanda's in with the Alliance."

Amanda was involved with the Alliance? For once in his life Bobby was truly shocked. Not because someone who was on the outs with the Ivory Nation had turned to another group for protection. But because this was Amanda. His Amanda.

She'd been as wed to the Ivory Nation as he was.

"You are a good woman, Adele," he said calmly, when what he wanted to do was cry out in agony. He had a God to serve. People to care for. "Keep this between me and you, okay?"

"Sure, Bobby."

"Did you tell Don?" It was a hard-and-fast rule that all women had to follow or be cast out. If they had a man, they reported everything to him. Everything. If they didn't, they reported to Bobby.

"Not yet. I was asleep when he came in last night."

"You've told me. That covers you."

She nodded, and Bobby knew she wouldn't repeat the story to anyone else.

"Hey, Bobby?" she asked as he hugged her goodbye a moment later.

"Yeah?" he asked, allowing his groin to push up against her.

"Is it a sin if I keep fantasizing about you when Don touches me?"

He didn't even have to think about that one.

"No. Everyone tires of a mate sooner or later," he explained. "It's human nature. It's like eating only steak and baked potatoes. No matter how good they are we'd start to crave something else. Why do you think God gave us imaginations?"

She nodded, and then squinted up at him in the bright sunlight. "What about you, do you care if I do?"

That was an easy answer, too.

"I'd be honored."

Adele smiled. And as he watched her tight ass walk away, Bobby made a vow to think of her when he got home and took care of his arousal. God was proud of him. Bobby was proud of himself. He'd just resisted the hardest temptation of his life.

He deserved a good come.

Bobby was halfway home when his cell vibrated against his thigh.

"Donahue," he said, recognizing the number immediately. It was a number he never ignored. No matter what.

"Jury's back." The voice was soft, barely audible. The voice of a man the world saw as a lowly janitor. The voice of a disciple.

"And?"

"They're getting ready to read the verdict. I thought you'd want to hear."

"Well done."

At first all he could make out was mumbling in the background, but his associate was an expert and soon Bobby could hear Judge Hannah Montgomery as clearly as though he were down in Phoenix, in the courtroom with her that very second.

And two minutes later, when he could speak once again, every part of his body was shaking.

First Amanda. And now this.

Challenges. Opportunities for growth. He could handle them.

"You make sure that boy's protected, do you hear me?"

"Yes, sir."

"And get him out of there. No matter what it takes. I want him free."

Bobby had given his word to certain people who were, in an earthly sense, more important than God. The Hills. Their compatriots. People with the money that supported Ivory Nation causes.

"Protecting you is my first priority," his contact said.

And Bobby didn't even hesitate. "Not this time, it isn't. Put all resources on him."

He didn't like the long pause. Or the question that followed. "Are you sure?"

"Do it."

He clicked off before another word could be said.

Bobby wouldn't accept insubordination. Not from anyone. Even from the man who'd become his most trusted follower.

* * *

"They came back guilty." Still in her robe, Hannah sat back in her desk chair and stared blankly at the wall across from her.

It was filled with law tomes. Diplomas and commendations. All valuable. Some saw them as a symbol of power.

But they couldn't protect her from the demons that plagued her in the middle of the night. They couldn't keep her safe.

And neither could Brian Hampton. Still, he was the first person she'd called.

"So justice was done."

Just hearing his voice calmed her unease. She'd had lunch with Joan that day, hoping for a dosage of real life. The antidote had had no effect.

"Yes. Justice was done."

"Congratulations." He didn't sound all that pleased.

"Thanks."

"You heading home?"

Home. Where she lived. Where her life was. Her routine and normalcy. Where darkness and the fears she refused to let conquer her seemed to roam at will.

"Yeah."

"I'm leaving now, too. You want me to swing by on my way?"

It wasn't really on his way.

"No. I'll be fine."

"Of course you will be. You always are, right?"

Was anyone? Really?

"Right."

"I'll be there in half an hour."

"This is stupid."

"So? Who has to know? And it's not like we've never done anything stupid before. Remember the time we drank that entire keg of beer, went up on the roof of Mandalay House and dumped flour down on couples making out on the ground?"

Mandalay House. The guys' dorm across from the sorority house she'd shared with Cara and Joan and six other sisters after Jason's death. Brian had lived in Mandalay House.

"I didn't dump flour."

"But you were there. You cracked up when I nailed Carrie Williams while she was kissing Jim Bailey. You liked him, as I recall."

She had. Briefly. When she'd been trying to run from the grief of losing Jason. Not that she'd have expected Brian to remember that.

"And I remember distinctly because you laughed so hard you farted."

"I did not!"

"Yes, Your Honor, you did. I was standing right behind you and saw you look around to see if anyone had heard."

"Brian Hampton, don't you dare go around telling such lies!" He was being outrageous. But she was smiling. And remembering. Those had been such bittersweet years. While all the other kids had been experiencing their first real taste of freedom, she'd been grieving for her husband. And yet, for the first time in her life, she'd been carefree, too.

"It isn't a lie, but you also notice I've never spoken of it," Brian continued. "In all these years, I've never told a soul. Which proves that you can trust me not to tell anyone if I see you home this once."

She didn't need him to do this. She'd be perfectly fine going home alone. But he was being awfully nice and…

"What about Cynthia?"

"She and Joseph had an appointment with a child psychologist this afternoon and she promised to take him for a hamburger and French fries at his favorite fast-food place afterward so he had something to look forward to."

"She's a good mom, isn't she?"

"Yeah. That kid is everything to her."

"Lucky kid."

"So will you take pity on me and let me stop by on my way home?"

"You're full of it, Brian Hampton, you know that?"

"Yeah. I'll see you in half an hour."

He said goodbye, but Hannah couldn't let him hang up yet. "Brian?"

"Yeah?"

"Thank you."

$\underline{9}$

William and her deputy escorted Hannah out to her car. And then, needing to leave while security could see her safely off the lot, she made her second call of the evening. To the man in the car right behind her.

He didn't know he was second. He shouldn't have been.

"I'm worried about you," William said as soon as they were able to speak freely, albeit in different vehicles.

"Whatever for?"

"The guilty verdict."

"Come on, Will." She spoke commandingly, pushing back her fear. "Kenny Hill is just the latest in a line of convictions for the Ivory Nation over the years. Not one judge has ever been touched."

"This case was different. Bobby Donahue came forward."

"Which is all the more reason not to try anything. The entire country would hunt them, if necessary, if they retaliated against a judge."

"Yes, but that might not stop them. These guys'll do anything for a cause, you know that."

"William!" she said, waving at him as their routes took them in opposite directions. "I can't believe this is you, talking! You've handled far more of these cases than I have. You even dismissed the threats against Francis a couple of years ago, and you were right to do so. Rather than overreacting and scaring your son to death, you took commonsense precautions and went on with your life. And, I might add, nothing happened."

His sigh was heavy, as though weights that used to be light to him, were suddenly hard for him to carry. "Times have changed, Hannah. Look at the judge in Chicago. And the courtroom in Atlanta. We aren't as sacrosanct as we used to be. These are the days of suicide bombers and terrorists. People are willing to die for their beliefs—and to take other people with them, no matter how random it seems to us. And all for a cause."

He was scaring the shit out of her.

"What's gotten into you?" she asked. "It sounds like you need a vacation. How about this weekend? We could drive up to Prescott or Sedona. You game?"

Getting away sounded good. Though even as she made the suggestion, she was a little uncomfortable. A trip out of town meant the awkwardness of deciding on one room or two. Until now, two rooms had been understood, but recently William had been sending out some pretty clear signals. He was ready for more intimacy than she was.

But was she ready to lose him over it?

She didn't think so.

"Just me and you?" His question fed her suspicions.

"Of course." She wouldn't deal with the sleeping arrangements yet.

"We could fly to Vegas," he suggested. "Now that's a city where a body can get lost."

And get a headache, too. But the shows were fabulous.

"Fine," she said, eager in spite of the possible impending change in their relationship. A couple of days away from Phoenix, from her empty house, were just the ticket.

"I'll make the reservations," he said before telling her to take care, his standard farewell.

It was only after she'd hung up that she realized he'd never offered to see that she was safe at home.

Brian was waiting in the driveway when Hannah arrived. He went inside ahead of her, walked around, checking all the windows, making certain that she was satisfied that not a speck of dust had been moved, and then he got the heck out of there before he could be tempted to stay.

He didn't even mention his visit from the Phoenix police earlier that day. He wasn't going to give it that much credence. Even to himself. And he sure as hell didn't want to give Hannah anything more to worry about.

Hannah and William stayed at The Mirage. One room with two double beds. William claimed that

was all they had left. One room. He'd been lucky
to get it.

Hannah applauded herself for having the fore-
sight to pack a pair of lightweight sweats and top to
sleep in. Just in case.

Funny how, when he'd called late Wednesday
night to give her their reservation details, he'd never
mentioned that there'd been only one room.

They had tickets to *Love,* the Grammy Award-
winning Cirque du Soleil show at the Mirage—one
of the few shows Hannah had not yet seen. They ate
dinner. And then they went upstairs.

Braced for a fight, Hannah let him kiss her good-
night while she was still fully clothed. And in the end,
slid into his bed willingly enough. William was gentle
and sweet and she'd been alone for a long time.

Pay dirt. Once again at his computer, naked, in
the middle of the night, Bobby Donahue sat up
straight, staring at the lines of details, phone num-
bers, times of day, durations, dates, his instincts
screaming. He'd found her.

Or at least, where she'd been a couple of months
ago. For at least ten minutes each day, three days in
a row.

Finding her had been easy, really, once he'd
started a search for all Alliance brothers who'd visited Arizona prisons recently. There'd been plenty of
those. But just one who'd also been receiving regular
calls from a pay phone. Only reason he could think
of for an Alliance brother to get calls from a pay

phone, a technology easily traced, was if he was talking to someone on the run. Someone who had no other choice but to use a cell phone. Someone who wouldn't be in the same location if the call was traced.

The guy was Alliance. He was visiting the prison where a friend of Amanda's was incarcerated. He'd received pay phone calls. The guy was involved with Amanda.

A quick phone call and he was certain. The Ivory Nation wasn't the only organization who'd ever had a traitor. Or a double dipper.

Another search in places he shouldn't be, and he had an address for the pay phone. In Apache Junction—just outside of Phoenix. A couple of hours from Bobby's Flagstaff home.

He knew the place. His first drug deal had gone down there, out in the desert, a couple of twelve-year-olds with edges that were way rougher than they should've been. And then, with a bagful of weed, he'd hitchhiked his way back up to Flagstaff, and the trailer where his drunken father probably hadn't known he'd been gone all weekend.

Or even that the weekend had passed.

That Monday, he'd come home from school with enough cash in his pocket to begin planning his escape.

All that was before he'd been called by God. Before he'd known that rotten kids from the wrongest side of the tracks could save the world.

Amanda being in Apache Junction seemed right somehow.

Dropping to his knees in front of his desk, the wood floor hard, even through his calluses, Bobby bowed down.

"Thank you, God. My heavenly God, once again You have blessed my righteousness and once again, I am in awe that You, the beloved, chose me. I love You, Father." He paused as tears streamed down his cheeks. "I am humbly Thine, my God, here to do as You call me to do. Anything, Father. I will do anything for You. I am Your servant. At Your command."

When the phone rang five minutes later, regardless of the fact that it was three o'clock Sunday morning, Bobby wasn't the least surprised.

"Yes?" *God always responded quickly.*

"It's done."

This was God's will, then.

Bobby Donahue would be their sacrifice. He would martyr himself to free God's people. To free Kenny Hill.

All was well. As God ordained.

"I'm ready."

The sun was still shining when William pulled into Hannah's drive Sunday afternoon. As eager as she'd been to get away, she was glad to be home.

After lifting her bag out of the trunk, William leaned in for a kiss. Not their usual peck on the cheek, but a deep, consuming, tongue-meeting kiss.

"I'll call you later," he said, heading for the driver's seat.

Hannah nodded, watching him as he backed onto the street. After the passion he'd been unable to contain the night before, the way he'd hardly been able to keep his hands off her all day, she'd expected him to stay over. Or at least to try.

But then, he'd been withdrawn since they'd landed at Sky Harbor. Was he having regrets?

Wasn't she?

Shaking her head as he turned at the corner, she headed up the walk. Too many questions. And no answers.

What had they started? And how would it play out at work?

Would they kiss there, too? And hold hands?

Would everyone know that she and Will Horne slept together this weekend? Finally?

Or did they all assume that had been going on for years?

Did she really care what people thought?

With the last question still in her mind, she let herself in the front door.

And stopped.

Not a single thing was where she'd left it.

Sick, shaking, turning her back on the wreckage that had once been her home, hardly able to absorb the tipped-over furniture, broken glass and unrecognizable debris, Hannah fumbled at her waist for her cell phone, and dialed 911.

She was still shaking half an hour later as she waited outside while Deputy Charles and his crew, after asking her all the pertinent questions, moved their way through the destruction in her living room.

This time, she called William first. Seemed like the appropriate thing to do, now that they'd become lovers. Or at least since they'd had sex.

And it was Sunday. She had no business bothering Brian when he was at home with his family. The last thing she wanted was to become a problem between him and his new love.

"What?" Will's clipped tone was indicative of his stress as Hannah told him what happened. "They weren't there when you went in, were they?"

The police dispatcher had asked her that when she phoned. She hadn't even thought of the possibility. Which, considering her job and the cases she heard on a daily basis, just showed how off her game she was.

"No. At least, if they were, they were gone by the time Deputy Charles arrived. I waited for him across the street."

And her neighbors, an elderly couple she'd met occasionally while wheeling out her big city-issued trash can, had offered to let her spend the night if she needed to. Or wanted the company.

"And you weren't hurt, right?"

His concern warmed her. "Right."

"Thank God for that," he said, with obvious relief. "How extensive was the damage?"

Hannah sat on the front stoop, tucking her long cotton skirt around her. "I have no idea. I haven't been all the way through, but it looks as though the living room is the only room that they touched. It was completely trashed. Stuff ground into the carpet, the furniture and paintings slashed, curtains shredded. I don't know…" After a minute of looking around, she'd had to leave. It was too much to take in all at once.

"It was the Ivory Nation," William said, his tone brooking no argument. "You know that."

"Charles doesn't think so." This news was the only relief she had, and she was eager to share it with William. "He says it was probably kids. Whoever did this didn't have a lot of strength. The slashes weren't deep, the furniture was turned over, but not with the force of a man flipping it since the frames were still intact. Nothing more than five feet off the ground was touched."

"So they're trying to throw off the cops," William said adamantly. "Don't ignore me on this one, Hannah." His warning was clear. Authoritative. As though he were addressing a defendant in his courtroom. "I know them and this is definitely their work. It's too coincidental that something like this would happen the exact weekend you send one of their brothers to prison."

"He hasn't been sentenced yet."

"Exactly."

"What does that mean?"

"They're out of patience. If you don't lean in their favor with the sentencing they're going to trash a lot more than your living room."

"Will, stop it." Hannah stood, a hand on her

forehead as she tried to think straight. "You're scaring me."

"Good!" His response surprised her. Until he continued. "I want you scared. It's the only way I can make you listen. Make you keep yourself safe."

"You didn't give in and you were fine."

"I've been lucky enough to have enough competent defenders to keep my ass out of hot water."

Was William glad the state had lost so many Ivory Nation cases? Surely not.

"But what if you hadn't?" she asked softly. "If the state had been able to prove those cases, you'd have ruled justly, and sentenced justly, too, wouldn't you?"

"Of course." His lack of hesitation satisfied her completely. And confirmed what she'd already known. William Horne was one of the good guys.

"And I'm going to do the same," she said with renewed conviction. It helped to know that the police were certain that her break-in was, indeed, a coincidence, and nothing more.

"No, you aren't." William's sternness was new to her. At least toward her. "You're a woman, Hannah. You live alone, and—"

"Will." Her own tone was stern as she stopped him. "You are not my keeper simply because we had sex last night, nor am I suddenly a helpless woman. I am your equal. I'll do my job just as you would. Get over it."

When he didn't respond she added, "Don't go all protective male on me, okay? No Neanderthal tactics?"

"I'm coming on that strong, huh?" He didn't quite chuckle, but almost.

"Pretty close."

"Point taken. Do you need help cleaning up? Or is that too pushy?"

"I'd love your help," she said. "But I can't touch anything until they're done in there. It'll probably be at least tomorrow. They need someone from the crime lab to come out and whoever's on call is busy someplace else."

This was the real world, not television, where there were always forensic people free to run to the rescue as soon as the plot called for them.

"Where are you going to sleep tonight?"

"Right here. The doors still lock. Charles boarded up the window that they broke to get in. And the rest of the house is fine."

"You're welcome to come over, if you'd like."

"Thanks." Hannah wasn't sure why she didn't jump at that idea. No matter what she said, she wasn't looking forward to a night alone in the home that no longer felt safe. "I might take you up on that if things get too creepy here after dark."

"My door's open anytime. You know that."

Especially now that she'd be sleeping in his bed?

Hannah didn't know where the thought came from, but it shamed her.

Brian's first call went right to voice mail. He didn't leave a message.

"Hannah's either on the phone, or she's turned it

off," he reported to his small family, the two members of which were sitting in the front and backseat of his Jag, one waiting expectantly.

"The kitty's crying." Joseph's voice, which could hardly be heard over the two pound animal's howling, was a welcome sound. He'd shown more reaction to Sunday afternoon's adventure, specifically, to the cat they'd purchased, than to anything Brian had seen so far.

"She just doesn't like being in that cage," Cynthia said. "She wants to be out playing with you. Try calling again," she urged Brian, her enthusiasm for their mission filling the car.

"Maybe we should have gotten one for him, too," Brian said, opening his phone.

"Uh-uh." Cynthia shook her head. "Not until we're more settled. If anything…happened…and we had to leave, he wouldn't be able to take it with him and that would be devastating."

"And you don't think it's going to be hard for him to give that cat away after the way it's taken to him today?" Holding his phone, Brian spoke softly, hoping the boy couldn't hear him.

"Life is hard, Brian." Cynthia's reply was just as quiet. "And we told him from the beginning that the cat was for a friend who needs one. He knows it's not his. If he learns how to handle little disappointments now, he'll be better prepared to let them roll off him in the future."

She had a point. He hit Redial.

"Besides, it's good for him to see that he doesn't get to have everything that everyone else gets."

Another valid point.

He was wishing he had a hand free to hold Cynthia's just as Hannah picked up on the other end.

Hannah insisted that she wanted them to come over, regardless of the taped-off crime scene in her front room.

Once Brian heard about the break-in, he had to see her, to assure himself that she was as fine as she claimed, knowing damn well she wasn't. So he allowed her to talk him into continuing with his family adventure and delivering her surprise.

He'd have liked to have gone by himself. To stay with her if she needed him.

"We can always take the kitten back home with us if it's too much for her tonight." He tuned a Winnie-the-Pooh CD to the speakers in the backseat so he could warn Cynthia about the scene they were walking into at Hannah's.

"You're sure she still wants us to come?"

"Positive."

As if anything could keep him away. Not when Hannah was in trouble.

Ready to meet her guests at the kitchen door as she'd prearranged, having just said goodbye to Deputy Charles and the detective he'd called in, promising not to touch anything in her living room, Hannah tried very hard to smile as she saw the young boy in Brian's arms. Joseph looked right there.

The sight hurt more than she'd expected.

As did the sight of the woman behind him. Cynthia was carrying something—presumably the surprise Brian had mentioned—but all Hannah could do was stare at the picture her old friend presented.

A dad with a young son.

A boy who had the most solemn eyes she'd ever seen. She couldn't look away.

And then, when she did, couldn't bear to look back.

"Come in," she said, stepping aside so Brian could enter and let Cynthia in behind him. He put the boy down and without another word went toward the living room.

"I'm sorry your house got broke."

The barely perceptible voice stabbed her heart and she couldn't find a word to say in reply. Would Carlos have sounded like that in another few years?

"We brought you a kitten."

Cynthia stepped forward, along with the tiny ball of fur that was curled up in the palm of her hand.

Accepting the tiny being, even while part of her protested its presence, Hannah snuggled it against her and used it to hide the tears she couldn't contain.

She wasn't going to keep it. She couldn't. She had no room left for love. And no trust in her ability to care for those who loved her.

But when Brian finally gave up trying to convince her to come home with them, she let the kitten stay. Just for the night.

10

Detective Angelo was back at Brian's office Monday morning. After hearing nothing all last week other than the medical examiner's report that Sammie Blanchard's death had been attributed to SIDS, Brian had assumed that the Phoenix police were focused on something more productive than chasing down unsubstantiated rumors.

Like solving actual cases.

Or tracking down real murderers.

Seeing the police cruiser in the otherwise empty parking lot as he arrived an hour before his first appointment, Brian wanted to turn the Jag around and head right back out. Instead, he parked in his usual spot, grabbed his coat and briefcase, straightened his yellow-and-blue Donald Duck tie, and strode purposefully toward the waiting police officer.

"Detective Angelo, what can I do for you?" he asked. Maybe the man was there to return the file he'd borrowed. Or to apologize for his attitude the week before.

No such luck. "Can we talk inside?" The detective's manner was impassive.

Brian led the man back to his office—a practice he most definitely did not want to become habit.

"You gave Sammie Blanchard a vaccine injection the week before he died," Detective Angelo said as soon as they were seated, without offering so much as a good morning.

"Yes."

"What exactly was in that shot, Dr. Hampton?"

Brian sat stiffly in his chair as he recited the generic and brand names for the vaccination.

"And you're certain there was nothing else?"

"I read the autopsy report, Detective," Brian said, leaning forward. "There was nothing in it about medications, toxic or otherwise, in that baby's system."

"And you know as well as I do that not everything shows up in a general autopsy, Doctor," the man returned. "Certain drugs won't present unless specific tests are done to look for them."

That was true. And irrelevant. Did they actually think he'd purposely and knowingly killed his own patient? Or anyone else? That he'd inject a child with something lethal...

The idea made him sick.

"Am I under suspicion?"

"No."

He stood. "Then if you don't mind, I'd like you to leave. Your insinuations are insulting and I have patients to see." He wasn't about to sit here and be harassed—even if this detective was the law. Brian knew his rights.

"We'd like to see the records of the other babies who've died this year."

"I already turned them over to the medical examiner—standard procedure at the time of death as you know."

"And they were returned to you."

"Yes."

"And now I'd like them."

"Then you'll need a subpoena, Detective," he said, one hand on the doorknob as he waved the officer out of the room.

Good riddance, he thought as he watched the man climb back into his car and pull off the lot.

"And don't come back."

By Monday night Hannah's living room had been returned to her. And the reports weren't encouraging. The forensic team had been unable to lift any usable prints. Whoever had desecrated her space had at least been enough of a professional to wear gloves.

And the fact that whoever had been there had targeted a localized area of her home, the fact that they hadn't touched several thousand dollars' worth of jewelry in her bedroom, made the crime appear more like a warning than a burglary.

"But then, your alarm system went off," Deputy Charles told her when she returned his call on her way home from work. "The intruder was in and out pretty quickly."

"Yesterday you said you didn't think this was connected to the Ivory Nation," she said slowly, giving the few cars on the road more concentration than they required. "Are you saying you've changed your mind?"

She could be cold in ninety-degree heat. She could look over her shoulder before walking alone, and check out her backseat before getting in her car. She could make sure her windows and doors were locked.

She would not be afraid. She couldn't allow that.

"We don't think so, Judge." As the detective's words registered, the panic attack she'd been barely avoiding dissipated. "The glass break was sloppy. Loud. Based on everything we know about them, the IN would only do that if breaking the glass was all they were going to do. And they'd shoot it out from a moving vehicle. They're well trained. If they wanted to physically invade, they'd have disabled the alarm system—as part of the warning. To let you know that they could get past safety measures. Trashing your home is not the end goal to guys like them. The violence is only a pleasurable bonus."

With her stomach feeling jittery again, Hannah turned onto her street. The tension in her neck was becoming a constant companion. "Thanks," she said, asking him about a mutual acquaintance—one of her ex-deputies who'd been put back out on street duty—before ringing off.

She needed a glass of wine. A guard dog.

Or at least a talented masseuse.

* * *

Sitting in front of the computer screen in her home office at nine o'clock that night, with Taybee (since she hadn't given the kitten back yet, she'd named it) curled into a tiny ball in her lap, Hannah considered the possibility of needing a new job. Briefly.

And then, knowing that she wouldn't really leave a career she loved, a life she loved, she considered a bodyguard. Except that her pay from the state of Arizona, not known for generous financial treatment of public officials, wouldn't allow her that particular luxury. And without any formal threat against her, which would allow the state to step in, she was nothing more than an overemotional female buckling under the pressure of a tough job.

Staring at the monitor in front of her, she zoomed in on the article she'd found, as though changing the font size would change what it said.

The article in the *Arizona Daily Sun* archives had been published in Flagstaff, Arizona, two years earlier.

Coconino County prosecutor Janet McNeil is safe tonight after a break-in at her home this morning in which a man was shot and killed. While investigators are not releasing any information a witness at the scene said that Ms. McNeil had been held at gunpoint and would have died if her neighbor Simon Green hadn't arrived and shot the intruder.

Earlier police reports show that Ms. McNeil, 33, has had other trouble in recent weeks, including garage vandalism, a broken windshield and mail threats.

Ms. McNeil just finished a case involving a member of Arizona's largest white supremacy organization, the Ivory Nation. The defendant was found guilty.

Ms. McNeil, who lives alone, has allegedly petitioned to adopt a child she prosecuted while working for the state in juvenile court.

Shaking, Hannah drew her sweater more firmly about the terry shorts and tank top—standard sleeping attire—she'd changed into after work, burying Taybee in the process. The kitten responded with a stretched-out paw, followed by a dig into an already faintly marked thigh.

"For that you get the floor, wretch," Hannah mumbled, making a mental note to get her new family member declawed.

And then realized what she'd just thought. Realized that at some point in the past twenty-four hours she'd become a mother yet again.

A mother to a cat. Not to a child.

An image of Joseph reluctantly leaving the cat in her care the previous night flashed before her and Hannah closed her eyes against it. She could only handle one crisis at a time.

Taybee scampered off, probably to hide under the wingback chair in the corner of the office, as she'd been doing a lot since she arrived, and Hannah fixed herself some hot chocolate. Turned down the air-conditioning. Thought about a hot bath, but didn't want to be naked. She didn't want to be that vulnerable. Not while it was dark outside.

Back in her office, she checked under the chair, just to make sure the kitten was safe. And left again, avoiding even so much as a glance at the computer screen.

She was not Janet McNeil.

Mug in hand, she turned on the hall light. And the spare bedroom light as well. She tried the back door, and even, with a pounding heart, made it to the front door, keeping her back to the destruction in her once beautiful sunken living room.

She was not Janet McNeil.

Yeah, she lived alone. And she worked for the state. She'd recently been involved with a case against the Ivory Nation.

She'd adopted a child.

But there the resemblances ended. Carlos had nothing to do with the state of Arizona, white supremacy or her job. She'd flown to a poor province in southern Mexico to find her son. She'd wanted a baby and the waiting list in Arizona was years long. Especially for an older single woman.

A tire iron was hidden between the molding and the door jamb by her front door. Her can of pepper spray was in her pocket.

On her way back to her office, planning to call Brian to offer a begrudging thank-you for Taybee, and to ask him to assure Joseph that the kitten was happy, she stopped outside the room she never entered. She knew she'd have to someday. If for no other reason than to give all the baby things behind it to a church or women's shelter.

Someday, she planned to have a sewing room behind that door. Someday. When she was ready.

Tonight, as she had every single night for the past year—except the couple of times deputies had been checking the place out—she moved on past. For now, until she was ready, she had to leave that door closed.

So she'd open others.

Hannah set her cup on the stone "believe" coaster on her desk. And risking limb, if not life, slid as far under the chair in the corner as she had to in order to retrieve her new housemate.

"You can't hide from everything," she told the precious bundle.

The kitten's stare reminded Hannah of the little man who'd said far more with his eyes than with his mouth the night before.

Life was hard. You lived anyway. Because there was no other choice.

With Taybee in her arms, Hannah went to the phone.

Ten minutes later she was counting rings, waiting for Janet Green, now married to the neighbor who'd saved her life, to pick up on the other end.

Hannah hadn't reached her position as one of the youngest female judges in the state without making a million contacts.

She didn't use them often. Which was why, when she did, she got results. Like a Flagstaff prosecutor's unlisted phone number.

"Hello?"

"Is this Janet Green?"

"Who's this, please?" The hesitation in the other woman's tone was still apparent even two years after her ordeal, and Hannah recognized, in that instant, that her life was never going to be the same again. The fear that followed her tonight was going to be there, in some fashion, for the rest of her life.

Just as the Ivory Nation intended.

"Thank God." With a grin so big his jaws hurt, Brian leaned back in his chair, phone at his ear, and let the relief filter over him. "Have you spoken with her parents yet?" he asked his friend and colleague, Jim Freeman.

"I have an appointment with them this afternoon."

"You are a miracle worker, my man," Brian said, his chicken sandwich forgotten.

"Not this time," Jim said, his voice equally light. This was what they didn't tell you in med school. That the high you got from partying back then would eventually be replaced by an unmatchable and much longer-lasting euphoria—one that came from saving lives.

"All I did was run tests and read results," Jim continued. "And she's not completely out of danger yet, but with any luck she will be by this time next year."

With an open invitation for Jim to bring his wife

and daughter over for dinner, Brian rang off, still grinning.

A miracle had happened. A diagnosis had proved false with further testing.

Felicia Summers was going to live.

Brian's grin faded when he recognized the unmarked car that pulled into his parking lot half an hour later. He'd just come in to grab a bite of his forgotten sandwich between appointments and caught the dark sedan in his peripheral vision as he headed to his desk.

"What now?" he said aloud, punching the interoffice phone line.

"Yes?" As always Barbara picked up immediately.

"Show the man coming in to exam room four," he said, winging it. "And tell him it'll be at least a half-hour wait."

"Should I have him fill out a new patient form?" Barbara asked. "Will he be bringing a child with him?"

"Nope. Just show him to room four before he has a chance to speak in front of anyone in the waiting room. And I'll need copies of the complete files of every patient we've had die of SIDS in the past year. Put them in the bottom of my credenza."

"Yes, sir." Barbara had to have questions. But she didn't ask them.

Calling on contacts he kept hidden, Bobby had a tap put on the pay phone in Apache Junction. And had members of the Apache Junction police force, the Phoenix police force and the Ivory Nation looking out for the young woman who'd stolen his heart.

And his son.

They'd get word to him. No matter where he was.

And he'd get her.

More importantly, Bobby thought, smoothing the clean sheets on Luke's mattress, he'd have his son back where he belonged.

Where God wanted him.

Once the camouflage comforter and the furry matching pillows were in place—the ensemble his homecoming gift to his son—Bobby unwrapped the pajamas, underwear, jeans and shirts, size-four T and replaced all of the smaller outfits in the drawers and closets. He made a call to ensure that if Luke was recovered before Bobby returned, his son would be well guarded, well taught, well loved. And then, though it was only midmorning, he set up his camera, opened the live chat program, scrolled down to see which of his lovelies was online, typed in a two-word invitation and within ten seconds, was unzipping his jeans at her command.

"I hope you have hours," he typed as her full breasts came into view, covered only by a minuscule bra.

One that he'd have her remove in due time. He wanted her to fondle her nipples through the fabric first. Just as he'd have done had he been making love to her.

"You have my life," she typed back.

The words satisfied him as much as the hand holding his straining cock.

They could come for him anytime now. Bobby Donahue—the living sacrifice offered for Kenny Hill's release. He'd be arrested. Charged. Probably jailed. It might be awhile before he had a chance for physical release. He owed it to God—to everyone who was counting on him—to make sure he was relaxed. Prepared for the physical drought.

Brian wanted to make the detective wait, but didn't have the guts to piss him off. Or the where-withal to concentrate as he dealt with the Anderson kids—all four of them—who were in for routine checkups, and were apprehensive about the possibility of shots.

Which three of the four were getting.

His job was to joke with them, make them laugh, so they couldn't think about what he was doing to them—so fun, not fear, was what they associated with trips to the doctor.

He'd just finished up with the younger two, one of whom, three-month-old Abigail, was too young to know that she was supposed to be afraid of the needle, when Barbara motioned that she'd done as he'd asked. Copies of the files were hidden in his office.

Without another thought, Brian asked Mollie Anderson if she'd mind rescheduling her two older children.

"I'd be glad to," the young mother said over the noise of her brood, smiling through the mass of arms and legs entangling her. "I think we've reached our limit on confinement here this morning!" Then, with the baby in a carrier on her chest and the tiny fingers of her two next youngest grasped firmly in her hands, she said, "How about a trip to the park before we head home?"

The discordant chorus of "yeahs" could have won a cheerleading competition.

"Judge, can I have a minute?"

Looking up from the files in front of her on a break from the courtroom Tuesday morning, Hannah nodded and waved Julie Gilbert in.

"Of course." She hadn't seen the prosecuting attorney since the reading of the verdict the previous Wednesday.

"What's up?" She shut the door between her office and the rest of her chambers. Julie's face was pale.

"We've got a problem."

She'd figured as much. With cat scratches up and down her arms and legs, and, a living room that was mostly bare and awaiting new carpet, Hannah had already had her fill for the week. Mercury must be in retrograde.

But she'd heard that morning that the police had caught the kid who'd trashed her house. A thirteen-year-old who'd been drinking with a buddy and had acted on a dare, not on orders from a dangerous brotherhood. Her house had been his first criminal offense.

And hopefully would be his last.

He'd end up in counseling and sentenced to community service of some kind, and his parents' insurance was footing the bill for her new living room.

"What kind of problem?" she asked after joining the prosecutor in the conversation pit on the far side of her office.

"Kenny Hill isn't guilty."

It was the last thing Hannah expected to hear. At least from Julie Gilbert. Staring at the prosecutor, Hannah waited for her to continue. The rumors of Ivory Nation infiltrations in politics, law enforcement and the justice system had been circulating for years. But Hannah would never have guessed Julie to be one of them.

She'd certainly done her job to convince the jury, and Hannah, that Kenny Hill was guilty. But then, the Ivory Nation had risen to such power because of their brainwashing tactics. Bobby Donahue and his cause had supporters that didn't even know that the Ivory Nation existed.

They were masters at making what was happening appear as though it was the opposite. Or not appear at all.

"I have an appointment with Robert Keith within the hour and I'm sure he's going to make a motion to have Kenny released," the prosecutor continued after a long, awkward pause.

"Based on what evidence?" She'd call a hearing. But only if she believed one was truly warranted.

"I was contacted this weekend by a Tucson police

detective," Julie said, her voice as shaky as the rest of her. "He knows who killed Camargo Cortes. And he has irrefutable proof."

11

"I don't have much time, Detective," Brian said, closing the door of the exam room behind him. "I have patients waiting."

"This won't take long, Doctor," Angelo said, holding an official-looking piece of paper. "That's a subpoena for the records of Mikel Sanchez, Jovan Cruz, Emmanuel Rodriguez and Carlos Montgomery."

The four infants who'd died of SIDS while under his care. One of whom was Hannah Montgomery's son.

Heart pumping overtime, Brian stared at the outstretched form. And then took it. He had nothing to hide.

"Let me see what this says." He pretended to read, stalling.

This whole thing was bizarre. He'd done nothing illegal. Ever. He paid ahead on his taxes and didn't take all the deductions coming to him.

He believed in God and in free speech and voted in every election.

Who was doing this to him? Who could possibly be after him? And why?

The parents of the children who died? Emmanuel Rodriguez was an only child of an unmarried indigent. Was it the Sanchezes? Or the Cruzes? Neither made sense, as both families were still clients, trusting him with their other children.

And where did whoever this was get the power to involve the *Sun News* and have the police take up their fight?

As he stood there, staring blankly at a bunch of legal mumbo-jumbo, Brian was comforted by the thought of the files in the closet in his office. If the papers he turned over were tampered with, he'd have his own clean copies as evidence.

Copies that he would be perusing as soon as he was finished with today's appointments. If anything was amiss, he wasn't going to wait around for someone else to find it.

"This appears to be in order," Brian said eventually, pocketing the subpoena. "What exactly are you looking for, Detective?"

"We won't know until we find it, Doctor." Angelo wasn't budging. And wasn't particularly polite, either. "Now if you could show me to the files?"

"Wait here and I'll have them brought in to you."

Sick to his stomach, Brian went in search of Barbara.

Robert Keith was pure professionalism as he handed Hannah the motion to revoke all charges against Kenny Hill and order his immediate release. Julie Gilbert stood with him, in front of Hannah's bench in the empty courtroom. Her afternoon calendar finished, Hannah was beat.

"Tell me what you know," she said quietly, looking first to Julie. The press was going to have a field day. She was hoping to get the defendant into court for a hearing and then read her decision into the record as quickly as possible.

"Detective Robert Miller of the Tucson police department contacted me at home over the weekend," Julie said, giving indication of the far-reaching sensitivity of this issue. "Last year he and his partner, Daniel Boyd, were lead detectives on that biracial rape case in Tucson."

Cold to the bone, Hannah remembered the case, which was saying a lot. The unthinkable crime had taken place the week after Carlos died.

Somehow she'd linked the two incidents in her mind. She and the Kendalls had both seen something precious die in bed at night.

"Miller, a veteran cop with a perfect record, had known Ivory Nation ties. He claims he received a call the night of the rape, telling him that two Ivory Nation brothers were responsible. He made certain that he and his partner got that case. His assignment from Bobby Donahue was to make Harry Kendall look crazy, and to have the rape remain unsolved."

A veteran cop. A man in a position of authority. Hannah swallowed. "You said this detective *had* Ivory Nation ties?"

Nodding, Julie stood before her, the shoulders of her navy suit jacket straight. "He knows those ties will be permanently severed when his testimony is made public. Last year he managed to work a miracle—sort of. He was a good cop. And a good IN servant as well. If not for him, Laura Kendall would have suffered another rape and probably death. He saved Laura, but he exposed a traitor to the Ivory Nation, too. Two of them. They were both killed. One by Miller."

Hannah stared intently between the attorneys, glad that she'd dismissed her staff. She was already determining that she would call for a closed courtroom for the official hearing.

"Turns out, Miller was a hero to Bobby Donahue," Julie said. "The rape had taken place without Donahue's direct orders or even knowledge." She grimaced. "The two dead brothers had put the Ivory Nation at considerable risk."

Remembering the horrific photos of the torture Cortes had suffered, Hannah figured Miller had done this traitor a favor by shooting him outright. A quick and relatively painless death.

"In the end, Miller managed to keep his job *and* remain a member of the organization," Gilbert continued, "which is how he came to be at the scene when Cortes was murdered."

"He was there?" Hannah needed to be sure.

"He says he was."

"How reliable is his testimony?"

"He says that while Kenny was present early in

the evening, as many of the brotherhood were, making a game of torturing the kid, he left before life-threatening damage was done. You know the imprints the coroner's report referred to?"

"The ones that were all over the victim's head and face, evidence of the strength of the blows that killed him," Keith interjected.

Hannah would have liked to reprimand the man for his unnecessary dose of drama in a situation that was already too grotesque to bear, but figured the resulting tension from a bruised ego wouldn't be worth the satisfaction.

"I remember," she said, hoping her tone communicated the message well enough.

"Miller said the imprint is from a ring," Julie continued. "A ring he has in his possession."

"It's his?" A cop witnessed—and allowed—the horrible torture they'd all been sickened by these past weeks? Would this crazy, messed-up world ever right itself?

Would anyone ever be safe again?

Julie shook her head, but the relief was short-lived. "It belongs to Bobby Donahue," she said.

"Donahue killed Cortes?" Hannah didn't know why she was surprised. Except that...

"He never gets his hands dirty."

"Apparently he does," Julie told her. "But the brotherhood line up for the honor of taking the rap for him."

"And Miller is turning his back on his career with the police force, putting himself at the scene of a horrendous crime, and betraying Bobby Donahue, why? I'm supposed to believe the man suddenly developed a conscience?"

"He's Kenny Hill's half brother." The surprises didn't stop. Hannah now understood why Julie Gilbert had been looking so sick all day. "Seems the elder Mr. Hill got a girl pregnant when he was in high school. Robert Miller was the result of that pregnancy. Kenny came along more than twenty years later. Miller was raised by his mother and eventually a stepfather but his father kept in touch and helped support him. The Hills eventually introduced Miller to Donahue's church."

"Donahue assured the Hills that if Kenny took the rap for this one, Donahue would pull strings and see that he got off," Keith jumped in. "Instead, they just heard their eighteen-year-old son be convicted of a crime that could get him the death penalty."

"And Miller is prepared to testify to all of this, here, in my court, on the record?" Hannah asked.

"Yeah," Keith confirmed. "The brotherhood rely on Donahue's ability to protect them. Hill's conviction has shaken a lot of faith. Miller has a wife and children. He's worried about them. Imagining the horrible things that could happen if Bobby's protective mechanisms fail again. We made a deal with him. His testimony for his freedom and their protection."

"And he'll bring the ring with him?"

"Yes," Julie answered while Keith rocked back and forth on his heels. "I called in some favors and forensics has already tentatively verified that the branding on Cortes's face matches the imprint of the ring."

"I assume you've got Miller someplace safe?"

"Of course."

"You've read the defense's motion, Ms. Gilbert?" Hannah kept her stare intense.

"Yes, Your Honor."

"And you agree to withdraw all charges?"

"Yes, Your Honor."

"I don't have to remind you that double jeopardy will apply," Hannah said, looking between the two attorneys. "If we set that young man free, he can't be tried again."

Keith nodded.

"I know." Julie's voice was hoarse, as though she hadn't slept.

"The hearing is set for eight-thirty tomorrow morning." The knot in Hannah's stomach was never going to go away.

Brian didn't know whether to call Hannah or not. This whole thing with Angelo was going to die a quiet death. It had to. There was no basis for any of the detective's insinuations. After a few more hours of work and a chance to think calmly, he knew that a year from now he'd be looking back on this with a shake of his head—and nothing more.

He'd done nothing wrong. He had nothing to fear.

There was no reason to upset Hannah's already unstable emotional equilibrium with reminders of

Carlos's death; with his own inconveniences. She had enough on her plate at the moment.

In the end, he called anyway. Ostensibly to check up on her. And the kitten. He couldn't just foist the thing off on her without making certain that the tiny feline beast wasn't too much for her.

And if it meant he got to hear her voice, so be it.

"It's only four-thirty, I can't believe you've left the office already," he said after finally reaching her on her cell phone. "I can't remember you ever leaving before five."

"I generally don't, but I had a rough day. I've finished my files for the morning, I'm not on search warrant duty this week and I was kind of worried about leaving Taybee alone so much her first few days at home. I don't want her to become antisocial."

She was mothering the cat already. Just what the doctor had hoped for. Now if only the rest of her life could settle down, bring her the kindness and love she deserved, Brian wouldn't spend so much time thinking about her.

"Any more news on the break-in?"

"They've taken the extra patrol off my house. They caught the kid who broke in—it wasn't gang related at all."

"They're sure about that?"

"Yeah, he's only thirteen. He and his friend were experimenting with alcohol and a dare got out of hand."

"Or maybe that's what the Ivory Nation wants you to think."

He could hear her turn signal and wondered how far she was from home. And had to fight the urge to turn the Jag in that direction.

"What would be the point?" Hannah asked. "The only reason they'd have vandalized my house would be to scare me. They wouldn't make up a lie that would make me feel safer."

"Unless they're lulling you." Brian had no idea what he was talking about, but he couldn't give it up. He was worried about her.

"Again, why? Their MO is to intimidate. A thirteen-year-old kid making a stupid mistake isn't intimidating."

With no answer to that, Brian frowned.

He should have gotten her a dog. A big one. With incisors that could take off a leg if need be.

"Besides," Hannah continued, "even if it was a warning, there'll be no need for it after tomorrow." Her voice had dropped, sounding small and defenseless.

Definitely not the Hannah he knew.

Taking the next exit, Brian headed away from his mountain community and toward her upscale neighborhood. "Why?"

"A motion's been filed to drop all charges against Kenny Hill."

"What!?" He swerved, barely missing the car he hadn't seen coming up beside him on the two-lane ramp.

She couldn't tell him nearly as much as he needed to know, not until the morning when everything became public—but she gave him enough to make him sweat.

"I'm on my way over."

"No, you aren't."

"Yes, I've already turned around."

"Then turn back, Brian. I'm not kidding. I'm tired and plan to have a quick dinner and then go to bed early."

"I don't want you there alone. Not with the hearing in the morning. You might be able to keep this from the press, but Kenny Hill will know. Which means the Ivory Nation brotherhood will know—including Bobby Donahue. You're a sitting target."

"I don't think so."

"A target that just had extra patrol removed from her home."

"Brian!" The firmness in her tone didn't faze him a bit. "You're being melodramatic. I've handled tough cases before. Last year, as a matter of fact. I had another Ivory Nation case. With a guilty verdict. Nothing happened to me."

"That case didn't involve their leader—either as a witness or a possible defendant." He wasn't budging. "Callie is mysteriously found dead outside when you know she'd never get out on her own, and then your home is vandalized, all while you've got this trial going on. I don't like it, Hannah. I'm on my way over."

"You can't stay here again tonight, Brian. You have a family to think about now. I've been living alone for almost twenty years. I can handle it."

"Not with the state's number-one criminal organization breathing down your neck."

"Stop it. You're scaring me."

"Good. Because I'm not going to leave you there by yourself."

"You can't stay here."

"Then I'll take you to my place. We've got the guest cottage in the back. You can sleep there. It's either that or I camp out in your driveway."

"I'm bringing Taybee."

Brian loosened his hold on the steering wheel, drawing his attention to the cramping in his fingers. He hadn't been aware of the death grip he had on the thing.

She could bring the whole damned neighborhood if she wanted to. "Fine."

"And I'm going straight to the guesthouse."

"After you have something to eat. There's not even bottled water out there."

"I'll stop for something on the way over."

"*We'll* stop for something," he said, turning on to her street in time to see her garage door close. "If you think I'm leaving you alone for a second, you're wrong. You won't come if I do and then I'll be up worrying all night. Now, do I wait in the driveway or in your living room?"

"In the driveway." Her response didn't surprise him. "I won't be long."

"I'm not hanging up."

"I'll be able to pack a lot more quickly with both hands."

"So put the phone down," he conceded. "But put it on speaker."

Sitting there, scarcely allowing himself to blink as he watched the house and kept one eye on his rearview mirror and the street behind him as well, Brian hardly recognized himself.

He didn't usually overreact.

Or smother someone who wanted to be free.

"Brian?" Hannah was back. And if she thought he'd let her change her mind…

"Yeah."

"I'm only doing this because I'm too tired to argue with you and I have to be sharp for the morning. You got that, right?"

"Absolutely."

He'd never been overbearing. Or even the slightest bit pushy with Hannah. She was fiercely independent. Her choice. He'd always respected that. Honored her need for personal space.

"Do I need to bring towels?" Her question broke his concentration.

"No. No soap or shampoo, either. And there are fresh sheets on the bed." The place was used on a fairly regular basis as he had a habit of offering it to business associates coming to the valley. And he had a couple of college buddies who still came back to Phoenix for golfing expeditions. His cleaning lady always kept the place ready for guests.

Still, he'd need to call Cynthia on the way home, to let her know that Hannah would be staying over. Maybe she'd be able to talk her into having dinner with them. Or to join them for a drink. Maybe he and Cynthia could take a bottle of wine out to the cottage and share a nightcap with her after Joseph went to bed. As long as the intercom Cynthia had insisted they buy reached that far.

If not, maybe she wouldn't mind if Brian went alone, just for a couple of minutes. It was a habit he'd started with his very first guest, years ago—taking out a nightcap.

Listening to the faint rustling coming from the other end of the phone—and then to her voice, faint and growing stronger, as she called for the kitten— he thought of the files in the trunk of his car. He was going to get through them tonight, too. Just in case.

And he'd left a message for the managing director of the company from which he'd purchased all of his infant inoculations over the past year. If they'd had any other complaints, any other deaths, and hadn't told him, there was going to be hell to pay.

"Okay, I'm ready."

Her garage door opened at the same time he heard her on the phone and Brian relaxed. He was getting her out of here safely. Backing down the driveway, he waited in the street for her to pull in front of him, and then, feeling amazingly better, he took his old friend home for a sleepover.

12

On the phone Tuesday night, Bobby Donahue sat at the desk in his home office, his gaze focused on a picture of Jesus Christ, God in the flesh. Son of God, just as Bobby was son of God. One of The Chosen. Brother.

"No, Dale, there's absolutely nothing you need to do," Bobby assured the owner of one of Arizona's largest private financial institutions—another son of God. A good man. "I wouldn't have called, but you'd see it in the news," he continued, calm. At peace. "As you can understand, the more people who know, the more likely it is that the state's money will go to waste, but I know I can trust you. I told my compatriots so."

He waited while the powerful man repeated avowals of loyalty to Bobby—who was one of Dale Longsby's largest clients.

"Thanks, Dale," Bobby said, and then added, "All I can tell you is that my arrest will be part of a statewide sting operation that will guarantee us safer neighborhoods and schools. A safer state."

And then he promised Dale that he would take care of himself. "My part is minimal," he said, fingering the cross around his neck. "I will be fully protected at all times."

He'd said what he had to say. And while he wanted to give Dale the time he needed, he was also working with limited hours.

His call waiting beeped, as though Bobby had summoned it, and he was able to ring off.

"Thank you, Father God," he said aloud, knowing full well that the Holy One had sent the interruption, and then clicked in.

"I've got the confirmation you asked for," the voice on the other end of the line said. "The Alliance contact in Apache Junction was right where you said he'd be. It took us an hour to get him to talk, but we got what you wanted. Amanda's in Phoenix. He doesn't know where—she won't say. She's doing a job, but not for them. He thought it was for us. He said to tell you he's very sorry he double-crossed you."

Adrenaline pumping through his veins, Bobby asked, "How sorry?"

"He's conscious. And burning."

Sometimes a man had to suffer the fires of hell on earth.

"Thank you. Now find her."

"Yes, sir."

Amanda was working? In their language that

meant serving an organization. She served the cause? Thank God something still made sense.

"And…if I'm not here…you know how to reach me."

"Yes, sir."

"Keep her alive. The Lord tells me I must do this one myself."

"I understand."

"Good. Great work. God is very pleased."

"Over the next few days…everything's in place. We've got your back."

"I know."

"I love you, man."

"I love you, too."

"I'm sorry Cynthia had to leave," Hannah said an hour past the time she'd hoped to be in bed that night—even though it was still not completely dark outside. She was sitting at the small kitchen table in the guest house with Joseph, watching his tongue dart in and out of his pursed lips as he colored a picture of a church. Or rather, painstakingly colored what she believed to be the landscape around the church as the square with the cross on the top of it was left completely white.

Brian was busy in the small kitchen, installing a garbage disposal he said he'd ordered months ago and forgot to put in. Taybee had disappeared under the bed and refused to come out. Even when Joseph had crawled under the bed with her and tried to coax her.

"Cynthia was hoping you'd have supper with us," Brian said beneath the sink. All she could see of him were the long legs he'd encased in a pair of nicely tight jeans. She averted her eyes before they got to his hips. Everyone had always said Brian had a great butt. That was no secret.

"I didn't realize she had any friends in town." Hannah purposely kept the topic on Brian's girlfriend.

And thought of the conversation she'd had with William on her way over. Rather than insisting that she come share his bed that night, as she'd expected him to do when she called, William had told her it was probably a good idea that she spend it someplace completely safe and unknown to anyone who might be looking for her.

"She's only got one friend in the area," Brian was saying, "which is why when she got the call saying her friend had been hurt, she felt she had to go."

Brian sat up. "But even as she was running out the door, she worried that you'd be offended."

"Of course I'm not!" Being able to count on a friend in a time of need was one of the great comforts of life. "I just hope she's not upset that I'm crowding you guys. This is the second evening I've taken up this month."

"Mama likes you."

The voice was so soft Hannah barely heard it. It was the first the child had spoken directly to her that night.

"She does?" she asked, mostly because she couldn't let the boy's effort go unnoticed.

She'd tried not to pay attention to Joseph. Three years older than Carlos, the child reminded her too harshly of what she'd almost had. What she'd lost.

But now when he met her eyes and gave her a solemn, silent nod, she couldn't look away.

"How do you know that?" she asked, her heart pounding in her chest.

"She told me."

Coming around the counter, Brian knelt down by the boy. "Your mother specifically told you she liked Hannah?" he asked. He seemed pleased.

"Mmm-hmm." Joseph's serious expression didn't change.

"When did she tell you that? Today?"

"Yes. So I wouldn't be scared."

Brian had told her about the child's nightmares. And about how conscientious Amanda was of Joseph's needs. More and more Hannah was growing to like the woman Brian had found to share his life with—and the more she liked her, the guiltier she felt for talking to Brian.

Which didn't make a whole lot of sense.

She and Brian had been friends for years.

She wasn't sure how she ended up in Brian's house, but an hour later there she was, sharing a glass of wine with him and Cynthia, who'd returned just as Hannah was, at Joseph's request, helping Brian put the child to bed.

"Please stay for a few minutes," Cynthia said as she took over at the stepstool in the bathroom, helping to squeeze toothpaste. "I'm really sorry I couldn't visit more with you."

Because of the confusing emotions she knew would attack her as soon as she was alone, Hannah had agreed.

But she regretted it almost immediately. The tenderness in Brian's touch, as he sat with Cynthia on the couch, his arm around her shoulders, hurt more than the fear of being alone.

She told herself it was because of Cara.

They spoke first of Cynthia's friend who was with family and would be fine. There'd been an explosion, some burns. Nothing life threatening, but Cynthia had needed to see for herself.

Hannah understood that completely.

"Brian said they caught the kid who broke into your house," Cynthia said with almost as much compassion in her tone as there'd been when she'd been speaking of her friend.

Hannah could see why Brian had fallen for this woman—and her beauty, while obvious, had little to do with it.

"They did," she said, trying to come up with an excuse to leave.

"But he's still not convinced you're safe—something to do with a case you've got in court?"

"Brian worries too much," she said, ignoring the man in question.

"Maybe, but it's nice, isn't it?" Cynthia nestled her shoulders deeper into the crook of Brian's arm.

And because she didn't want to offend her hosts, Hannah said, "Yes, it is."

"I really admire what you do." Cynthia's smile was kind as she met Hannah's gaze. "It must be frightening sitting up there, facing the dregs of society."

"I have protection," Hannah said. "Even a panic button by my knee."

"You do?" Brian asked, forcing her to look at him at least briefly.

"Yes. There's one at my desk in my office, too."

She drained the wine she didn't really want. "And we have a full staff of sheriff's deputies there, taking care of us."

"Have there been lots of retaliations?" Cynthia asked.

"Not against judges, no. Some threats. But nothing came of them." She thought of the conversation she'd had with Janet McNeil the night before. And, maybe because she really was slightly spooked about the hearing in the morning—a hearing that would see Bobby Donahue charged with first-degree murder—she asked for a second glass of wine and started to talk.

"This prosecutor in Flagstaff, this Janet McNeil, had her windshield broken while she was at work?" It took every ounce of control Brian had to stay seated as Hannah told her story, to keep his arm around his lover and not grab Hannah and run—as far and fast as he could.

Cara would expect him to protect her closest friend—the way he'd been there last year to comfort her after Carlos's death.

The things the Flagstaff prosecutor had told Hannah gave him chills. Not because of the violence perpetrated as much as the similarities.

Was he the only one that saw them?

"Yes, her windshield was broken, but…"

"Just like you had your car keyed."

"Yes, but—"

"And someone vandalized her garage?"

"Yes, Brian, but—"

"I'd say a trashed living room was a more serious warning than a garage, wouldn't you?"

"The Ivory Nation had nothing to do with my living room. And her garage wasn't trashed. A brick was thrown through a window. That's all."

"You just said that the detective in Flagstaff was certain Janet's garage was the work of neighborhood kids, too. They also ruled out Ivory Nation involvement."

"Yes, they did, but—"

"And it turned out to be the Ivory Nation after all."

"Sort of, but—"

"I'm telling you, Hannah, this is serious. I'm not going to sit by and watch you get yourself killed over a job. I—"

Brian felt Cynthia turn to look up at him, and tempered himself. He was overreacting.

And wasn't even sure why.

Except that Hannah was all alone. And she was usually so strong and capable.

Not that she wasn't now. But…

"I'm sorry. I'm behaving like an idiot."

"If you'd let me finish my story…" Hannah said when Brian was properly contrite, and had earned himself one of Cynthia's beautiful smiles.

"Go on," Cynthia said, sitting forward to refill his wineglass. Only halfway. To go with the half he'd just had.

One drink for him was all. He had patients to check on at the hospital early in the morning before heading to the office.

"It turns out that her younger brother was a member of the Ivory Nation. When he found out that his sister was prosecuting one of his comrades, he tried to get her to step down from the case. She wouldn't and he apparently lost control. He was the one behind the threats. He even set a fire at her house when he thought she was going to be out at some function."

"You're kidding." Cynthia's mouth hung open. Her face was pale.

"In the end, he broke into her house with a gun and would've killed her if her next-door neighbor hadn't gone over to check on her."

"I read about that case," Cynthia said slowly. "Didn't it turn out that the neighbor was an ex-fed? The brother—his name was Johnny something or other, I think—he's the guy who hanged himself in his jail cell here in Phoenix."

"That was Ivory Nation?" Brian asked. "That guy was completely whacked. Brainwashed. The news said he trained with terrorists."

"I heard that, too," Cynthia said. "They broke up a terrorist cell just outside Flagstaff. The guy who ran things skipped the country." Eyes wide, she stared at Hannah. "Oh, my God, Hannah, I had no idea. These are the same guys you're dealing with now? Brian's right, you have to be careful. Those guys stop at nothing to get what they want."

As fear shot through him, Brian had to fight the urge to snap at Cynthia. And was ashamed of himself. A classic case of shooting the messenger. One he loved.

What was the matter with him?

"That was an isolated case." Hannah's words didn't help much. She sounded like she was still in denial and that made her vulnerable. She'd lost some color, though. "It got so out of hand because of the family connection. There were other things going on there. Janet's brother blamed her for the fact that he grew up without a dad."

"Why would he blame her for that?" Cynthia asked while Brian was still processing the idea that terrorists were after his friend. Working out ways to keep her safe.

"Their father was an abusive drunk, and hit their mom regularly. One Sunday, when Janet was four, he apparently went after her brother, too. Johnny was only a baby then. Somehow Janet got hold of the gun their father had been cleaning. It went off and killed him."

"Oh, my God." Cynthia, her eyes filled with horror, turned back to Brian. "Oh, my God," she said again, wrapping her arms around her midsection the way she did when she was really upset. "A four-year-old child, living with that…"

Hannah's face was pinched as she continued. "Johnny didn't remember the man, of course, and somehow over the years, painted a far different picture of him. He didn't believe his father had been abusive at all. Maybe because he turned out just like him. Before Johnny went after his sister, he killed his mom. That had everything to do with punishing Janet, and nothing to do with the Ivory Nation. So you see, there's nothing to worry about here."

Brian wasn't convinced. No matter what she said, he wouldn't be convinced.

They talked for another twenty minutes or so and then, when Hannah stood to leave, Brian walked her back to the cottage, checked out the entire place—twice—and insisted that she sleep with her cell phone by her pillow.

He stopped short of hugging her good-night.

And knew that he had to get himself under control.

He'd lost Cara. He wasn't going to lose Hannah.

First, because she was a strong, capable woman who knew how to take care of herself. Second, because while the state of Arizona had prosecuted many bad guys over the past hundred years, not one judge had ever been harmed. And third, because she wasn't his to lose.

He had his own problems to deal with. His own crosses to bear.

Another woman and child who had to be his top priority.

He had files to read.

With tensions building to the point of affecting his blood pressure, William walked through the outer offices of Hannah's chambers the next morning. Susan would have stopped him in his tracks if he'd been anyone else, but with a brief nod, he continued on to the door of Hannah's private office, knocking softly before he let himself in.

"William!" Her surprised tone held a note of pleasure, too, and he honed in on that. "I thought you were downtown this week with the court of appeals."

"I am. But they don't start until nine and I needed to see you." Though he wasn't sure how welcome he'd be, William came around her desk and kissed her full on the mouth.

And when he felt her kiss him back, his world settled again. Enough for him to remember who he was and what he was about.

"I didn't like it that you were with Brian last night," he admitted. "You should've been with me."

"I wasn't *with* Brian. I stayed in his guest cottage. He was inside with his girlfriend and her son."

Thank God. Life felt better. More manageable. And he had much to manage.

"Francis sees the new psychologist this afternoon."

Her smile was comforting. Personal. "Your son

loves you, Will, you know that. Everything will be fine."

It would be. He knew it would be. "It should be already. Patsy wanted the divorce. Why the hell can't she just let me live my life?"

"She's not happy." Hannah shrugged. "She doesn't want you happy, either."

He knew that, too. But it felt damn good hearing it from someone else. From someone who cared about him. From Hannah.

She had her robe on already and looked impressive. Powerful and soft. William had never had it so bad.

"So…you ready?" he asked.

She stared down at the large file in front of her. "Yes."

"You're going to grant the defense's motion." He wasn't asking. She had to do this. Her safety depended on what she did in court that morning.

It was also the right thing to do.

"If the Tucson cop comes through and the testimony is as we suspect, then, yes, of course I will."

Satisfied, his blood pressure settling almost to normal, William moved on. "You're going to have to be very careful," he warned, knowing he had to scare her to keep them all safe. "The state's obviously going to charge Donahue and that won't go over well. Since you'd be the one who let Hill go, which inadvertently would have had Donahue charged, you could be a target. A message to whoever sits on Donahue's trial."

Her lips tight, she nodded. "Is that what happened to you?" she asked, her voice dry. Weaker than usual.

And while he hated seeing her suffer, he also knew that keeping her down was the only way to keep them safe. Sometimes Hannah was too strong, too independent for her own good.

And for the good of the man who loved her.

"Tonight, you come to my place, okay?" He asked the most important question of the morning.

"I'm staying at home, William. I live there."

"Then I'm staying with you." Permanently if she'd let him. They'd been seeing each other a long time. Had known each other even longer. And they weren't getting any younger.

"Fine. I'll make those chicken breasts you like. You know the ones with bacon."

Chicken and rice. It sounded so…normal. So right. And she hadn't argued.

A woman like Hannah—beautiful, successful, in a high-profile position—shouldn't live alone.

"And you'll let me spend the night?" He was asking for more than the opportunity to keep her safe. And he knew she knew it.

"Yes," she said.

She didn't look at him. Was she too embarrassed to do so? William needed so much more from her. He needed life from her. But he knew he couldn't push.

His time—their time—would come.

13

Robert Miller—who'd resigned only that morning from his position as a Tucson police detective—was taller than Hannah had expected. And thinner. With gray hair at forty-one, he looked absolutely nothing like what she'd pictured.

His wife and their kids were in a room with a sheriff's deputy, waiting to be taken into the state's protective custody. Hannah had seen the family on her way into the building that morning.

She could have done without the visual. The pretty woman with her gentle smile. The innocent little faces. Their lives would never be the same after this morning's testimony.

"Mr. Miller, please tell the judge first, as briefly as possible, about Laura and Harry Kendall." Kenny Hill's attorney, Robert Keith, stood at the table beside his client as he spoke.

The information would never be allowed during trial. But it helped establish, for Hannah, the validity of the witness.

"They were victims in a case my partner and I had last year. Their house was broken into in the middle of the night. Mr. Kendall was tied up and made to watch while his wife was raped. Twice. By two different men. She's white. The two men were white. Harry's black. They were being taught that white stays with white."

Miller gave horrendous details of the crime—much more than had ever been reported in the media—as though he was speaking of a traffic jam.

"And you knew who did this?" Keith asked next.

"Yes."

"Who were they?"

"Two college students, one undergrad and one in med school."

"Were you associated with either of these two men?"

"Yes."

"How?"

"They were members of the Ivory Nation, the church to which I belonged at the time."

Church. Just hearing the word made Hannah cringe.

"How close were you to these men?"

"Like family. They called me as soon as they left the Kendall house, told me what had happened."

"So when you found out what they'd done, did you immediately turn them in?"

"No."

"What did you do?"

"I did what I could to protect them."

"Including tampering with evidence?"

"Some."

"Yes or no, Mr. Miller."

"Yes."

"And were they arrested anyway?"

"One was."

"Did he stand trial?"

"No. He was released."

"Due to your tampering?"

"Yes."

"And then what happened?"

"I found out that David Jefferson, the leader of the two, had been acting without authorization. The rape wasn't sanctioned. He'd been disloyal to all of us. I was ordered to find him. That night I was at a fundraiser that he'd been expected to attend. Laura Kendall was also present, a guest of her parents."

"Laura Kendall? The woman who was raped by members of your organization?"

"Yes. Bobby Donahue, our pastor, was there as well, with his three-year-old son, Luke. We were all at the same table."

Names were dropping like flies. Disturbing, venomous, monster flies.

Hannah sat, stunned, as she listened.

"Jefferson's name had been taken off the attendance list, but he was there and Luke was kidnapped."

"What happened next?"

"I went after him. But he hadn't taken Luke. He had Laura Kendall, grabbed her while she was on her way to the bathroom. He believed Laura was pregnant with his child."

"Did you arrest him this time?"

"Before I could catch him, he'd been killed by the other rapist, Tony Littleton. When he wasn't in college in Tucson, Tony lived with Bobby Donahue, was like a kid brother to him. I knew Bobby would want me to leave Tony for him to deal with, but I came upon him just as he was starting to rape Laura and couldn't let him do it a second time. Especially when I knew that he wasn't acting on orders."

"Bobby's orders." Keith's gaze was shrewd. He was leaving no stone unturned.

And was putting himself, another member of the justice system, in danger of Ivory Nation retribution far more than Hannah had. He was putting justice before the protection of the leader. The defense attorney rose several notches in Hannah's estimation.

Unless, of course, he was playing a part in a twisted plan, too.

"Yes, Bobby's orders. He never would've sanctioned a cold-blooded rape like that. Bobby Donahue has a heart. He does a lot of good work."

"So you stopped Littleton. Arrested him."

"I attempted to, but he pulled a gun on Laura, so I drew my weapon and shot him. He was hit in the chest but somehow managed to run. I followed him. And was there to catch him when he finally fell to his death."

"You killed Bobby Donahue's protégé."

"Yes."

"You saved Laura Kendall, who'd been raped by two of Bobby's men, but without Bobby's orders."

"Yes."

"Laura Kendall, whose parents were with Bobby at the fund-raiser."

"That's right."

"So Bobby Donahue and Laura Kendall's parents are associated?"

"Laura's parents have been donating to Bobby's causes for several years."

"To his church?"

"No."

"To what?"

Miller didn't show any emotion at all as he hesitated, his eyes still locked on Keith's.

"Bobby is involved in many charitable works. He's a tireless worker, a believer in God. He'd sacrifice himself on a cross if he thought God wanted him to do so."

"What cause of Donahue's do Laura Kendall's parents contribute to?"

Miller hesitated again. Looked down. "To the political campaign of Senator George Moss."

Moss was Ivory Nation? They'd reached that far up the ruling chain of the state of Arizona?

Sick to her stomach, Hannah wanted to lay down her aching head and float away.

For as long as it took.

God told him to wear slacks and a long-sleeve dress shirt. No tie. And to stay out of sight.

And Bobby Donahue always did as he was told. He'd long since known that his life was not his own.

He was on earth, not to find himself, but to help God find His people. To save His people.

Even if that meant hiding in a closet in a jury room, barely able to hear the proceedings going on in the adjoining courtroom. Some might consider the position humiliating.

Bobby knew his calling was an honor. He was set apart from other men. He'd known that from the time he was a very small boy.

The darkness, the cramped space, even the tall metal easel digging into his rib, didn't bother Bobby as the hearing progressed. Robert Miller, God bless his soul, performed perfectly.

He especially liked the part about the ring.

"Is this the ring that Bobby Donahue was wearing the night he beat Camargo Cortes with his fist?" he heard the attorney ask.

"Yes."

Picturing every intricate detail of the ring, every groove and scratch, the settings of sparkling emeralds in a twist of his and Amanda's initials, Bobby squeezed his fly and started to rub.

"How did it come to be in your possession?"

I earned the right to wear it for a week. Bobby mouthed the words as his compatriot recited them for the judge.

"Earned it how?"

I impregnated one of the single sisters so that she could help to populate God's world with pure, chosen people.

As though singing a well-known song, Bobby spoke in unison with the witness in the next room.

Robert Miller was a good man. He'd faltered, killing Tony. But he'd just won his way back into God's graces.

Something everyone should do before dying.

Getting harder, Bobby tended to himself inside the dark closet. He wouldn't orgasm. But he could show a little love.

And when Montgomery made her ruling, setting Kenny Hill free to be loyal to the Ivory Nation for the rest of his life—Bobby wept.

Kenny's voice shook as he told the judge he understood her warnings to walk the straight and narrow. His "yes, ma'am," was properly respectful when she told him she didn't want to see him back in court again.

And then, just before court was adjourned, Bobby carefully left the closet door, moved silently to the far wall, watched for the raised hand that would tell him the inmates' passageway was clear, and slipped away to wait.

The five dead babies were male. They were Hispanic. Four of them, all except Carlos Montgomery, were patients he'd initially treated at the free clinic where he volunteered—and then added them to his regular caseload, still treating them at no charge.

And that was a crime? Caring enough to provide services free?

Brian sat at his desk early Wednesday morning, going over his notes from the night before. There was something there. Something he was missing.

He'd been in at dawn, personally checking his inoculation supplies. There was no evidence of interference. And when eight o'clock came and he knew the managing director of the company that provided his medications would be at his desk, Brian placed a nonsocial call to the man who'd been the best man in his wedding.

Barely bothering with hellos, he named the product in question, the series of newborn injections.

"Tell me you haven't had any notice about complications, Bruce," he demanded.

"Of course we haven't! Why, what's up? Is there a problem I need to know about?" His friend's tone was serious. And concerned.

"I'm telling you, Bruce, if you've had problems and didn't let me know, I'll take you to the Supreme Court and see that you never do business again," Brian said.

"Brian, what's wrong?" Bruce's tone lacked defensiveness. He sounded more concerned about his friend's state of mind than anything else.

And that's when Brian came back to reality. Came out of the fear-induced fog the night had produced.

"Nothing, I hope," he replied. And with a tired sigh, told his friend about the five infant deaths he'd had in his practice during the past year. Told him about the *Sun News* article. Detective Angelo. Bruce asked a lot of questions. The two men discussed angles. And came up with nothing new.

"Let me know if there's anything I can do," Bruce offered as they hung up. "A character reference, chemical analysis, whatever you need."

Bruce knew he hadn't done anything. The reassurance calmed Brian.

Maybe he was looking at this all wrong. Maybe the one out to get him was an aggrieved parent who *didn't* get free treatment—perhaps the child had died and this parent blamed Brian for a perceived lack of care.

But he hadn't lost any other patients in the past year.

So maybe it was someone from the clinic, a patient of one of the other doctors, who'd heard that Brian sometimes took his patients with him.

Word traveled fast in those circles.

And then a realization hit him with resounding force. There was another element common to those infants. Something that wouldn't be found in the babies' charts, but something he knew. Four of those dead baby boys were illegals.

The knowledge, and the possible ramifications, stopped him cold.

On Friday, the 19th of September, Bobby Donahue was arrested. And on Monday the 22nd, an Arizona grand jury indicted him on twelve counts, including first-degree murder. The state was going for the death penalty.

Hannah had spent three of the five nights between Kenny Hill's final hearing and the indictment of the Ivory Nation leader in bed with William Horne. A toothbrush and disposable razor decorated the once-bare shelf of her second medicine cabinet, next to the

second sink in her bathroom. The one that, hereto-
fore, had boasted a silk houseplant.

On Tuesday the 23rd, she arrived at work half an
hour early as usual. Susan was there early, too. Also
as usual. Hannah didn't blink unless Susan knew
about it. The thought generally comforted Hannah.

"Judge Horne hasn't called for the last few mornings," the young woman said from her desk as Hannah reached for the robe she kept hanging in the
small closet just inside her door. "Is he out of town?"

On occasion Susan's inquisitiveness irritated her.

"No."

"Oh."

"We're still friends, Susan," was all Hannah
would say to the unspoken question.

With what appeared to be a concerned frown, but
could also have been a mask for hurt feelings, her JA
said, "Your calendar for the rest of the week is on
your desk. Pay particular attention to tomorrow
morning," and left.

At which time, robe half on, Hannah walked over
to her desk to check it.

And sat.

Shit.

It couldn't be. It just couldn't be.

She'd been assigned the Donahue case.

On the way home that evening, Hannah continued
to hear the words that had been repeating themselves
in her brain all day. *Pay particular attention to
tomorrow morning.*

Bobby Donahue's arraignment was set for eight-thirty.

Hannah had been in denial, certain there'd been an error, until late this afternoon when Susan once again stopped in her office to confirm the next morning's calendar. Donahue was still first on the list.

Because she still hoped a miracle would happen—that she'd be recused in the morning—Hannah didn't even tell Brian about the case when he phoned to check up on her and Taybee.

"Is William staying with you?" he asked. There was a new distance between them these days—put there by him or by her she wasn't sure. Maybe by both. Life was changing.

Still she missed him.

"He's not moving in."

Which wasn't what Brian had asked.

"Cynthia and Joseph are at a counseling session with three other mothers and four-year-olds this evening," he said. "I'm stopping for some wings and wondered if you wanted to join me." He named one of their favorite haunts from their college days.

She wanted to go. Badly. It seemed more like years than the six weeks it had been since she'd done any SIDS work with Brian.

"I can't," she said, knowing it was best, though she didn't delve into why that would be. Brian had Cynthia now. She had William. "William's picking up Chinese and meeting me at the house."

Which meant he'd be spending the night. And wanting sex.

Tonight, Hannah wanted neither.

And needed both—company and a release of tension.

They were still at the stage of being more hungry than nonchalant, and shortly after dinner—and the one glass of wine Hannah allowed herself to try to relax—she and William were in the bedroom. His hands were planted firmly on her hips, pushing her against his hardness.

"Ah, what you do to me, woman." His hoarse confession was sweet. And she wished she was head over heels in love with him. That she'd felt anything akin to passion since Jason.

Her affection for Brian didn't count, not in that way. They didn't think of each other like that. Cara's memory was always there with them.

Concentrating on William's pleasure she unbuttoned his shirt, running her hands over his chest, flicking his nipples.

"You're the most generous lover I've ever had." She gave him total honesty—with what she gave him. "You make it easy to please you."

"Just being with you, seeing you, touching you, pleases me," he said. The sincerity in his voice brought a wave of fondness so powerful, it carried Hannah through the next half hour, undressing her lover, being undressed. And bedded.

William's entry was a little rough, but the action was so obviously heart-felt Hannah met him thrust for thrust, and prayed that some day, if their relationship continued, she'd experience the same amount of pleasure that she apparently gave. The amount of pleasure William was trying hard to give her.

"I'm not going without you." He half panted the words, but stilled inside her. He'd been about to come. She'd already learned his signals.

"It's okay," she told him, needing him satisfied.

Resting his weight beside her, his body still connected to hers, he looked her in the eye. "No, it isn't," he said. "If you can't get there, then we'll wait."

He was a good man. Some days she was sure she must love him. "I can get there," she told him, hoping she wouldn't have to fake it, but knowing that she would do that, rather than leave him feeling as though he wasn't enough.

As it was, she found space in her tired and frantic brain to reach a small release. And as much as she welcomed the respite from the tension that had been gripping her all day, she welcomed the arms that held her afterward more.

"I'm sorry we waited this long to make love." William's voice was soft as he leaned against the pillows cradling her to him.

Another thing she liked about William—he talked afterward. Any lover she'd ever had other than Jason—not that there'd been many—had fallen immediately asleep after orgasm, leaving Hannah alone in the dark.

"Why did we?" she asked, curious—and needing the distraction from her thoughts, as well.

"I didn't think you were interested."

She hadn't either.

And maybe she hadn't been.

Was she now?

Pushing away the question, Hannah forced herself not to move away from him. She'd been alone too long, guarded her private space too closely. Unless she wanted to be alone forever—and these past weeks had shown her she didn't—she had some work to do.

Opening up.

Letting people in.

14

"Rough day?" William asked, several lethargic moments later.

She knew what William would say if she told him about the news Susan had brought her. And she didn't want to hear it. She was nervous enough as it was.

But he was lying naked in her bed—at her invitation. She was starting to think about a more permanent relationship with him. She had to be able to talk to him.

She had to quit hiding.

"You're not going to believe this…." She tried for lightness. Nonchalance.

He hugged her a little closer. "What?"

"I got the Donahue case."

If it was possible for blood to freeze in a still-living body, if it was possible for a person being touched by those fingers to feel that chill, it happened right then. Everything about William stopped.

"That's impossible."

"That's what I said." Over and over again, all day long. Cases were randomly assigned on a first-come, first-served basis among the thirty criminal judges on the list. The statistical odds of her drawing this particular case were slim. "I had Susan do some checking and I am definitely the judge named."

"They'll recuse you."

"Keith has the case. He didn't. We're set for arraignment tomorrow morning." The state wasn't wasting money on settlement conferences—they weren't going to offer any kind of plea bargain. The Ivory Nation leader had to enter his plea straight up. "Not guilty" was a no-brainer. There was no way Donahue would skip a trial and proceed straight to sentencing with a guilty plea.

Letting her go, William sat up. And then stood, pulling on the slacks he'd worn to work, fastening the fly over a belly that wasn't quite as flat as it had been in law school—but was still more toned than most men his age.

"Then you have to recuse yourself."

"I do not." Hannah thought about getting up, too. About making herself less vulnerable.

"Hannah," he turned, his expression a curious mix of power and vulnerability. "You're crazy if you think they'll leave you alone on this one. These guys are insane. And have more power than God. Hell, Donahue thinks he's the Christ. He really believes that he walks hand in hand with the almighty. That they converse on a regular basis. But his god directs him to intimidate with fear, to manipulate, brainwash, even kill people when he deems the situation warrants it. If you don't get out, you'll be next."

"I'm not going to let some bully run me off the playground," she said, certain of that at least. "Someone has to sit on this trial. Why am I so special that I can't face the possible danger but someone else can? Who will it be—Dean? Or Whittier? Are their lives less precious than mine?"

"Donahue and his clan have it in for you."

"They shouldn't have. I let Hill go."

"You don't honestly believe Miller just waltzed in out of the goodness of his heart," William said, facing her at the end of the bed. "That was all orchestrated to get Hill off. This is Donahue, Hannah. I'm telling you, you don't want to mess with him."

"I don't intend to. I'm going to do my job. Period."

He sat on the side of the bed, taking her hand. "And that's the problem," he said, his voice softer now, cajoling. "You're black and white, Hannah. You won't slide, or use common sense when it's time to turn a blind eye. We all know this guy's guilty, but if you facilitate a conviction, your life is as good as over."

"They aren't that powerful, Will. I still believe in our justice system. And in our law enforcement."

"Everyone knows they have cops on the inside."

"So we're supposed to let them take control of our world? Let them scare us into submission? What then, Will? Does Donahue become the next Hitler? Do we find pockets of concentration camps throughout our cities? Piles of dead bodies along our roads?"

He stood again. Swore. Grabbed his shirt and slid into it, leaving it hanging open. "I can't believe you're doing this."

"I'm doing my job. Nothing more."

"You've just come off an Ivory Nation case," he reminded her. "No one would think any less of you if you passed on this one."

"I would." And that mattered far more than William seemed to understand. "My life isn't worth saving just so I can continue to eat and breathe, Will," she explained. "It's only worth the contributions I can make to ensure a better world."

Jason had taught her that. He'd seen something in Hannah that a life of abandonment and foster care hadn't ever shown her. And he'd made certain that she saw it, too. That she never let go.

"Stop this, Hannah. Take a vacation. God knows you've accrued enough time. You're still grieving for Carlos. No one would question it if you took some leave."

"I don't want to take a vacation," she said, starting to get angry with him. Weren't friends, lovers, supposed to offer support?

So why were hers hell-bent on tearing her down? Making her feel weak?

"Then think of me," he said, buttoning his shirt as his voice became more tender. "I love you, Hannah. Did you ever consider that? How do you think it makes me feel to know that the woman I love is putting her life in danger?"

He'd never said he loved her before.

"William, please." Her voice softened. She wanted to tell him she loved him, too, but at the hard look on his face the words stuck in her throat.

"They'll kill you, Hannah. You have to get out of this."

They weren't going to kill her. "As far as I know, there have only ever been two incidents of judges being targets of violence. Once in Chicago and once in Atlanta. Only two, William."

"We live in a different world now, Hannah. A world where anything goes. You have to get off this case."

Hannah wasn't sure she liked this sudden display of ownership. Not when William seemed intent on talking her out of doing something she knew was right.

"Not only is quitting wrong on many levels," she said, pulling on her robe as she faced him. "Showing them I'm intimidated would be more dangerous than taking them on. I'd be off that case but they'd know they had me. They'd exploit my fear and start blackmailing me for favours in the system. It's happened before."

"I can't believe you don't see the danger here! You're a smart woman, Hannah. Open your eyes."

Who said she didn't see? She was scared to death.

"My eyes *are* open. I have their attention now, Will. And I have two choices. I either show them my fear and risk having them use that to get what they need from me, or I stand up to them and risk the retribution. The first way, I get hurt for sure. The second one, I have a chance. And more importantly, I have my self-respect. I have a job to do and I'm going to do it to the best of my ability," she said. "It's all I know. It's who I am."

If she'd run from danger, she'd never have lived—never have had the love of her life. Or become the woman she was. A woman she could love. And live with.

If she'd run, she'd never have known Jason.

He'd shown her long ago that facing death wasn't nearly as frightening as being alive without fully living.

Somehow she'd forgotten that. She'd allowed Carlos's death to shut her down again.

In a twisted way, she owed Bobby Donahue and his brainwashed cronies her gratitude. They'd brought her back to the woman Jason had loved.

The only woman she wanted to be.

On Wednesday, September 24th, at 3:05 a.m., Crispin Garza died in his sleep. He was eleven weeks old. Hispanic. Seen at the free clinic. The son of illegals.

His attending physician was Dr. Brian Hampton.

"Dr. Hampton?" Brian turned toward the voice calling him as he left the building Wednesday night, not surprised to see Detective Angelo getting out of the only other car in the parking lot. He'd pulled up too close to Brian's Jag to be polite.

"What is it, Detective?" he said, too tired to deal

with the investigator's overzealousness. "If you're looking for Crispin's records, I've already sent them to the medical examiner's office."

Along with a piece of his soul.

That was the sixth baby he'd lost this year. The sixth grieving family who would never completely recover from tragedy.

And now, even Brian was convinced something was horribly wrong. There was no way six infant deaths in one year was a coincidence. Or natural tragedy.

Someone was murdering male Hispanic babies.

And Brian had no idea who. Or how. Or why.

"I don't need the records, Dr. Hampton," Angelo said briefly in an expressionless tone that set Brian's senses on edge. "I'm sorry, sir, but I need to ask you to come with me."

"What?" Keys in hand, Brian moved toward his car. Sanity. Home. Eventually. "If you need me at the station, I'll follow you down." He'd be stupid not to cooperate with the police, no matter how misled this particular officer appeared to be.

Angelo's grip on Brian's forearm was his first real warning. "You'll need to leave your car here, Dr. Hampton. You're under arrest for the murder of Crispin Garza."

"Wh…?" Brian's words caught in a throat gone dry. Shaking his head, he stared at the detective, only partially aware that a second man had exited the unmarked car he'd seen pulling in as he'd come outside. "We'd like to do this without making a scene," Angelo said. "If you'll come quietly, I won't handcuff you."

They were wrong. He couldn't possibly have killed that baby. He'd been working all afternoon.

"Dr. Hampton?" The pressure on his arm increased, and stunned, Brian got into the back of the car before they roped him up like an animal.

As soon as he was in the car, the cuffs came out anyway. And the second officer, whose name Brian didn't catch, slid in beside him and read him his rights.

He didn't even have a chance to relock the Jag before they were spinning out of the parking lot and heading down to the station.

It was one of the longest rides of Brian's life.

They booked him. Without so much as an hour in interrogation, they escorted Brian to a backroom facility, made him strip. Shower in an open room with no doors. No privacy. Put on elastic-waistband pants and a pullover short-sleeve top that looked as though they'd been through a world war and felt about as good.

"What about my phone call?" he asked the junior officer who was shepherding him through the humiliating process. Or was it only on television that a guy had that right?

Oh God, this couldn't be happening to him. He was no criminal. "I don't even jaywalk." Embarrassed that he was panicking, that the tight-lipped and heavily armed kid with him could see that and was ignoring his distress, Brian shut up.

And made a decision. Whatever happened to him, he'd take it like a man.

Once dressed, his feet clad in something akin to the paper sandals he'd worn during his stint in surgery during his residency, Brian was escorted, hands back in the cuffs, up the hall and shown into another room—not the cell he'd expected. The place looked more like an examination room.

And within minutes he knew why.

Knew, too, he would never be the same again.

An officer of the law had just forced him to suffer the indignity of having a finger shoved up his backside.

They had to make certain, he was told, that he hadn't smuggled any contraband in with him.

For the first time since Cara's death, Brian felt the urge to cry.

And he had a sickening suspicion that it was only beginning.

Hannah had been home over an hour—alone, as William had taken Francis to a Phoenix Suns basketball game and back to his house for the night—when her cell phone rang.

Recognizing the exchange as an official city number, she picked up right away.

"Help me."

"Brian?" Heart pounding, she leaned against the kitchen counter. "What's going on?"

"I need a criminal lawyer. The best one you know. I don't care how expensive. I need him now. Tonight."

"Talk to me. Where are you?"

"I'm in jail. Booking photo, handcuffs, the whole thing. I refused to talk to anyone without a lawyer. And I need out. Immediately." His words were succinct, with none of the usual tenderness she associated with Brian.

"Slow down," she said, rubbing her head as she assimilated the information. Brian? In jail? "Tell me what happened."

"They came to the office, arrested me, booked me and here I am. I need a lawyer, Hannah. Get me the best. And do it fast."

His plea sounded forced. She could hardly believe it was Brian talking. This wasn't the man she knew.

"What are the charges?"

"Murder."

"What? Murder? Who? Oh my God, Brian, what's going on?"

"One of my patients died today. They say I did it. I don't have a lot of time, Hannah. Just get me an attorney. Okay?"

The last word sounded more like her friend. It was enough to fire up Hannah's determination.

"Consider it done."

After finding out which of Maricopa County's six facilities they'd taken Brian to and promising she'd have him out that night, Hannah said, "Don't answer any questions until you've got a lawyer there." She was dialing from her home phone even before she'd hung up the cell.

"Thanks, Hannah," he said as the other line started to ring through. "And can you please call Cynthia?"

Agreeing to do so, Hannah ended the call just as the woman who was slated to be Arizona's second woman governor picked up. Tanya Clarion might be the most expensive defense attorney in the state, but she was also the best.

If anyone could have Brian home in his own bed by midnight, it would be her.

Sitting in the cell he had to himself, Bobby Donahue watched as the prominent-looking, clean-cut man was escorted down the hallway to another vacant cell, complete with bare cot and…nothing.

Only moments before, God had brought Bobby word via an earthly angel that the doctor was in the house.

He'd lived an easy life, this Dr. Hampton. Drove a Jag. Lived behind a gate on a hill. He was the worst kind of white man, as far as Bobby was concerned. He shoveled out money instead of taking action. Paid people off, and then turned around and served the other side. He kept up appearances, gave the impression of being a light worker, and then hid in his mansion and left God's real work to men like Bobby and his loyal brothers.

Brothers who didn't play both sides.

They'd see how Hampton liked living behind another gate for a while. A gate with no remote controls, no codes to type. Only a key hanging on a ring held by a man who didn't like pretty white boys who showed loyalty to the cause and then ignored their duty to keep God's earth pure. Hampton used his

God-given talents on children of the lesser race. Dirty children. Keeping them alive. Healthy. Raising them to shed the blood of God's chosen.

And now this...

If he thought killing six babies and then pretending he hadn't was suddenly going to endear him to God, to the brotherhood, he was grossly mistaken. Killing infants didn't serve the cause anymore than preserving their lives did. Babies of all races caught at the hearts of men. Dirty baby prevention was the key. Untreated natural health issues was the key. Not baby murders.

Many used their medical skills as Hampton did— caring for nonwhites. Most were ignorant. Hampton wasn't. He'd lost his wife to one of *them*. He supported the cause. He was a traitor.

If he thought he could get away with taking care of the dirty races and then keep himself in God's good graces by wiping out a few Hispanic babies, while continuing to care for those who made them, he was far more stupid than Bobby had thought.

The man should be killed.

But Bobby wasn't sure if the victory would be worth the risk. Now wasn't the time to draw attention.

God would tell him what to do. He'd just wait and see what the Good Lord had in mind for him. And for the sinner doctor.

In the meantime, what a pleasant pastime—at the end of a day that had bored him to hell—to imagine pleasing God.

In whatever fashion his Heavenly Father required.

15

Hannah tried to stay out of it, to let Tanya do her job, trusting that she'd do it well. She tried to stay home. Wait for the phone call to pick Brian up when he was released. Her presence at a local precinct would be topic for conversation.

She avoided conversation at all costs.

Bobby Donahue was in prison because of her. At least indirectly. She had to watch her back. Not drive on the streets of downtown Phoenix alone after dark.

Or walk them, either, she added to her silent narrative as she pulled into a parking space much farther away than she'd have liked, thanks to the Suns game in high gear a few blocks away.

Walking briskly with her head high and her hand on the mace in her pocket, Hannah **breat**hed a sigh of relief as she reached the door of the Fourth Avenue jail.

"Judge! I didn't expect to see you here." Tanya, looking fresh in her dark slacks, blouse and jacket, greeted Hannah as she exited a conference room. It was after nine.

"What's going on?" Hannah asked, nodding toward the hallway Tanya had left.

"They're planning to go to the grand jury for a first-degree murder indictment on up to as many as six counts."

Openmouthed, Hannah stared. There was just no way…

And because there was no way it could be true, no way this could be real, no way she could ever believe Brian was a murderer, she focused on practical matters.

"Planning to go. He hasn't been formally charged?"

Tanya shook her head. "True to form Angelo was a bit too aggressive. He hasn't said, but it's pretty clear that he had Brian pegged as one he could intimidate into a confession. While he probably has enough to get the state to indict, he's not nearly solid enough for a capital case. Too much is circumstantial. He put Brian through all the hoopla to scare him into baring his soul."

Angelo. Hannah knew the name. And the detective was good. While too rash, too fond of following his own rules instead of city or county code, he generally came through in the end. As detectives went he was smart, dedicated and had an instinct that could compete with that of any fictional detective.

"Has Brian said anything?"

"Yeah. He didn't do it."

Frowning, her arms wrapped around her middle, Hannah asked, "So what's Angelo's beef?"

"He says Brian killed at least six babies."

"How? Brian wouldn't do that."

"By putting HGH into their vaccinations. Brian has had seventy-five percent more patients die of SIDS this year than any other doctor in Phoenix. All boys. And all had just been vaccinated."

A vision of an empty nursery flashed before her mind's eye. A door in her home that couldn't be opened.

Oh, God, Carlos was one of those vaccinated babies. But…

"They do autopsies of SIDS babies. They'd have known if…"

Tanya shook her head. "Because HGH is a natural hormone produced by the pituitary gland, it doesn't show up with normal testing. They'd have had to look for it specifically to have found it."

"So they have no proof that that's how these… babies…died." Six of them. It was beyond comprehension. And too painful to accept.

Five other mothers, suffering as she had. As she still did.

"Angelo has been investigating Brian since the *Sun News* article." Tanya's next words were a complete surprise to Hannah.

Poor Brian. He must have been shocked when he heard about Angelo's activities. He'd dismissed that article, certain nothing would come of it.

"Investigating him how?" she asked. "Interviewing those who knew him? Or families of victims?" Then why hadn't Angelo talked to her?

Surely, if this were legitimate…

"He subpoenaed Brian's medical records."

Her son's records? Brian would have told her about that.

"How'd he get them without Brian knowing?"

"Brian knew. He handed them over. Angelo has questioned him a couple of times over the past few weeks."

Gray. All Hannah could see was gray. Gray walls. Gray floors. Even the defense attorney's face had turned gray.

"But those records wouldn't prove anything," she said, hanging on in the midst of the cacophony in her mind. Brian knew? He'd been interrogated? More than once?

Why hadn't he told her?

Especially since it concerned Carlos.

He would have told her.

Unless…

"No, but when Angelo noticed that all six infants had been inoculated just before their deaths he started checking into possible added substances that wouldn't show up on a normal autopsy. HGH was the most obvious. Yesterday, another baby boy died. Crispin Garza. He was a patient of Brian's. He'd been in for a shot on Tuesday. Angelo got an order for HGH testing in the autopsy and it was positive. In lethal amounts."

No!

Shaking her head, Hannah stepped back.

"That doesn't mean Brian did it."

"No, and this is where the evidence is too circumstantial for capital charges—and, I'm certain, why Angelo acted so brashly today. Brian administered all of the shots himself."

He always did. That was no crime.

"And he's the only one with a motive," Tanya continued.

"Which is?"

"Revenge for his wife's death."

"What does Cara have to do with this? And why, after ten years, would he suddenly be avenging her? That doesn't even make sense. He has a real girlfriend for the first time since Cara died."

"His quest for revenge isn't new." Tanya's look was sympathetic.

The attorney pitied *her?*

"Tell me what you've heard," Hannah said, a lifetime of emotional walls sliding into place.

"I'm assuming you know about the rallies he attended...."

"Of course." The *Sun News* had mentioned them, too. Surely Tanya wasn't buying into that old crap. "That was a long time ago. His wife was killed by an illegal immigrant who hadn't been able to take a driver's test or get a license. He wanted stricter border laws. But it's not like he's done anything since."

"He's almost broke, Hannah. He just applied for a second mortgage on his home."

"Brian? What are you talking about?"

"He's been supporting any and every political

move in the past ten years aimed at strengthening the border and deporting illegals. I have a long list of campaigns he's contributed to."

He'd never said a word.

Brian was in financial trouble? She'd never have guessed. A man would have to be at least a little bit emotionally unbalanced to give away his financial security in support of a cause, wouldn't he? Donating was normal—but surely not this much.

"Most recently, he gave more than a quarter million dollars to help elect Senator George Moss."

A quarter of a million dollars? To Bobby Donahue's senator?

Cold to the bone, Hannah didn't react. Didn't betray that the name meant anything to her.

"It doesn't look good," Tanya said. "Except for Carlos… I'm, sorry, Hannah, I know this has to be hard for you…."

"No…go on. Brian's my friend. I need to know."

After a pause, Tanya said, "All of the other babies were illegals. And Brian brought all five of them to his office from the free clinic. He treated all of them free of charge."

Sick, head pounding, Hannah couldn't think.

"However, they've found no trace of HGH in Brian's office, no record of it in any of his paperwork, nor in his suppliers' invoices. There's nothing to link the drug to him. The deaths were all ruled SIDS except for today's and it's not illegal to have given a vaccine to a child that died of HGH overdose."

"Then it sounds as though they don't have enough to hold him, if the state isn't ready to press charges."

"That's what I said. I'm waiting to hear, but I think he'll be released within the hour."

"I'll wait."

She was standing. Breathing. Carrying on. While her mind silently screamed two questions over and over. Louder and louder.

Was Carlos murdered?

Was Brian in with the Ivory Nation?

The questions reverberated until she was going crazy with the sound.

Nothing had ever looked more beautiful to Brian than Hannah Montgomery did when she walked down the hall of the Fourth Avenue jail just before eleven Wednesday night. She was tired and wrinkled. Her hair had lost its bounce and her makeup had long since worn off.

She wasn't smiling.

"You ready?" she said, stopping a couple of feet in front of him when he'd expected to feel her arms around him, returning a sense of rightness to the world.

"Yes." The single word stood in for all of the thoughts pounding at his brain. The questions he had to ask.

First, what was wrong with her? Followed quickly by what was in store for him? What were the cops going to do and how could he protect himself? How did he prove his innocence?

Falling into step beside her, Brian had to resist the urge to hold on to her arm—ostensibly to assist her, protect her as they walked out into the rough downtown neighborhood. And also to hold himself upright.

It hadn't been an easy night.

One thing he knew for sure. He couldn't wait around for the state to be unable to prove his guilt. His life would be in shambles. Not to mention what might become of his body if he'd stayed much longer in the godforsaken place he was leaving behind.

The looks he'd received, the catcalls as he'd been escorted out of his cell only moments after being locked up—shown to the interrogation room he'd expected to see when he arrived—had left him no doubt that he looked like dinner to someone. And breakfast and lunch, too.

It was an image he wasn't going to get over soon. If ever.

"You shouldn't have come down here alone. Not at night."

"I couldn't sit at home. And if things hadn't gone smoothly I might've been able to throw my weight around. If nothing else, I'd know who to call and have the clout to get the calls made."

There was no sound of braggadocio in her voice. No inkling that she was impressed by herself.

It was simply fact.

"Still, I hate to think of you walking by your-self—"

"Unless I was followed, no one would expect to

find me here, which made me anonymous. And if I was being followed, it wouldn't matter where I'd gone. They'd get me at some point. As you see, I made it just fine."

As she always did. Why that irritated Brian, he had no idea. Perhaps because he was the man, she was doing the rescuing and at the moment, he felt so damned weak.

Needy.

"Any woman down here alone isn't safe," he insisted when he should have shut his mouth and let her lead his grateful ass. "But at least your godforsaken trial's over. And that you gave them what they wanted."

"I upheld justice," she said, staring straight ahead. She hadn't looked at him since he'd come down the hall toward her. "And that's all old news anyway. I drew the Bobby Donahue case."

Stumbling, Brian hoped he hadn't heard her correctly, and knew by the resolute set of her chin that he had.

She tried to stay closed to him. To remember what she'd heard about him, not who she knew him to be.

"Looks like the Suns game got out." Groups of casually dressed people were slowly filtering into the area.

Distracting herself from the man at her side, Hannah scanned the pedestrians for William. Or for any father and son walking alone together.

"You didn't just say you're doing Bobby Donahue's trial."

"If it goes to trial."

"Which it will."

His usual astuteness where her job was concerned no longer disarmed her as much. If he was in with Donahue, he'd know the intricacies as well as she did.

They'd reached the Lexus, parked under the streetlamp where she'd left it. Pushing the remote opener, Hannah let him in, while climbing in on her side. She started the engine, which automatically locked the doors. Then dropped her hands into her lap.

"Tell me what's going on, Brian."

"I wish to God I knew."

She turned, peering at him with help from the light coming in through the window, trying hard not to feel betrayed. Had her son been murdered?

Had her friend known?

Did he know Bobby Donahue, too?

She couldn't even consider that Brian had murdered her son. And more. At the behest of a madman.

That would make Brian a madman, too.

She tried not to feel anything as she searched for the magic words that would make this all go away.

"Tell me everything. For real."

Frowning, he stared back at her. "What does that mean?"

"What have you done?" Had he been so blinded by grief that he'd lost sight of reality enough to get himself into financial trouble? If that was all, she could listen to his explanation. If that was all, she could help him.

"I've done nothing."

The Minnie Mouse tie he was wearing brought tears to her eyes.

"Were those vaccinations tainted?"

"If they were, it wasn't by me. I was on the phone with Bruce Browning last week and…" His words faded away. He was watching her still, but more warily, defensively, than openly. "You think I did it."

"I can't believe that," she admitted, tears in her eyes. "Over the past hour, I've tried to step back and look at the facts as though I was hearing them in court, but I can't see beyond the man I know you to be."

To see a man that might exist, but behind her back?

"So what's the problem?"

"Why didn't you tell me you were financially supporting illegal-alien legislation? Or that five of those babies were illegals? Or that you brought all of them to your office from the free clinic? Why didn't you tell me Angelo has been investigating you for weeks? Why didn't you tell me you're an Ivory Nation supporter?" Every time she thought of that her heart missed a beat. "My God, Brian, I'm your best friend! You know how scared I've been and all along you—"

His face was suddenly hard, his eyes pinning her with a stare. "What do you mean, I'm an Ivory Nation supporter?"

He would never have hurt her. Not Brian.

Would he?

William would be home soon. He'd call. She wouldn't answer. And he'd want to know why.

What was she going to tell him?

"George Moss has ties to Donahue."

"To Bobby Donahue." His flat tone said far more than his words. As did the sudden ashen hue to his face. And the way his jaw hung limply.

He appeared as though the entire world had gone mad and he was left with nothing to hold on to.

"My wife died at the hands of an illegal immigrant," he said, sounding like he was giving up rather than defending himself. "I can't bring her back, but I could give my money to changing a world that allowed her to die. Every election since she died, I've contributed to the campaigns of anyone who was in favor of stronger border laws. That's it. I don't even know most of them. Including George Moss."

The dread gripping her eased. It didn't go away. But it gave her hope. Dangerous hope. That sounded more like the Brian she knew. Throwing himself in with everything he had, not knowing all aspects of the situation.

He trusted far too much.

Or at least he had.

She never had. And she couldn't afford to be soft. Period. Evil lurked all around her.

Had Carlos been murdered?

Angelo seemed to think so.

And if her infant son had been murdered, why? Because of Brian?

She'd sentenced an Ivory Nation brother the week before Carlos died. Brian had known about that. He'd had access to her. He'd inoculated Carlos that week.

"You're telling me you've never met Bobby Donahue. Never met George Moss."

"Never."

"And you didn't know they were connected?"

"Absolutely not." His chin taut, he bit out the words.

She'd hurt him. Guilt wasn't going to distract her. "Why didn't you tell me Detective Angelo had been visiting you? Why didn't you tell me you were under suspicion? Most importantly, why didn't you let me know your records had been subpoenaed? They had to have substantial enough evidence to get that subpoena."

This was her territory. She issued subpoenas on a regular basis. She knew first hand what it took to get one.

"Angelo was an overzealous cop trying to use me, by way of the *Sun News* article, to climb the professional ladder. You were already under tremendous pressure. Why would I worry you with something I wasn't worried about myself? Especially when the man was spouting lies about Carlos. You've suffered enough."

"But he had to have more than just the *Sun News* stuff to get a subpoena."

"As far as I knew, he had suspicion. Period. Now, I'm not so sure. What if I'm being framed, Hannah? I want stronger border laws because I want those living here to do so legally, not because I hate Hispanics. But if Moss does have ties with Donahue, I don't know…I don't know what to think. I don't know how Angelo got the subpoena. But I'm guessing you could find out."

She could.

And, of course, because it was Brian, she would.

16

"Do you think Carlos was murdered?" Hannah asked.

She was driving, her face stark in the over-brightness of oncoming headlights, and then shadowed. Brian couldn't read her expression, but he knew she was struggling.

Hurting.

Just as he was. If he had to guess, he'd say they were both scared shitless.

And there was more.

Still reeling from his humiliating experience with Angelo, from the taste of incarceration—and the threat of a more permanent stay—Brian was having trouble ignoring the sting of knowing Hannah had doubted him. And an even harder time holding himself apart from her.

How had she become so connected to him that she had the ability to comfort even his darkest moments? That she was the one he instinctively turned to for support.

Why could he overlook her doubts, understand them enough to still feel better when he was with her than alone?

When had she come to mean so much?

Had it been over the years of communal gatherings, always with the two of them gravitating to each other, sharing a silent understanding of grief? Or over the past year, as they'd spent more time together on the SIDS outreach program, and grieving again.

Or back in college when they used to debate everything on the planet.

He hadn't answered her question about Carlos. "I don't know if he was or not," he finally said.

At the moment, he didn't seem to know much of anything.

Parking her car next to the Jag in front of his professional building, Hannah looked at him for the first time since she'd pulled out of the Fourth Avenue parking space.

"I'm sorry I doubted you."

He nodded. "I don't blame you," he said, accepting the truth of the words even if he couldn't feel it in his heart. "Angelo tells a convincing tale."

"Angelo's a good detective, Brian. One of the best. He has a tendency to skate a bit close to the edge, but if he says it, there's always some truth in it."

Her words added a new element to the fear coursing through him. "You're saying you still have doubts?" Pretty soon he was going to begin doubting himself.

Hannah shook her head. "The doubts were mostly because of those few key pieces of information you hadn't shared with me—things I would've thought you would."

He could understand that.

"But we can't dismiss Angelo's presence. I'm telling you Brian, the man doesn't strike unless he's onto something. And Crispin's death has already been ruled a homicide."

Was panic going to be a constant companion now?

"I didn't have anything to do with it, Hannah. I swear to you. I would never—*could* never—kill anyone, let alone a baby."

"I believe you." Her voice was soft, but sincere. Her compassion touched him as surely as if she'd reached out a hand.

"So how do they prove that the HGH they found in Crispin came from the vaccine?"

"The first thing they're going to do is check the product you have on hand. I'm sure, if you went up to your office, you'd find the door cordoned off with yellow tape. Right now it's a crime scene."

"I'll have to call Barbara in the morning and have her cancel my appointments for the rest of the week." Weary, Brian could see the writing on the wall. The ramifications came crashing down on him. "It's going to be in all the papers. And as soon as my patients' parents see that, they'll be leaving me in droves."

He'd done nothing wrong. But he was going to pay.

"Tanya's good, Brian. She'll prove your innocence."

But the doubts would already have been planted.

"I need to know why," he said, ashamed of the moisture in his eyes as he turned to Hannah. "Who's doing this to me? And why?"

"You really think you're being framed?"

"Don't you? If someone was out to hurt babies, why target one doctor?"

"Tanya's going to be looking at everyone in your life, searching for anyone new, changed, or anything different. She'll go over every move you've made over the past year, every bill you've paid, every patient you've seen. You're going to lose your privacy, but, God willing, you won't lose your freedom again."

Overcome by emotion he couldn't seem to push away, Brian stared at the building he'd been so proud to consider his professional home, thinking of all of the children he'd treated, the lives that had been protected, and then he nodded.

"Hey." Hannah's hand on his arm brought him back from the edge of an abyss that seemed too deep to survive. "We'll get you through this."

Exhausted, unable to find his usual strength, Brian soaked up the warmth of Hannah's touch, needing it to go on and on.

He covered her hand with his and said, simply, "Thank you." And then, "If Carlos *was* murdered, we'll find out who did it, and why."

As he saw the shocked, fearful, expression cross

Hannah's face, Brian suspected they'd both just been struck by the same thought.

"You were not the target, Hannah. You absolutely were not."

"I'd just finished an Ivory Nation case." She sounded ghostlike. "Earlier tonight when I thought you might've been involved with Donahue, I thought—but—" Her voice dropped to a whisper. The look of horror in her eyes increased. "Oh God, Brian! What if I'm the reason my son died? What if this is me, not you? What if they're going after you because of me? What if I caused this?"

"No." Reaching over the console Brian took her hands in his. Her fingers were icy cold. "Stop right there." Somehow he found the ability to be firm. "Carlos was one of six," he reminded her. "If you were the target, they wouldn't have hurt the others."

His brain had been reeling all night with possible scenarios, searching for any enemies he might have made, for anything that could explain the nightmare his life had become.

"Unless they're using you to get to me. It's no secret that you're the closest friend I have in the world."

God, that sounded good. Even now.

"It seems like we're fairly convinced that there's a link between these deaths and the Ivory Nation."

His words hung, cold and scary, in the confined darkness.

Hannah's hands moved inside his, turned, until their fingers interlocked. "We'll figure it out," she

said, her gaze deep and unsure as she looked into
his eyes.

He wanted to believe her. Needed to believe her.
And needed her to believe, too.

"Try to get some rest, okay?" she said next.

Brian didn't want to leave her.

"Cynthia's waiting."

Dear sweet Cyn. He'd called her before leaving
the station. And forgotten all about her since. A testimony to his lost state of mind.

"I'll follow you home," he said, gathering himself
up as he opened the door of the Lexus.

"You don't—"

With a finger to her lips, Brian silenced her. And
envied that finger.

"Don't argue. I'm following you home. I won't rest
until I know you're inside safe and sound." His words
were maybe harsher than he'd intended. He needed to
break the intimacy that had developed around them.

He had to get their relationship back where it
belonged, with Hannah taking care of herself and
him watching from a distance.

Smart woman that she was, she didn't argue.

On Friday, the 26th of September, at four in the
afternoon, Susan once again appeared at Hannah's
door. The frown marring her brow matched the
anxiety in her eyes and the purse of her lips.

"What now?" Hannah asked her JA. They'd had
a quiet week. No trials. No courtroom drama.

Hannah had a headache. Had been counting the

minutes until she could go home. She was covering search-warrant duty for Donna down the hall and had to stay until five.

And then it was home to a soak in the tub followed by a lazy night in front of the television with Taybee purring on her chest.

The world could wait until Monday.

"I just heard the ring's missing."

"What ring?"

"The one taken in as evidence from that Tucson detective, Robert Miller."

"Who told you that?" Susan was the keeper of all court secrets. Probably because she could be trusted to keep them well.

"Martha was downstairs checking on some evidence for her judge when some cop came in asking for the ring." Martha, Donna Jasmine's JA.

"What cop?"

Shrugging, Susan dropped into one of the chairs in front of Hannah's massive desk. "Martha hadn't ever seen him before, but he was in uniform. City police, not a deputy."

"And she knows for sure the ring wasn't there?"

"Yes. She checked. I guess the clerk, Leslie, was kind of flustered. She's been having a really hard time at home. Her husband emptied their bank account and took off with his secretary, leaving her with three kids under four."

How Susan managed to know everyone who'd ever taken a breath in the East Mesa facility, Hannah couldn't imagine.

"Anyway, they think Leslie made a mistake after Kenny Hill's trial. She was covering for someone and had to give Kenny back his stuff and was also checking in the ring. She thinks she gave it to Kenny."

"Who else knows about this?"

"I don't know. The sheriff sent a deputy to find Kenny Hill."

And the chances of the Ivory Nation brother turning in key evidence against his pastor were less than Hannah's chances of living forever.

"I'm figuring if he did have it he'll have 'lost' it by now," Susan said, echoing Hannah's thoughts.

"We'll see."

Susan leaned forward, frowning again. "What'll this do to the trial? Bobby Donahue won't get to walk, will he?"

"The ring was important," Hannah said, circumspect as always. "But they've got Robert Miller's testimony. They can go to trial with that."

Smiling, showing a feigned lack of real concern, Hannah told Susan she could leave, and to have a good weekend. And then, cradling her aching head in her hands, she picked up the phone and called William.

"I'm afraid the Ivory Nation has someone working here in the courthouse," she said as soon as he picked up. He was in his car already, on his way to pick up Francis for what might be their last visit for a while.

They were due in court on Monday for a final

hearing on his ex-wife's request to have his visitation revoked.

"What makes you say that?" he asked slowly.

She told him about the ring. "I suppose it could've been an honest mistake," she said, playing her own devil's advocate. "I'm just uncomfortable with anything that seems even remotely coincidental right now."

"That's what these guys do to you, my dear," William sounded almost as tired as she felt. He'd stayed over again the night before, had been asleep by ten, and hadn't moved until the alarm went off at six.

And he'd been looking forward to his weekend with Francis.

"They rule by fear, chipping away at you until you start to second-guess everything. Until they've convinced you that they are all-powerful. And then they've got you."

He'd mentioned that before her first Ivory Nation trial. But she hadn't succumbed to it until now.

"I'm telling you, you have to recuse yourself, Hannah, before this gets the better of you."

"I'm not backing down, William." And she didn't want to talk about this again. "I'm fully capable of doing my job."

And if he didn't think so, then...

"I know you are." He sounded resigned. "And while the ring was good evidence, a visual that would help sway a jury, it's not crucial."

"No, they've got Miller's testimony and that's all they need."

"And he's in protective custody, right?"

"Yeah." She didn't remember telling William that, but, then, they'd been spending a lot of time together. There were a lot of things she didn't remember saying.

"You said, when you were talking about him, that his wife and kids are with him."

"Right." She remembered now. She'd told him about Miller when they'd been discussing Francis, and his ex-wife's claim that her son was unsafe when he was with his father.

"I'm getting nervous, Hannah," William said. "What if we're wrong? What if Molina takes away my right to see Francis?"

Uberto Molina, the Cochise County judge who'd been appointed to oversee William's custody case because it would be difficult to ensure impartiality from a Maricopa County judge, was someone neither of them had met.

"How many threats have there been against your family since you've been on the bench?"

"One."

"And how long ago was that?" She was repeating what they both already knew, not to tell him anything, but to remind him. That's what lovers did for each other.

"Two years."

"Right, and what happened?"

"Nothing."

"So, William, what's your verdict?"

"Patsy's nuts. She's doing this to get back at me.

Any court in the country would see that. She's going to lose."

"Of course she is." Hannah stared at the large clock hanging on the wall across from her desk. Ten till five. She watched the second hand tick around.

Tick. Tick. Tick.

"Think of the precedent it would set," she continued. "Take a judge's son away because of job hazards and every divorced cop would lose custody. Every attorney who ever had a threat made against him…"

William's chuckle was pleasant. "You're very good for me, Hannah, you know that?"

"And you're good for me," she said, hoping she meant the words as much as he did.

And that her feelings for him would last. Grow stronger. William Horne was a good man.

She could do far worse.

"What have you heard on Hampton's case?"

"Tanya's doing her job, trying to find out who else could be responsible, but hasn't hit on anything yet. Angelo's like a dog with a bone. He searched Brian's home, his office, confiscated his computers, both personal and business, but he hasn't given the state enough to press charges. He's exhuming bodies to have them tested for HGH. I gave him permission to exhume Carlos. He'd have been granted a subpoena anyway and while I know Brian had nothing to do with it, I want to know if my son was murdered." She'd cried after she'd signed the form, not that William had known. He'd been with Francis that night. And she'd sat by Carlos's crib the entire night afterward. Making herself face the truth. Carlos was gone forever. If she'd failed him, if she was in any way to blame, she had to know.

"And he found a ledger of sorts, that Brian kept, detailing his private fight against illegal immigration," she continued shortly, bringing her focus back to the moment at hand. Something she could handle. "Brian catalogued every pamphlet he sent out, every penny he donated, every dinner or lecture he attended, every piece of legislation he voted for."

"Nothing illegal in that," William said slowly. "And yet, put that together with his financial problems, his support of Moss, a soon-to-be known Ivory Nation supporter, and you could sway a jury."

He was right. She'd had the same thoughts. So why did it make her angry to hear him say it?

Or was it the very real fear he'd elicited that pissed her off?

"Except that he didn't do it. Brian still believes laws are the answer. Not breaking them."

"But if he's donated every dime he's got, he's not going to appear all that stable. He's also going to appear more desperate. He went to the free clinic and found those kids. He knew they were illegals. Desperate people do desperate things."

She didn't want to hear any more.

"You think he did it." William knew Brian. She thought he'd liked him.

"No, I don't think he did it. I'm just taking the state's approach so we can see what he's up against. Tanya has to find rebuttals to those things."

"And the best way to do that is to find someone else to point the finger at."

The Ivory Nation.

"Someone with a better motive," William agreed. "And access to HGH and the vaccine."

Maybe Brian should move to Canada. The whole thing was just too surreal. Her best friend being investigated for murder? Her Carlos murdered? By that same friend?

Or had someone else, a sick man who considered himself a Christ, framed Brian and killed her son, too?

Hannah's head throbbed.

"I'm here to get Francis." William's voice came over the line, interrupting her disturbing thoughts. "Take care of yourself, okay?"

Tick. Tick. Tick.

"Of course. Call me Sunday?" She'd already told him that she was planning to lie low all weekend, to catch up on her rest.

"As always. And, Hannah?"

"Yeah?"

"About that idea that there's an Ivory Nation sympathizer working on the inside at East Mesa?"

"Yeah?"

"I don't think so. I mean, if there were, there would've been some sign of it before now, don't you think?"

"Yes." Probably. Unless they were just really good and no one knew they were there. Or what they were doing. Or unless he or she had only recently been hired.

"An inside guy would've forestalled Kenny Hill's conviction."

Probably.

Tick. Tick. Tick.

"Besides, the sheriff's guys are the best. There's no way they'd let a supremicist work under their noses."

He was right about that. Unless it was someone they knew and trusted. Someone no one would ever suspect. Unless the sheriff's office supported white supremacy efforts. Turned a blind eye to things that had to be done in the name of the cause....

Her mind spun so rapidly it made her dizzy. Which was exactly what Bobby Donahue and his cohorts wanted. Assuming they were out to get her at all.

The real problem here, the only problem where she was concerned, was that she was giving control over her mind to someone who might not even be trying to take it.

And if he was trying...she was allowing him to succeed.

If she stopped worrying, stopped being afraid, he'd lose all power over her.

Really, the whole situation was within her ability to command.

Hannah hadn't even completed the thought before she jumped out of her skin, pushing the panic button under her desk.

The outer door to her chambers had just slammed.

And she was supposed to be there alone.

Her staff, minus Susan, had all left following their afternoon calendar. And an hour later, Susan had locked the door behind her when she'd gone. No one else had a key to her chambers.

Trembling, listening, Hannah stared at her solid wood door. She couldn't hear any footsteps on the carpet outside. But security should be there soon.

She grabbed her phone.

The doorknob jiggled.

And Hannah stifled a scream.

17

The knob jiggled again.

"Judge?"

Susan.

Hannah pulled open the door. "Yeah?" She hoped she didn't sound as shaky as she felt.

And let this be a lesson to you, she added silently. She was allowing them to get to her, rattle her, unsettle her equilibrium. She hadn't done that in a lifetime of challenges.

As of now, it stopped.

A sheriff's deputy ran through the outer office door. "Judge?"

Another humiliation. Another lesson. "It's okay, Sam," she told the young man. "False alarm. I didn't realize Susan had come back."

"You sure?" He had his hand on his gun.

"Positive."

He insisted on searching the area thoroughly, in case someone was lurking there, forcing her to send him away.

When he'd satisfied himself that all was well, he returned to his post, leaving her feeling more stupid than she had in a long time.

"Sorry," Susan said. "I forgot to tell you I talked to my friend Sara." Sara was a clerk in the prosecutor's office. "She said that she heard that they went through the injection disposals from Brian's office the day that Crispin Garza was in. They tested the syringes and found one with traces of HGH."

Which didn't mean Brian had done anything. Anyone with access to his office could have tainted that vaccine.

But it wasn't good. By all appearances, he'd given a lethal injection. The question was, had he known it was lethal when he'd administered it?

"Sara better be careful about what she repeats," Hannah said, tense once again. "She could lose her job."

She *should* lose her job. She was spreading crucial evidence around.

"I know," Susan said. "That's what I told her."

Nodding, Hannah wanted to thank her assistant for caring enough to keep her informed.

And she wanted to tell her that it was wrong for Susan to do so.

Instead, another indication that she needed to pull herself together, she heard herself say, "Susan?"

"Yeah?"

"What do you tell these people that talk to you?"

"What do mean?"

"About us? Do you give tit for tat?"

"Of course not!" The horrified look on her JA's face shamed Hannah. "I don't know why people talk to me, but I don't tell them anything. I only talk to you."

"That's what I thought," Hannah said, softening her expression, her tone. "But with everything going on, I had to ask."

"I understand, Judge," Susan said, smiling again. "Your job alone is a huge responsibility, and then with Carlos and your cat and the break-in… I don't know how you do it. Handling so much. Anyway, don't worry. I've got your back, totally." And giving Hannah's wrist a brief squeeze, she wished her a safe and restful weekend and left a second time.

"I understand if you want to take Joseph and go," Brian told the beautiful woman lying beside him in bed Friday night. Instead of making love, like they'd done most nights, they'd been talking about the babies who'd died, analyzing every move Brian had made over the past year. Looking for connections. He'd thought of little else since his arrest.

They'd spoken of little else.

Though she'd been lying on her back staring at the ceiling for almost an hour, Cynthia turned toward him, her fingers brushing his cheek.

"Of course we aren't leaving you," she said gently. "I *know* you didn't kill those babies, Brian. I know you. This is my chance to show my mettle and stand by my man."

"But you have Joseph to consider."

"Exactly. And his best chance at a decent future is right here."

Brian lay there, watching her, wanting to find the words of love and gratitude and relief that she deserved.

So why was he reminded of the night before? Why was he filled with a bittersweet longing to have heard that same avowal of faith from Hannah?

Because, in his mind, Hannah had somehow come to represent Cara?

Even as the thought occurred to him he rejected it. Hannah was Hannah. Always had been. Always would be.

And what that meant was a complete mystery to him.

On and off for the past forty-eight hours he'd been besieged with bouts of panic—a condition he'd never experienced before. Had his patients really been murdered? Could Angelo pin the murders on him? Visions of himself locked up like an animal chilled him. Without warning, his heart pounded as though he'd run a marathon.

And each time, thoughts of Hannah were all that could restore him to a semblance of calm. To reality. Rational thought.

Hannah wasn't the woman in his life.

Brian pulled Cynthia to him, kissing her deeply. Thoroughly. And over the next hour he loved her the same way, showing her with his hands, his body, what he could not tell her with his heart.

* * *

True to her determination not to be bullied, Hannah went home Friday night, made some toast for dinner, took a hot bath and went to bed. She was out immediately. And slept all night.

Of course, that might have been a result of the over-the-counter sleep aid she took with her toast.

Regardless, she woke up Saturday morning alive, unharmed and rested. Her home was intact.

And when she ventured outside, to get the paper and check yesterday's mail, everything was fine there, too. No stray bullets came whizzing down the street, no cars sped toward her across the yard, no bogeymen or bombs fell from the palm tree.

Bobby Donahue had been in jail for a full week and nothing bad had happened to her.

And even if it had, she wasn't going to let them intimidate her. If she died, she died. In the meantime, her life was her own and she was going to live it.

Starting with a phone call she'd been debating making. Her job was important. Upholding justice even more so. But most important were loved ones.

Brian deserved every opportunity he could get to prove his innocence.

And passing on gossip wasn't against the law. None of her information was official.

"Hannah? What's up?"

"Am I interrupting anything?" she asked, curled up on the couch in her winter robe, though it was in the sixties outside, with the newspaper and a cup of coffee at her side.

"Not at all. Joseph is watching Winnie the Pooh on the Disney Channel, and Cynthia just ran to the grocery store. She prefers not to take him with her. Says there's too many germs."

"I didn't realize she was that protective." *Shut up, Hannah. Don't criticize.*

For that matter, don't find fault. Brian loved Cynthia. And she was a charming woman. End of story.

"Actually, she doesn't take him much of anywhere," Brian surprised her by saying. "Except to counseling. And on occasional outings when we're all together. The little guy's had such an unsettled life and until the bed-wetting and nightmares stop, until he opens up a bit more, it's best for him to be home as much as possible, in a safe, secure, unchanging environment. He actually takes a bag with his special things in it whenever he leaves the house, in case he doesn't get to come back."

"Wow." Hannah's eyes filled with tears as she thought of the boy she'd helped put to bed. "I had no idea things were that bad."

"They're starting to get better. We had two dry mornings this week."

God, she envied him. A child to care for. To love. "He's very lucky having you," she said, meaning every word.

And then remembered why she'd called.

"How are you doing, otherwise?" she asked, thinking of how he'd been Wednesday night. Beaten down. Lost.

"Okay. Considering."

She hated herself for doubting him. Even for a second. That's what the Ivory Nation had done to her. Made her doubt her own heart. Her friends. Made her doubt that there was good in life.

Not everyone had a dark side, evil secrets. Not everyone was capable of horrendous acts.

"Have you heard anything from Tanya?" she asked, determined to be there for Brian, no matter what.

"Nothing substantial. She's pretty much looking everywhere but my underwear drawer, and I'll turn that over to her, too, if she asks."

That sounded more like Brian.

Hannah hated to bring him bad news. But she couldn't very well pass gossip to his attorney. To a woman who appeared before her in court.

"I heard a rumor yesterday, Brian."

"What?" The wariness was back, as she'd known it would be.

"Angelo got the results on the used syringes from your office."

"And?"

"There was a trace of HGH in one of them."

The long pause hurt her heart. "I guess that was to be expected," he said finally. "It had to have gotten in the baby somehow."

Yeah. But she'd been hoping someone else had injected him, before or after Brian's vaccine.

"This still isn't proof you did it," she reminded him. "Only that someone tampered with the syringe or the vaccine itself."

"It's pretty convincing circumstantial evidence, though," he said. For once, Hannah wished he hadn't paid such close attention to her and her work over the years. She had a feeling that the less Brian knew about the process, the better it would be for his peace of mind.

"Even if we accept that Donahue is behind this, he's obviously not doing the work himself. Who could he bribe or blackmail into helping him? Someone with access to you, your office, your supplies," she said as she sat up, taking a sip of coffee. Her mind was clearer than it had been in days.

She was reclaiming herself.

"I've been trying to figure that out," Brian told her. "Who has it in for me? Who's doing this? Why?"

"What have you come up with?"

"Not much. I've had a couple of families leave, but mostly because they were moving away, or couldn't pay a bill."

That caught her attention. "Let's go with that. Those that couldn't pay, what happened after they left?"

Was there someone out there whose child had died from an illness after they could no longer afford Brian? There would have been other care available to them—state care—but if they thought it had somehow been inferior, that if only Brian had been there…

"As far as I know, they're fine. There was only one that I can think of," he admitted. "And I didn't cut them off—they refused to come without paying."

Unfortunately, that left her back where she'd been, without a solid motive they could pursue.

Not that she wanted any other children to have died.

"And there's no one else you can think of who's ever been angry with you, Brian? Come on. Everyone pisses someone off on occasion. No woman who read more into your attention than you intended? Someone who feels jilted?"

"If anyone did, she didn't let on to me."

Or he hadn't read the signals. After all, Brian was a guy. It happened.

"And no angry husbands?" She had to ask.

"The only woman I've dated in the past year is Cynthia."

"What about neighbors? Anyone want to build something that you objected to?"

"Nope. And I wasn't rude to the grocery store check-out clerk, either." Brian's dry chuckle lifted her spirits.

"Okay, I'm fishing here," she conceded, but it felt so damn good to be back. Even for a moment. "But if Crispin Garza was murdered—" She decided not to bring Carlos into this. Not until she knew for sure "—someone did it."

"So maybe someone needed him dead and I was a convenient scapegoat. Maybe this has nothing to do with me at all. I was just in the wrong place at the wrong time, with the wrong baby as a patient."

"What are you saying? That someone was targeting the Garzas?"

"I don't know." He sounded tired again. "And that wouldn't explain the other babies."

"If they're really a part of this," she said, her mind honing in on everything she knew about Brian. "I've met most of your employees—" she used to be a client, after all "—but refresh my memory. Tell me about them."

He named Barbara first. Hannah knew her better than the rest. She'd been with Brian at a couple of the SIDS seminars, handing out copies for them, taking names and addresses for the mailing list they'd compiled.

"Then there's Lila," he said. "She started with me about a year ago—"

"Wait!" Warning bells went off in Hannah's head. Just as they had when she'd been working cases for the state all those years. A feeling of just knowing…

"Did she start with you before or after…Carlos?"

"Just…before," Brian said slowly. "You don't think—"

"I don't know," she said. "Hang on while I get a legal pad. I want you to tell me everything you know about her."

18

While Brian went to take Joseph some juice, Hannah retrieved a pad and pen from the drawer of the end table. She had them stashed in every room in the house, a habit left over from her trial attorney days.

"First off, give me her full name, age, marital status," she rattled off when Brian returned to the phone. Her robe fell open as she sat back on the couch.

"Lila Whitehall. She's in her mid- to late-twenties. Married with one son."

"What does her husband do?"

"I'm not sure. I've only met him once. I think he works for ASU, something to do with athletics. A trainer, maybe. They moved here from Flagstaff a couple of years ago."

More alarm bells. The horror story she'd heard from Janet McNeil about her experiences with the Ivory Nation had included reports of terrorist training at a ski resort in Flagstaff. The prosecutor had described rigorous physical workouts on the side of the mountain.

"Lila got her degree from NAU."

The same university Donahue's missing wife graduated from. Amanda's degree was in business, not nursing, but that didn't mean the two weren't acquainted. The ages were about right.

"Has she ever said anything about what she did in Flagstaff? People they knew? Places they went?"

"No…" Brian spoke carefully, as though searching his memory. "The only thing I remember is a neighborhood pub they used to hang out at. She's complained about not being able to find one like it here. It's right on Route 66. The Museum Club. Ever heard of it?"

"No." But she wrote down the name. And would be calling Ms. McNeil again as soon as she got off the phone with Brian.

"How sure are you about this Tanya Clarion?" Brian asked, clearly getting caught up in some of her own irrational worries. "Can we trust her?"

"I don't know." She had to be honest with him. "I'm not sure I can trust anyone right now."

"I gave her a key to my office and access to all my personal records."

"We have to trust someone," Hannah said, wishing she could reassure him. "I feel more sure about Tanya than I do about anyone else."

Tanya, who'd seemed to believe Brian was connected to Donahue.

"Who else is there?" She dropped the question

into the heavy silence that had fallen. They'd been going through his staff. Needed to focus.

"Tracy, my file clerk. You've met her. She's been with me forever."

Tracy was sixty. Widowed.

Brian named a couple of part-time employees, including a young man who handled all of their IT needs, from computer maintenance to programming the Web site.

And then he was back to the babies. Trying to find common denominators other than him. And the vaccines he'd given them. "The only thing they all have in common is that none of them were breast-fed. But that wouldn't affect a vaccination. And I have a lot of patients who grow up on formula. With today's working mothers, nursing is becoming more and more rare."

Which brought Hannah right back to Carlos. He'd been formula fed. Her adorable baby boy with big dark eyes that looked at her as if he couldn't quite believe she was real.

She'd struggled to accept that he was real, too. A baby of her own. In her home. Waiting for her every morning…

Until the morning he hadn't.

Because someone had killed him? Someone she knew?

God, please stop me now, she prayed. *Please give me back my mind. Don't let them do this to me. Don't let them take me to the point of no return.* She was not going to see their power, their vindictiveness in every aspect of her life. She was not going to believe that her son had died because of an Ivory Nation guilty verdict.

She'd brought the boy with her. Sitting outside the downtown courtroom Monday morning, William smiled at his twelve-year-old son, looking far too solemn, in the chair across the hall. Francis nodded. Patsy stared off in the opposite direction. She hadn't looked at William since she'd arrived, Francis in tow, half an hour before.

But William knew she was aware of him. He'd seen her grab the boy's wrist as he'd made a move toward his father.

It wasn't right, what she was doing to their son—using him as a weapon to get back at William. Patsy knew him well. Knew how to hurt him, a price he paid for having once loved her. She knew that Francis meant more to him than anything.

You're the one who asked for the divorce, dammit, he wanted to say to her. And might have. If not for Francis's presence. He refused to bring him into this. Patsy was his mother. Francis needed to respect her. And someday, when he was an adult, to look out for her. Protect her.

It's what boys—and then men—did.

The courtroom door opened. William's attorney appeared. With Patsy's lawyer right behind him.

With one look at their faces, William took his first easy breath in more than a year.

And five minutes later, after speaking with Francis, giving the boy a hug, he was in his car driving back to work, to his Monday afternoon calendar, and calling the second most important person in his life.

Hannah picked up on the first ring, as though she'd been sitting by the phone, waiting for him. "I won."

"Oh, that's wonderful. I mean, I knew you would, but I'm so glad it's over. And that justice was done." Hannah's words, coming in a rush, were sincere.

And suddenly, as joy flowed over him, a darker emotion spiraled through William. For every good there was a corresponding bad. And while he'd fought hard for his son, had rejoiced in his new relationship with Hannah, he couldn't help but wonder what he would do if he lost either one of them.

Monday didn't always suck. Smiling, Hannah pushed the first number on her speed dial as soon as she'd cleared the court building at lunch. William had had good news, and so did she.

Brian didn't pick up his cell, but she reached him easily on his home phone.

"Hi." She didn't bother introducing herself.

"Hi, yourself." The catch in his voice tore at her.

"Don't worry, it's not bad news," she added quickly. Whoever was doing this to Brian was going to pay. "I just heard another rumor."

And didn't feel the least bit guilty about passing it on.

"And?"

"There was no trace of HGH in any medicinal

product you had in your possession. None was found among the personal belongings at your home, either. Nor can they trace any orders of it, legal or not, to you, your license or your office."

"Thank God. Oh, Hannah, thank God." The emotion in his voice brought tears to her eyes.

"This doesn't mean you're off the hook," she warned. "There's still at least one murder that must be accounted for and you're a suspect."

"I understand." At the moment he didn't sound like he cared all that much.

"There's something else." This wouldn't be as easy for him to hear. But it helped his case.

"What's that?" The wariness had returned.

"That place where Lila hung out, the Museum Club. According to Janet McNeil, Amanda Blake, Donahue's missing girlfriend, worked there. That's where Simon Green, ex-undercover FBI and also now Janet's husband, met Amanda. It's where Amanda first agreed to work with law enforcement to bring down Donahue and his organization."

"Lila's linked to this. I should've known."

Hannah didn't say anything. She'd met the woman. Couldn't picture her in the room with Carlos. Couldn't picture her period.

"There has to be someone on the inside," she said when she could.

"I'll call Tanya. Let her know to start checking. What do you suggest I do with Lila in the meantime? Fire her?"

"Ask Tanya what she thinks, but my gut reaction

is no. These guys aren't stupid. You don't want to give any indication that you're on to them. They'll vanish and you'll be left with a conviction."

"There's no way I'm exposing another child to her, conviction or not."

"Isn't there some seminar you can send her to?"

"I'll find one."

Brian sounded better. Energized. The angst would return, Hannah knew that. But she was glad to have been able to give him this respite.

"How do you keep hearing these rumors, by the way?" he asked.

"I'm not at liberty to say," she told him. And silently thanked her judicial assistant.

There was no way Susan had just happened to hear about Brian's case. She'd called in a favor for the information.

It was a favor Hannah hoped to be able to return someday.

On Tuesday morning, while Joseph was still asleep, Brian crept quietly past his door, peeking in long enough to see the bed covers rise and fall with his even breaths. "Tell him good morning for me," he whispered to Cynthia behind him.

Cynthia nodded. And a minute later reached up to straighten the knot in his *Toy Story* tie as he faced her before he headed out to the garage—and his Jag. "I'll be here all day," she told him. "Call me if you need me."

"I'll need you even if I don't get a chance to call," he said, knowing the words were true on some level.

He did need her. She was a friend. A loyal friend. He cared about her. Wanted her to be happy.

He just wasn't sure he was in love with her.

But he wanted to be.

The past several days at home would have been excruciating if not for her and Joseph. The four-year-old hadn't had a single nightmare in five days. And he'd only wet the bed once.

"Good luck." With one hand on the back of Brian's neck, Cynthia pulled him down for a kiss.

The strikingly obvious yellow caution tape was gone. And inside Brian's office looked, surprisingly, just as he'd left it. As long as he didn't open file drawers or go through his desk. Fresh paper still covered the tables in the examination rooms. Utensils filled the glass canisters on the counters. Instrumental renditions of kids' songs played over the sound system when he turned it on.

His appointment book sat open on Barbara's desk, as always, though the police had taken photocopies. His medicine cabinets were full and locked.

He might, technically, be under suspicion for murder, but no formal charges had been filed. Nothing formal done at all, other than a too-hasty booking that he could probably sue for if he chose.

All Brian wanted was to put it behind him and get on with his life.

He came armed with a seminar for Lila in Washington, D.C. It was a SIDS symposium and since he couldn't leave the state…

She wasn't the least bit upset to hear that she was to take the day off to get ready, or that he'd booked her a flight from Phoenix's Sky Harbor airport the next morning. Because she was being kind to a boss who'd had a rough experience? Or because she was guilty as hell and eager to get out of town?

Brian didn't know. And at the moment, didn't care. Tanya was investigating. It was out of his hands.

And because she'd worked a solid year without a vacation, Brian insisted she take at least one of the two weeks she had coming to her. Overworked nurses weren't healthy choices in a doctor's office.

"I can understand why you'd want to be extra cautious right now," she said with an agreeable nod. "I'll see if Zane can get some time off… Maybe my mom can watch the baby, so he and I can have a few days away somewhere. It's football season, but ASU has a bye next week…"

Lila chattered on, seemingly happy and at ease. Not at all like someone who'd just murdered her sixth infant.

But then, what did he know? He'd never been personally acquainted with a murderer.

Brian's first patient, Allie Barnes, was due in at eight. Which left him an hour to wait and see if she showed. In the meantime, he opened drawers, closed up space left by missing folders, collected the medical files he'd need for the day, adjusted a couple of boxes of tissues.

He had his stethoscope in his ears, the base on his wrist, was counting absently as he stood in the middle of examination room one, when Barbara arrived.

"Hi," Brian said, letting the stethoscope go to hang around his neck.

"Good morning, Doctor," she said, her eyes concerned as she scanned his features. "How are you?"

"Fine," he said, with the false optimism he'd been practicing for the past hour. "Ready to get back to work."

Barbara studied him so long Brian knew she didn't believe a word he said, and then, settling her sweater on the back of her chair, she pulled the appointment book forward.

"I've already collected the charts," he told her. That was something she would have done before leaving the office the previous day, if they'd worked. And he informed her of Lila's trip and the temporary nurse who would be starting that morning.

"Oh! Well, that's fine then." She peered up at him. "I'm sorry, sir, but I have to say this. I know you didn't hurt those kids. And what's more, everyone I've talked to knows it, too. You've been around a long time. Helped a lot of people. That kind of stuff isn't forgotten."

Biting his lips against the sudden emotion building in his throat, behind his eyes, Brian nodded. Tried to thank her.

"I just wanted it out in the open. Nobody here suspects you in the least. We're all just tense as anything, waiting for them to find whoever did this. It's creepy to think that someone's been here in the office, tainted our supplies…"

"We don't know that," Brian said, focusing on the case that had consumed his thoughts. "We only know that a syringe with traces of HGH was in the trash receptacle," he clarified. "We can't tell for certain when or how that HGH got there."

"You think someone might've tampered with it after it went out in the safe box?" she asked, giving his name for the locked container he used to dispose of needles.

"I sure as hell hope so," he replied. And then looked back at the calendar.

"How many were you able to reach?"

"All of them."

"And how many can we expect to see today?"

When she repeated the same three words, Brian stood up a little straighter, adjusted the knot in his tie.

It was time to work.

Hannah was the first one in chambers Wednesday morning—a common occurrence. Sometime over the past year she'd developed the habit of collecting her paper from the porch as she was leaving in the morning, hitting the drive-through for coffee on the way to work, and having a few moments of solitude in the peace and quiet of her office before the day began.

In another world, another life, she'd enjoyed those moments at home.

Flipping on the lights as she passed through the

well-insulated suite, her footsteps barely audible on the carpet, she set her coffee down long enough to exchange her sweater for the robe hanging in the closet inside her personal office, and, paper under her arm, headed over to the desk.

Pray to God there was nothing about Dr. Brian Hampton in the headlines—though he'd surely have called if there had been.

And no more SIDS deaths in the city, either.

She had to look twice at her desk, at the pile of files front and center that she'd left there the previous evening, ready for her morning calendar, before she realized what was wrong.

The files were as she'd left them, neatly lined up, one atop the other, but there was a difference, too. A sheet of regular typing paper was sticking out from the middle of the pile—marring the symmetry of the stack.

Without thinking, or rather, thinking that Susan or the janitor must have left her a note, Hannah picked up the piece of paper.

And felt every nerve in her body tighten as she shivered.

There was no note. No words at all.

Only a very clear, enlarged picture of the ring that had gone missing from the evidence locker.

A crucial piece of evidence in the *State v. Bobby Donahue* case.

Still holding the paper in her shaking hand, Hannah sat. Stared at the offensive message. And dropped it as though it burned her.

She meant to press the panic button under her desk. She meant to phone Donna's office next door, in case her deputy was already in. She meant to call the cops. Susan. Or William.

Instead, she carefully picked up the paper, trying to touch it as little as possible. Sealing it into an envelope, she deposited it in the fireproof safe she'd had installed in the closet when she'd first taken office.

She'd have the paper analyzed for prints. D.N.A. Any kind of identification.

As soon as she had an idea of who she could trust.

She'd just had absolute confirmation that the Ivory Nation had someone working inside the Maricopa County East Court Complex. What if it was one of the deputies? Someone in Susan's confidence?

Susan herself?

Hannah shook her head. Surely not. No. She couldn't go that far.

And William? There was no way he was the infiltrator. Though she still didn't call him. She wasn't convinced he'd keep the information quiet. He was getting panicky about her work. And now that he had access to Francis, had more at stake by being connected to danger, he'd be even worse. He wasn't involved with the Ivory Nation; she just couldn't count on him to be rational.

Maybe it was a clerk. Or a janitor. Or Donna's JA, Martha, who'd told Susan about the missing ring.

Names, faces swarmed through her mind until

she felt dizzy. She didn't know who among them was a traitor. But she knew someone was.

No one but a fully vetted county employee, be it a cleaning person or a judge, had access to the inner sanctum.

Ever.

Wednesday had been even better for Brian than Tuesday. If not for the investigation looming—and the fact that he'd had to hospitalize a five-year-old girl with meningitis—it would have been close to perfect.

He called Cynthia as he drove home. She and Joseph had counseling, but maybe they could meet for hamburgers before they had to go. There was one thing that had become very normal about Joseph—his love of French fries.

"I'm sorry," Cynthia said when she heard his suggestion. "I've already fed Joseph and I told Linda that we'd come early tonight so Tyler and Joseph could play together in the toy room before our session starts."

Linda and Tyler—names he recognized. And maybe she'd told him about the pre-session playdate. He'd been a bit distracted lately.

And thinking back to a week ago tonight—the worst night in recent memory—Brian dialed another number.

He'd spoken to Hannah again briefly the day before when she'd called to see how his first day back at work had gone. But he hadn't seen her since she'd picked him up from the police station.

"Brian?"

He didn't like her tone of voice when she answered. "What's wrong?" Had she heard something else about the investigation?

Looking in the rearview mirror for signs of Angelo on his tail, Brian felt his palms start to sweat.

"Nothing, why?" She spoke a little too quickly. Or maybe her voice was too tense.

Or maybe he still had some recovering to do.

"Because I can tell something's bothering you," he said. "What's happened?"

"Nothing."

And then it hit him, probably would have come to him immediately if he hadn't been preoccupied with the threat of life in prison.

"You're scared."

"No, of course not."

Was someone listening? In her office? On the line?

"Okay, sorry, I guess I'm feeling jumpy," he said, giving up far more easily than she should expect.

"That's understandable." Her chuckle wasn't quite natural.

"Hey," he said, thinking quickly, "I'm at loose ends tonight. How about we meet at that bistro on Mill Avenue and have a beer and some wings?"

Reminiscent of their college days. She'd passed the last time he'd offered.

A return to yesteryear, when they'd felt more in control of their lives and had faith in the world around them, appealed to him.

Even so, Hannah's instant reply surprised him. "That'd be great," she said, sounding as relieved as he was. And that's when he knew something was seriously wrong.

"How soon can you leave work?" he asked, needing to be with her. It was just before five.

"Now. I've finished my files for the morning."

"Great, I'll meet you on Mill in twenty minutes."

He didn't want to wait that long.

19

Odd that Brian had called right when she was sitting at her desk, staring at the closet door, trying not to think about the message concealed behind it. She'd been wondering whether to go home and leave the offensive piece of paper where it was, without telling anyone about it—and yet was afraid to leave, to walk out of her chambers and into the world alone with that photo haunting her.

She didn't believe in omens, or signs, and yet felt, as she answered Brian's call, that she'd just been pushed out of her stupor and toward her future.

Walking stiffly, watching her back every step of the way, Hannah made it out of her office without incident. She rode the elevator with a couple of attorneys and another judge, talking about the unusually warm October weather.

The Lexus was just as she'd left it—no notes, no marks, the mail she'd collected on the way out that morning still on the passenger seat. Funny how traffic could be so normal, too, so many people zipping in and out of lanes, desperate for that extra car length—while others muddied the whole system by staying stubbornly in one lane at a slower speed, oblivious to the race they were interrupting.

Didn't they know that, more than likely, on that very road, was an Ivory Nation supporter? A white supremacist who advocated killing innocent people if their skin was a different color? Or their religious affiliation not Christian?

Didn't they know that they could be the next victim? Or that their baby could be murdered in the safety and security of his own nursery while they were right there, sleeping while he died?

Supremacists were everywhere. Doctors. Lawyers. The next-door neighbor. Even an Arizona state senator. There was no way to identify the danger.

Or to know if one was safe.

Hannah made it to Mill in record time. And then spent fifteen minutes circling the block until a parking space opened up. She didn't even consider the covered garage where she normally parked. Too dark. Deserted. Too many posts behind which someone could hide.

And when Brian met her at the door to the restaurant, she fell into his open arms and hung on for dear life.

"They're waiting to see what you do with that photo," Brian said, hating the lines of fear on Hannah's brow, the shadows beneath her eyes. The glint of panic he caught when she met his gaze over the draught beer she'd ordered.

"But who's waiting?" she asked, her elbows on the tall table for two, a basket of uneaten wings between them. "And for what? How do I play this? I'm stuck here," she said, "powerless."

"No." He couldn't allow that. If he'd learned nothing else from his ordeal, he knew that everyone had power. They had to recognize it, choose to use it, but it was there. "You always have the ability to make choices," he said, thinking back to the previous week, the humiliating examination. "Even if it's just to choose to smile or cry. To be silent or to yell. The trick is not to let them get to you," he said. "And I'm talking to myself as much as to you. Kind of odd, isn't it," he added, sipping from his own beer, "that we're both being harassed by unknown people?"

Hannah's smile was weak, but it managed to warm him. "Kind of like we're meant to be each other's strength?"

"Maybe." He could think of worse things.

"Or that we're in this together," Hannah said. "Whether they're out to get you and using me, or out to get me and using you, they're hitting us both."

He'd loosened his *Beauty and the Beast* tie, unfastened the top button of his yellow dress shirt, and still couldn't quite breathe easily. He didn't disagree with her.

"So what am I going to do?" Hannah's blue eyes were questioning.

He wished he had an answer for her. One that he could live with. Moving to Jamaica probably wasn't it.

"What does William say?"

"I haven't told him." She toyed with a wing, as though fascinated by the sauce. The sleeve of her cream-colored blouse was only inches from sporting a brick-red stain. "This case has become such a sore spot between us that I don't mention it anymore. He wants me to quit—not because it's right, but because he's afraid. I can't let fear rule my life." She grimaced as she looked over at him. "I mean, I know I'm not doing such a great job of staying calm, but at least I'm fighting. If I quit, if I run, I'm giving the Ivory Nation control of my life. I'd rather be dead."

Brian wanted her alive. Period.

And he understood. "You've made your decision," he said.

"I have?"

Nodding, Brian took the wing she was desecrating but not eating from her fingers, motioned to the top she'd just barely missed with the sauce. "You're going to show them that they can't manipulate you by fear. You're going to go back to work, and turn that photo over to the proper authorities."

"But if they're the ones who're crooked?"

"You'll find that out sooner or later, right?"

"Yeah."

Hannah studied him grimly. "Will you come with me?"

Try to stop him. "Of course."

And he'd follow her home afterward, too.

Wednesday nights were quiet. Church night. Confinement was getting to him. He'd be released in the

Lord's time. Bobby knew that. His stillness was serving God. He knew that, too.

He saw again the face of the new guard who'd visited him earlier. Earnest. Serious. Adoring. As he'd offered Bobby a white female guard for his pleasure.

"You name it, brother—blonde, brunette, blue eyes, brown, long hair, short, big tits or small…"

It hurt Bobby to look at the red laces in the man's boots. A top honor. Sign that he'd shed blood for the cause.

Laces he'd been awarded the same night Bobby had confessed to the brethren that the Lord God had appeared to him with the instruction to remain celibate for the rest of his life.

And here this man was, two years later, offering Bobby a woman.

Like Jefferson last year, he just didn't get it. Didn't understand that love of God was higher than any love of woman. That passion for Christ surpassed all earthly, human passions.

What was happening to them? Why were brethren changing the message? The messenger didn't change.

Nor did the Sender of all messages.

Bobby's Bible had been open for more than an hour, but the thin, rich, worn pages weren't offering the solace he normally found there.

And the cell walls seemed closer tonight. Trapping him in a hunting trailer with a man who thought fatherhood meant owning another human being. One there to serve whatever purpose you needed served. Be it cooking, cleaning, stealing, being a punching bag.

And more.

Closing the Bible, Bobby leaned back against the wall behind his cot, closed his eyes and recited the entire first chapter of Mark. The exercise consumed every part of him, his skin open to God's touch, his mind hearing God's word, his heart touched by the love he found within the sacred verse.

The cell hadn't changed when he opened his eyes. He'd arranged to have himself moved to the end of a row of unoccupied cells. A solitary confinement of sorts. Mostly a place he could use his laptop—brought to him folded in a blanket and kept hidden on his cot—during the day without question or explanation. The camera that was supposed to monitor him had been turned slightly, so that his calves and feet were in plain view.

The authorities knew he was here.

That was all they knew.

Or needed to know.

Calm again, he opened the laptop powered by batteries that came in and went out with his food tray, accessed the county's wireless network, a bit disgusted by the ease with which he circumvented all rules and regulations, all security measures that were meant to keep citizens safe. If he'd been an ungodly man he could have done so much damage.

A couple of quick seconds of typing and he was

in a private community on the Internet—one that he'd designed himself. Space he owned.

Scrolling down, he read through the postings, all seemingly innocuous chatter between high school girlfriends on the other side of the country. Giving him the reports he expected twice a day during his sabbatical. Reports in code from trusted members of the brotherhood.

At the bottom he saw an image that made his heart pound.

God, she looked good. Even with that hair, those clothes—even with the twenty extra pounds, she stirred his blood. One of his brothers had found her. It was the only way she'd be here. No one else had permission to post to the site.

She was in a room—a hospital room by the look of it. Bobby clicked, zoomed, captured. There was a dated clock through a window behind her. It was missing a corner of the decorative scrolling around it. That clock hung outside a hospital in Mesa. And it displayed yesterday's date.

Amanda was still alive. In Phoenix.

With shaking fingers he opened his imaging software. And within seconds, had an enlarged picture staring out at him.

"I'll be damned," he whispered as he quickly took in details. Amanda was at the bedside of the Alliance bastard who'd sent his apologies. He knew the man's eyes. The Judas had burns over most of his body, if the bandages were any indication. The picture had been taken from a cell phone outside the room, he'd guess, based on the pixels, resolution and the situation.

Amanda was gazing at the man as she'd once gazed at Bobby.

And beneath that first photo was a second. In that image she was kissing the man as she'd once kissed Bobby.

This image had been widened, letting him view the entire room. Enough to see that Luke wasn't with her.

Trembling, he saved, converted, zoomed. Still no child.

What had she done with his son?

Left him alone in a hospital hallway, where anyone could speak to him? Teach him? Snatch him? Left him with, God forbid, a babysitter?

No, the faithful brother who'd been watching the room and taken the picture would have Luke if he'd been there.

And Amanda had obviously managed to slip away from anyone who tried to follow her. She'd been trained by the best.

So where was his son? With a black man? A Hispanic woman? A Jew? He'd kill her. He'd kill her again and again.

He'd follow her to hell and obliterate her soul.

Arms around his chest, Bobby rode the pain as he'd learned as a child, purging through silent tears that which he could not bear.

Brian was at work again early the next morning. Before the crack of dawn, actually. He'd woken in a cold sweat, sitting straight up in bed, and after assuring Cynthia that he was fine, he'd showered, checked on Joseph and left the house.

Driving like a bat out of hell, all he could think of was his patients. And saving their lives. If six of his infant patients had been murdered, and the killer hadn't yet been caught, there could be a seventh. Today, even. He should have thought of this before. Should have thought of this first.

If another child died, because of him…

It took him an hour to go through the charts for patients under a year old. And another two to make the necessary phone calls.

By the time his staff began to arrive that morning, he was no longer pediatrician to any children under the age of one.

The following week was relatively, blissfully, uneventful for Hannah. A week without threats. Without trauma.

Without William.

She would have liked a week without fear, but she'd yet to manage a day free from panic.

She missed William. He'd had Francis since Saturday—part of a makeup plan for days he'd missed—and needed the time alone to forge a new relationshiop with his son.

He'd called Hannah every day, but when the conversation repeatedly turned to his pleas for her to recuse herself on the Bobby Donahue case—even going so far as to invite her on a Mediterranean cruise, his treat—she'd begun to cut the calls shorter and shorter.

She understood that William was worried about her. Frightened for her. She was frightened for herself.

But she could not quit. Quitting was tantamount to declaring her support for a cause she abhorred. To giving up her freedom.

Brian still had his. Tests had come back positive for HGH on one of the five exhumed bodies. They were still awaiting results on the other four. Carlos included.

The idea that her baby boy, so carefully entombed in the tiniest casket imaginable, so mournfully buried, was now a test sample in a morgue made her heartsick.

And physically sick as well.

She'd lost six pounds over the past two weeks.

There'd been no identifying marks on the photo left in her office, nor had anyone claimed it.

"Donahue's on the calendar for tomorrow." Susan delivered the bad news on Thursday afternoon, a week and a day after Hannah's beer-and-wings date with Brian.

It was a capital murder case. There would be many pretrial hearings. Mostly attempts by his lawyer to get the case thrown out. The charges dropped. Or lessened.

"A motion from Keith?" she asked.

Susan nodded. "He's objecting to one of the state's witnesses."

"Who?" The judge was usually the last to find out.

Whether because paperwork was slow, or because she didn't need to know before she heard it in court, Hannah had never completely decided.

"Courtney Moss."

"The senator's daughter?"

Susan nodded. "One and the same."

"Camargo Cortes's girlfriend," Hannah said, to confirm. The senator had more than one daughter.

"Yep."

"Another interesting morning," she said, trying to stay calm as she reached for the file.

She would not be intimidated.

She would not.

The words spent the night with Hannah. And accompanied her in to work the next morning.

I love Thee, Lord God, with all my heart. I love Thee, Lord God, with all my heart. I love Thee, Lord God...

Dressed in his Sunday-night-meeting best, Bobby sat next to Robert Keith at the defendant's table, his litany blocking out most of what was going on around him.

The courtroom was closed to the public due to the sensitive nature of the upcoming proceedings.

I love thee, Lord God, with all my heart.

Courtney Moss, sitting with her father behind the prosecutor's table to his left, looked fresh and pure in her white blouse and navy skirt. Bobby loved the child—God's child. He loved the judge they were waiting for as well.

I love Thee, Lord God, with all my heart.

The judge should be home having a white man's babies, serving God with the tools He'd given her, but Bobby still loved her. As God did. As God wanted *him* to. He wondered how he could tell her so.

And wondered, too, how much longer his Father in Heaven would have him remain here, this space of waiting, until His purpose was served and Bobby could breathe fresh air again. Work by doing, rather than by faith.

I love Thee, Lord God, with all my heart...

Courtney would have her chance today. She had penance to do. Amends to be made to the Father who'd given her soul life, as well as to the earthly father who'd raised her. But she was young. She'd bear them good children.

Bobby already had a man picked for her. One who would be able to control her. Teach her God's plan for her. Keep her pregnant and nursing—white babies, and him.

I love Thee, Lord God, with all my heart...

Tonight sweet Courtney would know how it felt to have a real man between her legs. Filling her with clean seed. By tomorrow she would be speaking of love and telling her father she wanted to get married.

Bobby's penis grew hard, thinking of how pleased God would be, knowing that one more of His precious children was set for life. Serving Him. Protected.

One at a time.

Bobby was to bring them home one at a time.
I love Thee, Lord God, with all my heart...

"Judge, they're ready for you."

With her shoulders back and her stomach relatively calm, Hannah looked up as Susan appeared in the open doorway, and nodded. She wasn't going to think about this, wasn't going to leave any room in her mind for anyone else. She would simply do her job.

She was good at it.

Her morning files were already on her bench. Standing, she reached into her top drawer for the pen she always took with her to the court and—

"Oh! Ow!"

"What?" Susan was there instantly, staring down to the open drawer.

"Oh, my God."

Hannah, her middle finger at her mouth, stared, too. A scorpion, an inch long, lay curled next to her pen. She slammed the drawer shut.

"I was stung!" The pain was intense. Making her dizzy. Hot and cold at once, she fell back into her chair, trying desperately to think. To remain calm.

"I'm calling for help." Susan already had the phone in her hand. Hannah heard her talking.

Only the very young and the very old ever got seriously ill from a scorpion sting. She knew that. She'd lived in Arizona her entire life. Knew several people who'd been stung.

"They're on their way," Susan said.

Eyes closed, Hannah heard her assistant leave. And moments later come back. The rest of her staff were all still in the courtroom. Presumably waiting for her.

"A friend of mine was stung in her bed in college." She could hear her own voice as if from afar, her burning hand lying limp on her lap. "And another one when she got her mail."

Both had been fine. Sore, but fine.

"My sister was stung on her shoulder one night as she slept," Susan's voice sounded louder, closer.

Opening her eyes, Hannah focused. Cooled.

Held the ice-filled plastic bag that Susan had just put on her injured hand. "Security said ice would slow the venom."

"I think I'm more panicked than hurt," Hannah admitted, trying to chuckle as she sat with her right hand still lying limp on her knee. She'd pushed her chair back a couple of feet from the desk.

But Hannah was keeping her eye on the drawer.

And everywhere else. Was there only one? Or had someone infested her office?

A paramedic arrived within minutes, checked her pulse and her eyes, examined the sting, and instructed her to keep ice on it to reduce the pain.

It took him slightly longer to find the scorpion in her drawer, but, when he did, he removed it immediately.

She was lucky, he said. The offensive creature was bigger. The worse stings were from the little ones.

"Give it another ten minutes or so and you'll be able to carry on with your day. Your arm will probably feel numb until tomorrow, but you're going to be just fine."

Hannah believed him.

As far as the sting went.

20

Brian was with a patient Friday morning when Barbara knocked to tell him he had a personal phone call.

There were only two people for whom he'd given his receptionist permission to interrupt him when he was with a patient.

Cynthia. And Hannah.

Leaving ten-year-old Simon Adler and his mother with Jamie, the replacement nurse he'd brought, he hurried into his private office to take the call.

His heart pounded the second he heard her voice. She was sick. Or scared. "Hannah?"

"I hope I didn't interrupt anything. When I left my name with Barbara she told me to hold on and—"

"She has orders to come get me if you call," he said, standing with his feet apart, ready to run. "What's up?"

"I got stung by a scorpion." She told him about reaching for her pen, not seeing the thing until it was too late.

"Put ice on it," he said to pretend this was a medical call.

"I did."

"Your arm's going to be numb for a day or two," he warned her.

"I know." A paramedic had been there. Called by her JA, she said. Good. Measures were in place to protect her. At work at least.

"You may feel a bit nauseous," he added, more because he didn't want to let her go than anything else.

"Brian?"

"Yeah?"

"Do you think I'm nuts for thinking that someone put that scorpion in my drawer?"

He wanted to tell her not to worry. That he wasn't concerned.

"You aren't nuts." He chose his words carefully. "You've been under a lot of pressure, odd things happening. Someone was in your office once before. It's not unnatural for you to assume that."

"But is it illogical?"

Yes. Yes, there's nothing to worry about. "I don't know."

"I called maintenance and had them check the whole office. And my bench area, too. I've got a hearing waiting to begin, but I'm not taking any more chances."

"I think you're safe now," he said, rubbing the ache along the back of his neck. He lowered his head to give him better access, and his vision rested on the multiple images of Cinderella on his tie.

If only life were a fairy tale.

"If the scorpion was put there deliberately, it served its purpose," he finally said. "You've been warned. You're scared, bordering on paranoid. If someone is trying to intimidate you, I'd say it worked."

The long pause at the end of the line was difficult to endure. Never in his life had Brian felt so helpless—for Hannah and for himself.

"I'm afraid to ask, but you don't happen to have Bobby Donahue on today's calendar, do you?"

Another telling pause. "He's in the courtroom. It's his hearing that's waiting."

It wasn't the answer he wanted.

"What are you going to do?"

"Do my job."

"Meaning?"

"I'm going to hear the testimony and make the decision that justice demands."

He'd known that. It's what he'd have done, too. And it scared the hell out of him.

"But based on what I know so far, I'll probably be taking it under advisement. I want to give a written opinion," she added. "I want Donahue in jail when he hears the news, not sitting in front of me. I want the witness safely away."

"So that won't be until Monday?"

"Yep."

"Come spend the weekend in the guest cottage. Please? For me?"

Hannah hesitated, as though actually considering

the request. "I would, but I'm supposed to be seeing William," she said. "And besides, I won't live my life in fear. They've delivered their warning, right? What more can they do until I render my decision?"

Okay, he'd buy that. She was safe as long as things were under advisement. Could she just leave them there permanently? Let the man rot in jail waiting for his trial?

"And no, it isn't something I can draw out indefinitely," she chuckled, as though reading his mind. This seemed to be happening a lot lately. "Every defendant is entitled to a speedy trial. If I wait too long the charges would be dismissed."

And Donahue would go free. They most definitely couldn't have that.

"Take care of yourself, my friend," he said after dismissing at least three possessive statements that were completely inappropriate.

William was her man. Her "protector." Not Brian.

"I will."

"And call me, okay? Let me know you're all right?"

"Yes, sir."

Brian had to be satisfied with that.

But he didn't have to like it.

As it turned out, Courtney Moss's testimony and the hearing were uneventful. If one ignored the shock on Julie Gilbert's face when the girl claimed to have been with her parents the night her lover, Camargo Cortes, was brutally tortured and murdered.

She knew nothing about the attack.

"Camargo and I weren't really all that close," she said. "We only dated a few times."

The girl was staring at her hands.

"But you slept together," Julie pressed, moving closer.

"Well…" Courtney looked at her father. "No." The answer was emphatic.

And, Hannah was certain, a complete lie.

She finished the hearing, writing as best she could with her left hand. Gave her spiel about taking the matter under advisement. But before she adjourned, called the attorneys forward.

"I'm not sure why we're here today." Hannah was a judge, not a prosecutor. She couldn't do the attorneys' jobs for them. But…

"She's lying, Your Honor." Julie kept her voice low.

Hannah turned to Keith. "That's not what she told me when I questioned her," he admitted, though the testimony didn't hurt his case any. It just made his motion to suppress pointless.

She looked from one to the other. "Either of you have a suggestion?"

"Can we clear the courtroom?" Julie asked. "Including the defendant?"

"A defendant always has the right to be present…" Keith said with a forceful whisper as the two attorneys stood side by side, just their heads and shoulders visible to Hannah.

"Unless he waives his right and has his attorney there in his stead," Julie finished.

"Why would I agree to that?"

"Because you know I'll get the information anyway and it'll be better for your client if the witness testifies than if I prove that she refused because she was so afraid."

"That's assuming the judge allows the testimony to come in."

They both looked to Hannah.

"Talk to your client," she said to Keith. "We're going to take a five-minute break," she announced to the courtroom and then, turning, stood and left through the back door.

Within ten minutes, Hannah was on the bench, and the proceedings were on the record, minus all spectators, including the defendant and the witness's father who'd agreed to leave at Donahue's request. Only Hannah's necessary staff members, the two attorneys and Courtney Moss were present.

Hannah had no idea what Keith had said to get his client to leave, but Donahue had appeared entirely at ease, confident, as he'd been led away.

Hannah's right arm, which had throbbed for a while but was now numb to the shoulder, hung limply at her side.

"You want to tell us what's going on?" Julie Gilbert asked the witness as soon as Hannah motioned her forward.

"Nothing." Courtney didn't seem to have much trouble lying.

If you didn't count the way her lips trembled.

"You do realize the penalty for perjury, don't you, Courtney?"

The girl shook her head.

"If you lie, and it affects the outcome of the trial, it's called obstruction of justice and you could be charged and tried as an accessory." Not likely in this case, but true. "Is that what you want? To go to prison along with whoever tortured your boyfriend?"

Courtney's silence was telling. The child was obviously more frightened than Hannah had been earlier that day—and she was only seventeen. And, until recently, had lived a privileged life. Hardly as equipped as Hannah to deal with these kind of pressures.

"Talk to me, Courtney," Julie said. "Like you did before when I came to your school with your mom. It's just us now, and everything that's said here today will be kept confidential."

The girl's apparent struggle tugged at Hannah. It took everything she had to remain professional, when what she wanted to do was haul the child into her arms, cradle her, promise her everything would be all right.

Or at the very least, take hold of that fist clenching and unclenching on the other side of the table.

"Have you ever heard of Amanda Blake?" the girl asked the prosecutor.

Bobby Donahue's former lover. The mother of his child.

"Yes," the prosecutor replied.

Courtney's stare was almost bitter as she

glanced over at Hannah and then back to Julie. "What do you know?"

"That she kidnapped their son last year and hasn't been seen or heard from since."

"And that's it?"

"Yes."

"Why do you think Bobby had custody of Luke to begin with?"

"I don't know, but I suspect you're going to tell me."

"Two years ago, Amanda wanted out."

"Out of the Ivory Nation?"

"Right." The girl wet her lips and then, as though having come to a final decision, started to talk so fast Hannah could hardly keep up with her.

"She knew Bobby wouldn't ever let her go, and more, that if she did somehow convince him, she'd never get to take her son with her. Well, Luke was one of the biggest reasons she had to go, don't you see? Amanda could handle pretty much anything for herself, but the idea of Bobby raising her son, once she'd seen all the things he did, how crazy he was, well, that was just too much. So she went to the feds."

Janet McNeil had told Hannah the same story.

"Amanda agreed to work with them, to be a snitch, and they guaranteed her they'd get Bobby and then, even if she died in the process, at least her son would be away from him."

Thinking of Carlos, Hannah could understand the desperation that must have driven the young mother.

"How do you know all of this?" Julie's question drew Hannah out of her thoughts.

"I know Amanda," Courtney said. "We met at one of my father's rallies and she took me under her wing. She was like a big sister to me, telling me that I wasn't a second-rate citizen, that I had as much right to control my life as men had to control theirs."

"So Amanda turned traitor," Julie said. "Then what happened?"

"Bobby put a hit out on her."

"On the woman he claimed to love more than life?"

"Yeah. That's what makes him so scary, you know? That cause of his, his God, it's bigger than anything else. He'd kill himself if he thought God told him to."

"I take it you don't believe in his God?"

"After what happened to Camargo? And Amanda?" Courtney's eyes filled with tears. "I don't believe in any God."

Hannah's heart cried out against the loss of innocence.

"If Bobby put a hit out on her, how was she able to kidnap her son a year later?"

"The guy who was supposed to kill her told Bobby she was taken care of, but he really kept her for himself. He was a sick guy. Amanda called me once from a pay phone. She needed information about Bobby's schedule but my mom came in and I hung up. The guy she'd been living with broke into a couple's home and tied up the husband and—"

"I know the story," Julie cut her off, as Hannah sat

there listening silently, feeling sicker by the second as she saw all the threads of evil coming together.

"Yeah, well, this Jefferson guy, he kept Amanda a virtual prisoner, his sex slave, for almost a year, promising her that he'd help her get her son. In the end, he didn't, but through him she was able to track Bobby's activities and whereabouts and when she saw her opportunity, she got Luke herself."

"Do you know where she is now?"

Courtney shook her head. "I'm sure she's dead," she said softly. "I was told she was…killed. Her and her little boy."

"By the Ivory Nation? Surely Bobby wouldn't have killed his own son?"

"Luke wasn't his son, really."

"What?"

"That's what Amanda told me. It was our secret. Bobby's sterile. Something to do with the beatings he took from his old man when he was a kid. He made Amanda get pregnant by some other guy while he watched, making sure no one enjoyed it, like that made it okay and medical or whatever."

The bitterness in the teenager's voice was a crime in itself. Hannah wondered if Courtney had grown up too young long ago? Or if this was a new development, since she'd fallen in love with a boy in her class who happened to be Hispanic?

"Do you know where that guy is now?"

"No."

"Maybe Amanda's with him."

"If she was, they're both dead. No way Bobby

would allow that. And it doesn't matter anyway," Courtney said, glancing at the deputy who'd been leaning silently against the wall by the door as if only now realizing he was there.

"The point is, there's no way I can go into court, with Bobby Donahue listening to me, and say anything other than what I've been told to say. I can't tell the truth about what happened to Camargo or I'll end up like Amanda. I'd rather go to prison—at least there—if I've done what I was told like a good little girl—I'll be safe. And I'll get out someday."

"You don't want to go to prison," Julie said as Hannah's mind reeled with options—none of them good. "You have rights, Courtney."

"Tell that to my dad."

Her dad. George Moss. The state's newest senator. The one who was supported by Bobby Donahue's money. And Brian's.

Hannah wanted to snatch the girl and run.

William took Hannah out to dinner as planned. Francis was with his mother, and even so, William had considered canceling. Too much was at stake.

Francis's safety. William's heart.

But he couldn't stay away.

Just one more time, he told himself. Once more. They'd have dinner. He'd kiss her goodbye and get on with his life.

After he noticed her favoring her right hand and found out why, he knew he had to steer clear of her. At least until the Ivory Nation threat was gone.

And then, over lettuce wraps and fried rice, she laughed at something he said. Told him about Taybee batting at herself in the mirror while Hannah was getting ready in the morning.

He had an instant vision of her standing at the double sink in her bathroom, a wall of mirrors in front of her. She was fresh from the shower, beads of moisture on her breasts and...

"Any development on the Donahue case?" he asked, bringing himself back to reality in the nick of time, but not before he'd filled her lettuce wrap for her—and taken care of anything else she might have needed both hands to do.

Hannah took too many chances. Her refusal to compromise endangered her life. And if nothing else, the worry was going to give William high blood pressure, send him to an early grave.

He had to finish this.

"I had a pretrial hearing today. Defense moved to have a witness struck."

She didn't say any more. Didn't reveal any of the specifics of the hearing. Palms sweating, he set down his chopsticks. "What are you going to do?"

She sipped her wine. Examined him as though measuring her words. "I'm not sure."

Not the answer he wanted.

"Grant the motion," he said. "Come on, Hannah. This is pretrial. You've got a jury coming in. Let them do the dirty work."

He hated the look she gave him, as though she'd tasted something bad. She hadn't taken a bite in several minutes. "This is me talking," he said, taking her uninjured hand. "You know how I feel about the law, about justice. But sometimes you have to play the game. Sometimes a greater justice is served by turning a blind eye."

He knew he'd made a mistake when she pulled her hand away. "What greater justice, William? Personal justice? You want me to save my ass, by letting that monster get away with terrorizing an entire state?"

He was losing her. "You're one woman," he tried. "You can't beat terrorism by yourself. Hell, the federal government has whole departments working on this sort of thing and even they can't wipe it out."

When and how the world had gone so insane, he didn't know. He only knew that he had to live in it. To keep his son safe in it.

"I'll rule whichever way serves the law," she said, standing. "I think I need some time alone, William. Call me tomorrow, okay?"

He meant to go after her. Instead, William sat back, ordered another glass of wine, and figured it was for the best that they'd driven to the restaurant separately.

"Brian?"

With his arm around Cynthia, Brian turned back to look at the tiny shape beneath the Blue's Clues covers on the twin bed in his spare room. "Yeah?"

"I love you."

The words were whispered. A secret. And nearly made Brian come unglued.

"I love you, too, Joseph," he said, taking his cue from the small, emotionally bruised child who'd captured his heart.

The four-year-old closed his eyes, hugging his Blue dog to his face, and rolled over.

Brian turned and caught the stark, bald love in Cynthia's eyes as she watched her son.

"He's going to be okay," she said, as though just now daring to believe it. They closed Joseph's bedroom door, headed to the master suite.

"You wait," Brian said. "In another year he'll be racing around making so much noise we'll be wishing for some peace and quiet."

Her silence met with Brian's as he heard himself. He was talking as if they were already a family. Or were going to be one.

And he'd yet to ask Cynthia to marry him.

Or even talk about their relationship. Their future. He'd asked her to live with him and left it at that.

She was a wonderful woman. A fabulous mother. Sexy. Smart. She'd stood by him in his time of crisis.

And there was something missing.

Brian searched for words. Searched again. Felt Cynthia's hand take his, pull him along to their room, to their bed.

He cared for her. A lot. It wasn't her.

It was him. Cara. When she'd died, a part of him had died, too. That had to be it.

Without speaking, Cynthia stripped him, caressing his body as she bared it to her touch. And then she stripped, too, slowly, putting on a show that would've made him hard if he hadn't already been aching for her.

Or for sex.

Take care of yourself, my friend. His words to Hannah earlier that day popped into his brain. As did her softly uttered, *I will.*

He hoped to God she was okay.

Cynthia pushed him back on the bed, and Brian let her, giving her the lead as she explored him with her tongue. And then he rolled over on top of her, pleasuring every inch of her, showing her with his body what he couldn't tell her out loud.

Showing her that she was precious. Valuable. That she deserved love in her life.

And when he closed his eyes, visions of another woman, another face appeared in his mind. He entered her. He moved in and out. He rode the waves.

But it wasn't Cynthia beneath him.

And it wasn't Cara, either.

21

When the phone woke her early Saturday morning, Hannah jumped for it. She'd talked to Brian during cartoons the previous week. Her right arm bumped the bed table as she grabbed the phone and when it didn't hurt, because it was numb, memories of the previous day came flooding back.

"Hello?"

"Hi, hon." William.

"Hi."

"You're still mad. Okay, I deserve that," he said. Pulling the covers up to her chin, she nodded. And said nothing.

"I'm sorry, Hannah. So sorry. I don't know, it's just…ever since Las Vegas, you drive me crazy, you know?"

"Yeah." She didn't want to understand. But she did.

"It's like all of a sudden I feel possessive. I'm in deeper than I bargained for."

He was going to tell her he loved her again. And Hannah didn't want to hear it.

Not this morning anyway.

She was too raw. From too many things.

"It's okay, Will, seriously. I understand. I know you're worried and it's hard to sit there and do nothing. If it helps any, I'm in the same boat. I'm also worried and feel like there's nothing I can do." She was talking too fast. And she kept talking.

"And before you say it, no, I can't do what they want. Not only because I have to do my job, but because to do so would give them power over me. Will, can't you see that? If I buckle under their pressure even once, I'm facing a lifetime of the same. I can't live like that."

William was a good man. She cared about him a lot.

"Can you understand that?" she asked softly, rubbing her numb arm, as if she could make herself begin to feel it sooner.

"Yes." His response, especially after his silence, surprised her. "Unfortunately I can see it," he added. "And I'm not sure where that leaves us."

Hannah wasn't sure, either. She hadn't shed a tear the night before. Not one. If she loved him, she would have, wouldn't she?

Unless she was just as numb as her arm?

"Let's just take things as they come," she suggested slowly, as she realized she wasn't ready for life without William, either. "So much is going on right now, for both of us. You've just got Francis back, so that was bound to change things for us again, anyway."

"Are you breaking up with me?" His genuine horror at the idea tugged at her heart.

"No, William, I'm not," she said, certain about

that much at least. "We've been through a lot together. And we haven't given this a chance to settle in." She hoped that was true. "I'm just suggesting that we not ask any more of ourselves and each other than we're comfortable with."

"Are you comfortable with seeing me tomorrow? Francis called and I'm taking him to a Suns game tonight."

"As long as you're comfortable with pork chops and a movie at home. I'm having a quiet weekend."

"That sounds wonderful."

"And, William? Don't worry, okay?"

"Yeah." He wasn't convincing.

As Hannah hung up, she wondered if staying in implied asking him to spend the night at her house. And hated herself for hoping he wouldn't.

Brian did the grocery shopping that week, leaving Cynthia at home with Joseph. He'd been insisting on pulling his share of chores since she'd moved in.

He'd also welcomed the chance to get out alone. Breathe. And just be.

And after an hour of wandering up and down aisles, comparing brand-name prices against generics, finding everything on the list he and Cynthia had made earlier that morning, he felt better. More in control. He'd been letting life get to him.

Wasting energy on things he couldn't control so much that he'd lost sight of those things he could. Focus was the key. He knew that. Had always known that.

Keeping that thought in mind, he walked into the kitchen, grocery bags in hand, ready to tell Cynthia the truth. That he was confused. But that he cared about her and wanted her in his home. That he'd take good care of her and Joseph.

She wasn't in the kitchen.

Or in the family room, either.

Setting the bags on the counter, he frowned, listening for the sounds of a television. Cartoons. Joseph. A mother speaking to a child.

All he heard was silence.

Odd.

He'd left the Jag in the drive and come in the front door, so now he checked the garage for Cynthia's old Chrysler.

It wasn't there.

And she hadn't left a message.

Odder yet.

There was no sign of injury. No drops of blood on the floor, towels lying around, plastic bags for ice. No signs of a hurried exit.

As he turned back, looking for any activity Joseph might have left in a hurry, the cleanliness that met his vision bothered him.

Where was Joseph's new booster chair?

And the plastic box that held his toys?

Brian took the stairs two at a time, hurrying to Joseph's room. The bed was stripped. The drawers and closet bare.

Cynthia's side of the master closet, her vanity in the ensuite were also empty.

As empty as he felt.

He found the note last—though he should have seen it easily propped in clear view against his pillow. And it eliminated any doubt he might have had.

She'd left him.

Because she felt so guilty for the hell she was putting him through, on Sunday Hannah broke down and told Will about Courtney Moss's confidential testimony. Putting their personal issues aside, William was the best judge she knew. And she'd struggled all weekend with what she should do regarding the girl's testimony.

She knew her legal options were severely limited. Will could only confirm that.

Still, it felt good to share the angst with someone who understood.

"I'm going to have to make her testify if she's called," she told him, though she was pretty certain the state wouldn't do so now. There wasn't enough to be gained that couldn't be brought in another way. And the danger to the minor child was immense.

For once, William agreed.

And on Monday morning, she informed Susan of her rulings, adding that she'd have a judgment written up that afternoon to file with the clerk of courts and pass on to the attorneys. Until then, if anyone should ask, no decision had been rendered.

Because she wanted time to change her mind?

"You're going to make her do it?" Wearing a

denim skirt and checked sweater, Susan looked almost as young as their witness.

"I have no reason not to," she said. Then added, "With luck, no one will call her. Why would they at this point?"

"But if they do," Susan said, following Hannah to her door, "she either perjures herself or her life is as good as over."

Hannah stopped. "How do you know that?" she asked her assistant.

Susan pointed to the speaker above her desk. "I heard the testimony," she said. "I didn't want to leave in case you needed me."

The sound system allowed Susan to hear into the courtroom.

"That was a confidential hearing," Hannah reminded her employee.

"I always watch your back, Judge. It's my job."

Relenting, Hannah nodded and went back to her desk. She was truly overwrought. Being too hard on everyone. William. Susan. The people who'd been supporting her for years.

She hoped to God this Donahue case went to trial as scheduled. The sooner this one was over, the better.

Angelo was back. Coming into the waiting room after an appointment Monday afternoon, Brian saw the detective enter and his heart sank.

What now?

He soon found out.

"We had an anonymous tip this morning," Angelo

said when they were alone in Brian's office. "I have a warrant to search your residence."

"You were already there," Brian said. He was wiser this time around—experienced. He didn't cower with fear.

"And we're going again," he said. "Because you're friends with Judge Montgomery, we're here to give you the option to be present."

Brian could refuse. And they'd go anyway.

"I'll have my receptionist reschedule the rest of my appointments," he said.

And then, when it seemed the detective was going to wait right there, Brian asked, "I'm assuming I can drive myself?"

Angelo conceded with a single dip of the head.

Riley Constance, the east complex presiding judge, was waiting in Hannah's chambers, chatting with Susan, when Hannah came off the bench that afternoon. Unless it was time for Judge Performance Review scores, a visit from the presiding judge wasn't generally positive. October wasn't time for JPR scores. Or transfers, either.

"Riley, how are you?" Hannah shook the other woman's hand. "Come on back." She led the way to her office.

"Fine," Riley's reply was short. Succinct. Never a good sign.

"What's up?" Hanging up her robe, Hannah took a seat behind her desk, rubbing her right arm, happy she could feel it again.

"I'm concerned about your decision to rule for testimony that could put a seventeen-year-old child at risk," Riley said. "Especially considering the circumstances." Riley's hair, always well coiffed, had turned grayer over the past several months. But her sixty-year-old body was as slim and stylishly dressed as ever.

Hannah felt a bit underdressed in her slacks and sweater, although these days, some judges even wore jeans under their robes.

"The circumstances?" she asked. No one knew—with the exception of Susan and William—that she'd made her decision. She hadn't even written it yet.

"The girl admitted she'd perjure herself. Her testimony won't be worth anything once a jury finds out. And if she tells the truth, she's betraying not only her father, but according to her, the Ivory Nation as well. They don't take that lightly. If something happens to her when she testifies, and it comes out that you knew of the potential danger and did nothing…well, I'd hate to see what the papers would do with that one."

Hannah sat unmoving, slowly freezing from the inside out.

"Her father's a senator, for God's sake, Hannah! You shouldn't have taken this kind of risk with such a high-profile case. Hell, I wouldn't be surprised if he sues the state for putting his daughter at risk."

Was Riley suggesting that Hannah *not* do what the law required? Which was to allow the witness? Because of who her father was?

"Based on what Courtney said in front of the defendant and her father, the only way to protect her is to allow the testimony. To do otherwise would raise suspicions." She told her superior what she'd realized herself.

"I'm banking on Julie Gilbert not calling the witness. The state's case wouldn't benefit from the testimony," she added.

"I don't like it, Hannah."

"Are you writing me up?"

"No. Of course not. You're within the boundaries of your job. I'm just concerned."

"About the press. And the state's money."

"And you." Clearly Hannah was a distant third.

"How did you know about my decision?" Hannah heard herself ask. As numb inside as her arm had been.

"I'm sorry, but I'm not at liberty to say. I promised to keep my source confidential."

"I understand," she said. And repeated the words several more times before the presiding judge ran out of steam and left.

Left Hannah sitting at her desk, afraid to move.

"Judge!" Susan stood before her, eyes wide. "I have no idea how she heard about your decision. I didn't tell her. I swear I didn't. When she came in, she asked me what I knew and I told her that she'd have to talk to you. But I couldn't help overhearing what she was saying and… Oh, Judge, I'm so sorry."

Sorry because she'd made a mistake? Betrayed her boss? Or sorry because she'd been caught?

"Did you put the scorpion in my drawer?" Hannah asked, staring hard at her young assistant. "And leave the picture on my desk?"

It all made horrifying sense. Susan had a key. She knew everyone. Talked to everyone. If someone wanted to get to Hannah, Susan would be the obvious way.

And if someone as powerful as Bobby Donahue threatened her, blackmailed her, she'd cave. She had a husband. Young kids. She was vulnerable.

"Of course not! I would never do anything to hurt you. You have to know that!"

The wringing hands were a smart move. As were the tears. "I wouldn't hurt you, Judge. I love this job. I love working with you."

Hannah didn't know what to believe. If Susan hadn't done this—and in spite of herself, she was inclined to believe her—that left only William. He was the only other person she'd told of a decision that wasn't even official yet.

"Am I fired?" Susan asked, choking on her tears.

"No," Hannah said. And then, "I don't know. Go home for now."

"Yes, ma'am." Susan had never called her that before. "Should I come in in the morning?"

"Yes." If nothing else, the young woman would need to collect her stuff.

Brian counted the rings. Just counted. He didn't worry. Didn't sweat. Just counted. And when she didn't answer on her office phone, he dialed her cell.

"Brian? What's up?" Hannah sounded beat. Defeated. And then he remembered that she had to file her opinion on the Donahue case. Unfortunately he only had a few minutes.

"This is my one phone call," he said simply.

"You're downtown again?"

"Yes."

"Why? What happened?"

It seemed like years since he'd talked to her, instead of three days. He should have called when Cynthia left—would have—except that their friendship had somehow started to color his relationship with Cynthia. Crying on Hannah's shoulder had just seemed wrong.

"Angelo got a call this morning saying there was HGH in the guesthouse, behind a paneling board in the bathroom."

"What!?"

"He served me with a warrant this afternoon. And went right to the spot."

"There was a hiding space behind the paneling?"

"Filled with HGH."

"I can't believe it."

That made two of them.

"Was Cynthia there? What did she say? Did she see anything? Someone could've posed as a landscaper maybe…"

"Cynthia's gone. She left me on Saturday."

"Oh, Brian. Oh, my God. I'm so sorry. Why? I thought she was one-hundred-percent supportive. Why didn't you call me?"

"I don't know. I figured you'd be with William." Conscious of where he was, and the time, he quickly told her how he'd found the house empty when he'd come home from the grocery store. "I think it might've been because I didn't ask her to marry me. It had kind of come up the night before and I dropped the ball."

It seemed so long ago now. And while he'd missed Cynthia on Sunday, he'd missed Joseph a whole lot more. Had worried about the boy all day, concerned with how this change would affect him. At some point, he wasn't going to be able to bounce back.

"Joseph had just told me he loved me," Brian said, mostly because he had no one else to share his thoughts with.

And they were jumbled. Confused. Overwhelming.

"Well, if she managed to pack up and leave in the time it took you to grocery shop, it's obvious she'd been planning to go," Hannah said.

He didn't think so. "She didn't have much." And at the moment, Cynthia's leaving was irrelevant. "I'm in deep trouble, Hannah." He'd already been booked— again—the whole procedure. So far, he was in a cell by himself, but there was no telling if that would last. If he'd have even that security. "Please, do what you can to get me out of here."

"I'm assuming, since you only had the one call, you haven't spoken with Tanya?"

"No."

"I'll call her. And then I'm coming down. We can talk more in person."

The promise was a lifeline. He held on to it rigidly as he was shown back to the cold hole of cement with a skinny excuse for a cot and absolutely nothing else.

He had no possessions. No freedom. And no dignity left, either.

Hannah didn't get to sleep until early the next morning. She'd canceled her dinner with William as soon as she'd heard from Brian—telling him only that something had come up. She still needed to deal with her long-time friend—and recent lover. But in light of Brian's crisis, her own upsetting day had seemed trivial at best.

She'd spent the evening with Tanya, and in an interview room speaking with Brian.

And then, after crying most of the way home, she'd poured herself a glass of wine and sat in the living room with Tay, with every light on, and tried not to think about her gentle friend, hunched over in handcuffs, or the stark, lost look on his face as they'd led him away from her and back to his cell.

And she prayed that Brian would be kept safe. Hard. As hard as she'd prayed when Jason took his final turn for the worst.

Tuesday morning, for reasons completely unknown to her, Hannah turned on the news as she waited in the kitchen for her coffee to drip. She wasn't a news watcher, preferring not to hear sensationalized versions of the evil in the world when she spent her days with the real thing. But this morning she needed company.

This morning, bad news seemed to be all there was. Having it on the television set as well as in every other aspect of her life, was almost comforting.

She and the rest of the world were in the same boat.

She wasn't alone.

Brian wasn't alone.

She poured a cup of coffee and took a sip. A second. Was contemplating possibilities for injecting the hot liquid directly into her veins when a name on the television set caught her attention.

"Robert Miller," the male announcer was saying, "a former Tucson police detective, who was rumored to have been in the state's protective custody waiting to testify at a trial in Phoenix later this month, was found murdered this morning, shot at close range outside a Wickenburg motel room…"

Hannah's coffee cup shattered against the cool tile floor at her feet.

22

By five o'clock Wednesday afternoon, Bobby Donahue was free. With no evidence, and their key witness dead, the state had to drop all charges against him.

There were no clues in Miller's shooting, but Hannah knew as well as anyone that Donahue had had something to do with it.

The only bright spot was that the D.A.'s office had managed to get Miller's family safely out of the state. Whether or not they'd stay safe was anyone's guess.

Hannah had no idea how she made it through the rest of the week. She did her job, stumbling her way through paperwork with a temporary court-appointed JA after having put Susan on leave. She went to dinner with Maggie Murphy and Donna Jasmine, the only other two judges she'd ever felt a kinship with. Another night she had drinks with a couple of her and Brian's mutual college friends. All were stunned by the turn of events in Brian's life. All wanted to help.

She visited Brian daily. Nagged Tanya incessantly. Avoided William completely. And waited to be murdered.

As melodramatic as that sounded, even to her, that was precisely what she expected. Even to the point of telling Maggie and Donna about Tay, and asking Maggie to take her in if something happened. While Maggie had assured her she'd be fine, she'd also agreed to take the cat.

While the evidence against Brian was still circumstantial—there were no fingerprints or DNA to definitely tie him to the HGH found in his home—on Friday the state charged him with one count of first-degree murder, with other charges possibly to follow.

The one good note of the week—they weren't going for the death penalty.

Hannah knew it was because they didn't have enough on him to prove his guilt beyond the shadow of a doubt. In a non-capital case, they only had the burden of reasonable doubt.

The semantics could cost a man the rest of his life.

"Funny, really," she said to Brian on Friday afternoon, having left work immediately following her afternoon calendar. "I lived in fear all those weeks, and now, with Donahue out, I'm not even afraid. He can do his worst. What have I got left to lose?"

"Don't talk like that," Brian said, sitting with her at a table in a private consultation room usually reserved for attorneys and their clients. She'd shamelessly pulled strings. And didn't care about that anymore, either.

"Your life is precious, Hannah. You've got so much ahead of you, so much to do."

"As do you," she said, tears in her eyes as she looked at him, cuffed wrists on the table between them. "So why does life keep turning us down?"

Brow furrowed, he stared at her. "Maybe because we weren't aiming in the right directions."

"What does that mean?"

"How long have you been seeing William as more than a friend?"

"I don't know," she said, thinking back. And trying not to. She hadn't told Brian about her visit from the presiding judge the previous week. It didn't even seem to matter anymore. "We've been partnering up for social events for a couple of years, I guess. Ever since Patsy first left him. But it didn't really get romantic until recently."

"And I was considering asking Cynthia to marry me."

She wasn't sure where he was going with this, but his intent expression was making her heart pound.

"Yeah. So?" Her mouth was so dry she almost choked on the words.

"How long have we been friends?"

She didn't need to count. "Twenty years."

Brian held her gaze. "My time in here has done one very good thing for me." His words weren't what she'd been expecting.

"Oh? What's that?"

"It's shown me that the happiness I've been trying to find all these years has been right in front of me.

I was just so caught up in who we'd been, in Cara's death, in carrying around the guilt for her death…"

"But, Brian, it wasn't your fault! That kid crossed over into your lane and—"

"I know," he said, sounding oddly at peace now. "But I was the man, the husband, the driver. I'd sworn to love and protect her. I lived and she didn't."

"Oh, Brian, Cara wouldn't ever have wanted you to feel badly about that, to waste one second of your life thinking you could've done anything differently."

His gaze grew momentarily distant. "Well, that's the other part of it," he said. "I know that I was told I wasn't to blame. I know I wasn't charged or ticketed. But I can't remember the actual impact. I remember approaching the intersection. And then I remember sitting in the car and hearing Cara cry out—"

"The bastard who hit you was convicted of aggravated vehicular manslaughter. He went to prison. You know that."

"Yeah." Staring down at the table, he grew quiet and Hannah thought they were done, until he raised his head again and looked her in the eye. "At first, my sense of guilt was very real, incapacitating, but over the years, when it would've dissipated, I think I subconsciously held on to it. I used the guilt to protect myself," he said.

Confused, she frowned. "From what?"

"You."

"Me?" Hannah drew back, shocked. "Why?"

"Because how could I possibly chance falling in love again when I knew how horribly it hurt to lose it?"

"Falling..."

"You see, Hannah, with nothing to do this week but think, with no one to listen to but myself, I've had to stop running and admit that I've been in love with you for years."

Her heart raced. Her mind couldn't settle. "But you never said..."

"How could I? Even to myself? We were set in our roles. I was Cara's husband. You were her best friend. We'd both lost our true loves. We were comfortable. It worked."

He was right, of course, but...

"But then it didn't. It doesn't work for me anymore. I know now that's why I couldn't love Cynthia. I told myself it was because my heart died with Cara. When, in truth, it's because I'd already given it to you."

Hannah didn't know what to say. What to do. Receiving a declaration of love in a jail conference room from a man in handcuffs wasn't in her repertoire.

Receiving one from Brian, even less so.

"Anyway," he said, waving through the window to the guard, signaling that he was ready to return to his cell, "I won't bring this up again. I have no expectations. I don't want it to change things, or make it awkward between us. In light of all that's going on, with both of us, I just wanted you to know."

The door opened, the guard entered, and Brian was gone before Hannah could form a coherent thought.

It took Bobby Donahue four days to find the only woman he'd ever loved. To find his son. Because, during his search, he found far more than he'd been expecting. Another Ivory Nation job that hadn't been ordered by him. Hadn't been handed down from God. What he found made him sick at first. Until he realized what it meant.

Bobby was being called home to his Maker.

At last.

Everything came and went in cycles—the planets, the suns and moons, the civilizations. They rose and then they fell. For every good there was a bad.

The Ivory Nation had been good. The Heavenly Father's tool. But power corrupted. Greed and hate took the place of service to God. Greed and hate twisted faithful followers until those followers believed they were more powerful than the Father who'd called them. Thanking his Heavenly Father that he'd been spared such a fate, Bobby spent hours on his knees, seeking direction for the coming days.

Ivory Nation brothers were no longer listening to God. They were acting on their own initiative and hurting the cause in the process. Killing babies was not the way to white freedom. They'd used God's tool for senseless destruction.

And so the tool must be delivered up.

If he'd ever imagined this moment, Bobby would have expected to be saddened. He loved the Ivory Nation. It had been his salvation.

But he wasn't sad.

This earthly life of pain and turmoil, of despair and betrayal, would be traded in for paradise. He'd finally earned his rest.

Or he would very soon. After he fulfilled God's final orders.

Bobby would have said, if ever questioned about finding Amanda, that he'd be racing as fast as he could to get her. To do his duty to God once and for all. To rescue his son. Another very special soul.

Luke. One of God's most special chosen.

Much like their brother, Jesus.

Instead, as calm as a summer afternoon, Bobby sat at the desk in his home office, the wood from the serviceable chair digging into his back in a way that was familiar to him, comforting, and dialed his cell phone.

Didn't matter that it was Saturday. The man would answer. Some things didn't change.

Anybody else might have been amazed that he could remember the number after not using it in almost a year, but Bobby knew from whence his thoughts came. Bobby hadn't remembered the number on his own. The Lord had been putting thoughts in Bobby's head for almost two decades.

Just hang on, son. He'll pass out soon. I love you. He'd been ten when God had first whispered to him.

And another time. *It's okay, son. You aren't alone. I love you.*

He'll pay for this, son. You have my assurance. I love you.

You aren't bad, son. You're one of my special souls. I chose you....

I chose you, Bobby. Don't ever forget that. I have plans for you....

The words went on and on. Replaying themselves, a ritual Bobby had been repeating for years...until they were interrupted by a voice on the other end of the line.

"Boyd."

"Detective, how are you?"

"Donahue? Is that you?"

"You saw my number on you caller ID, Detective. You knew it was me when you picked up the phone."

"You think I know your number by heart?"

"I know you do."

The cat-and-mouse game was kind of boring now that Bobby was filled with light.

"What the hell do you want?" the grizzled detective grouched.

"Marriage apparently hasn't improved your disposition," Bobby drawled, just because it was expected of him.

"You fucking bastard. If you've done anything to my wife, I'll—"

"Calm down, Detective." The games were over. "I have no beef with your wife. I'm calling on official business."

"Right."

"I'm dead serious, Detective."

"About as dead as my ex-partner is, right? We both know you ordered Miller killed. I even know why. You tricked him. You let him think he was working for you when, all along, you were planning to kill him for betraying you last year."

"You have a vivid imagination, Detective."

"You just bided your time until his death could benefit you," Boyd continued. "You courted him, let him think that he had earned God's favor by ridding your 'church' of two traitors, but in truth, you hated him for shooting Tony Littleton. You should've had the right to do that yourself."

Bobby couldn't get upset. None of this mattered anymore.

"You lured him up to Phoenix to use him as a pawn in your game, knowing you were going to kill him before he could testify. He got Kenny out and then, by dying, got you out, too."

The man was good. But Bobby already knew that. Hence the phone call.

"You're going to die, Donahue. You mark my words and when you do even hell will reject your sorry excuse for a soul."

"I love you, too, Detective," Bobby said, feeling his heart expand as he spoke. "And I want to help you."

"Help me how?"

"I'm going to hand you what you've been wanting for years."

"Your head on a platter?"

"Better." He was ready. Peaceful. There was no pain. "What could be better than that?"

"I'm going to help you bring down the Ivory Nation."

And all he wanted in return, though God had expressly instructed Bobby to keep this last to himself, was to take his son with him. Their earthly work was done.

Hannah spent Saturday at home alone. While she screened calls in case of emergencies, she didn't take any. Or return a single one, either. Not even when William's frantic tones came through her answering machine just after noon.

"Hannah, please pick up. I have no idea what's going on with you," he said. "I understand you're spending time at the jail, trying to help Brian, but there's only so much you can do. I need you, Hannah. Please at least let me know you're okay."

She thought about answering. Almost did. Compelled by guilt and a relationship that spanned most of her adult life. And then she heard Susan's words as she'd tearfully packed up her belongings Tuesday morning in preparation for her perhaps permanent leave.

"It's not me, Judge," Susan had said, hurrying through the office in an effort to be gone before the rest of the staff arrived. "I'm careful. I never repeat a word you say to me. Not unless you specifically tell me to pass it on. Not even to Tammy or Jaime when it's about our chambers. I wait for you to tell them."

Hannah had been struck by the truth of that statement. Many times over their two years together Hannah had assumed that the others knew something—vacation days, plans for their annual Christmas lunch—only to find that Susan didn't pass on the information without Hannah's instructions to do so.

Even so...

"Judge Constance couldn't have gotten that information any other way," Hannah had told her.

Susan had stopped, her eyes filled with tears, but no longer crying. "Did you tell Judge Horne about your decision?"

Hannah had said nothing. Her conversations with William were none of her assistant's business.

"If you did, there's your answer," Susan persisted. "I've seen him lurking in the halls, Judge, more than once, and then later he acts as though he just arrived. And a couple of times the expression on his face changed completely when you turned around. He'd be all smiles, and then the second you couldn't see, his face straightened and he looked, I don't know, almost depressed. Or cold..."

Hannah had still sent Susan home. She'd been frightened, felt betrayed by her assistant's possible culpability. And even more disturbed by the fact that her lover, a fellow judge, could be stabbing her in the back while he caressed her. The ramifications were too awful to contemplate and reached far beyond personal betrayal.

Afraid that William might really get worried and

turn up at her home, Hannah dialed his cell that afternoon, relieved when her call went straight to voice mail. She told him she was fine. And that she thought they needed some time apart, time to figure out how her career choices and his son, could fit together.

She just couldn't believe, or perhaps didn't want to believe, that William was working for the Ivory Nation.

Much easier to think she'd been double-crossed by a young woman who gossiped too much, but only in her own relatively small circle. Without as much clout or public trust. Without as much power.

One thing was certain: there were only two people who knew that she'd decided to grant the state's motion to allow Courtney Moss's testimony and one of them had sold her out.

The blow was equal no matter who had dealt it.

Brian considered not calling Hannah. But free or not, he'd changed during his days in that small gray cell. Life was worth more to him. Time was no longer a commodity, but a gift.

Personal honesty was a must.

There was no more running. No more hiding.

In jail. Or out.

Being caged by bars was one thing—being imprisoned by the fear of living was a fate worse than death.

"Brian, hi." Hannah sounded welcoming when he called Sunday before noon. Welcoming and reticent, as well.

She wasn't sure what to do with him.

That made two of them.

"Are you free?" he asked simply though his mind was reeling.

"Yeah, what do you need? I was planning to come this afternoon. Can I bring you something?"

Brian was fully aware of the relief that swept through him with the knowledge that she'd been planning to come see him. After his confession on Friday, and her absence at Saturday's visitation, he'd been unsure.

He acknowledged the relief—and moved on. She thought he was calling from jail.

"I need a ride," he told her, both exhilarated and focused. He had much to do.

"What? You're out? What happened? Where are you?"

The rapid questions made him smile, briefly. And the stiffness in his face reminded him of how long it had been since he'd done so.

He'd spent he didn't know how many hours of the past twenty-four locked in a conference room at the jail with Tucson detective Daniel Boyd, Detective Angelo, and, of all people, Bobby Donahue, leader of the Ivory Nation.

The man who'd been stalking Hannah for more than a year.

He'd had a little sleep. They all had. But not much.

"I'm free and will be ready to go within the hour," he said. After one last briefing. "I'd rather wait and explain when I see you."

At this point he didn't trust anyone. Or anything. Including the precinct phone.

"I'm leaving right now."

Brian almost repeated the release instructions he'd been given, but then remembered there was no need.

Hannah knew the drill.

23

"Tell me what's going on." Hannah faced Brian, a changed man, at his kitchen table. He'd insisted they wait until they were safely behind his alarm system before he'd tell her anything.

She still wasn't sure why.

But she was scared to death.

"Yesterday afternoon Bobby Donahue contacted a Tucson detective who'd helped him, briefly, when his girlfriend, Amanda, first disappeared. He's turning himself in—and turning in the Ivory Nation, as well."

She didn't believe it. It was another ruse. A game. "What? Why?" Who were the pawns? How many would there be this time?

"He received word, while in jail, that Amanda was still alive. And still in Arizona."

"God help her."

"Yeah, well, of course as soon as he got out he was hell-bent on finding her. But when he started digging, he found something else, as well. Something bigger than his own domestic troubles. He discovered the 'kill them before they grow up and pollute' project. Officially known as the Save Resources for God's Babies project."

Cold and shaking, Hannah couldn't speak. Could hardly breathe past the lump in her throat. Here it came.

And she wasn't ready.

"It took Bobby a little longer than usual to find out the details because, not knowing who was involved, he was working on his own."

She didn't believe that, either. Bobby Donahue sat in his castle and gave orders.

"The person responsible for the deaths of all six babies is a guy named Steven Brown. He's a doctor at the free clinic. I've worked with him. And he's a member of the Ivory Nation, though I certainly didn't know that. I think he initially planned to kill his own patients, but then he met me. And recognized my name from some campaign-funding list. With his IN contacts, it didn't take him long to figure out that I'd be the perfect target, the perfect frame, and suddenly his plan changed. The Alliance, a rival supremacist organization, heard about the plan through an acquaintance of Brown's and had wanted in on what was supposed to be not only the biggest single supremacist operation in Phoenix, but was to control a judge—you. And if that failed, would teach you a lesson and use you as an example for anyone else who dared to cross them. Word had spread that you refused to buckle. Which made them nervous."

So they'd been after her all along.

How had she ever imagined, even for a second, that she was strong enough to take on these fiends? The lump in her throat had spread to her stomach—a cancer that was never going to go away.

Brian, with a frightening lack of emotion, continued to relate disturbing details as though he were reporting on a baseball game—a fact that betrayed the toll the last week had taken on him.

The original scheme had been so simple Hannah didn't want to understand it. For every male, non-breast-fed Hispanic baby who'd been vaccinated in Brian's office, there'd appeared a free, professionally wrapped sample of formula in their parents' mailbox. A sample that had been tainted with HGH, with the help of a supremacist at the packager.

Amanda Blake, in exchange for Alliance protection from the Ivory Nation, had broken into Brian's office, gotten hold of his records, his calendar, kept Brown up to date on any new Hispanic patients from the free clinic and reported inoculation appointments.

The one piece of vital information they'd been missing was something Brian had considered irrelevant—the fact that none of the babies were breast-fed.

Five of the six babies were the offspring of illegal's who were poor enough to have to rely on free health care. That they would use anything that arrived without charge was pretty much a given.

And in Hannah's case, she'd been out of formula

and seen the envelope as a godsend at the end of a very tiring day of judging and single parenting. She'd just returned to work the week before, after her personal family leave. She'd still been adjusting to interrupted sleep and full-time work.

She'd been the only question mark. Carlos might not have died.

But they'd tried.

And they'd gotten lucky.

In the end, her fatigue had killed her son.

Baby ate. Baby ingested HGH. Baby died.

End of story.

Oh, God. She'd killed her son. Panic filled her. Choked her. And her mind ran on.

People were so easily manipulated. Smart people. People who should know better.

She hadn't known. Couldn't possibly have known. She hadn't done anything another parent wouldn't have. Even conscientious parents used mailed samples. Right?

But wouldn't a conscientious parent have known, first and foremost, that she had enough sustenance on hand to feed her child?

While Hannah sweated and chilled, while she fought nausea, Brian continued to relay information. No one from the Ivory Nation had known about Amanda's involvement.

And no one knew, still, how she'd managed to get in and out of Brian's office.

Hannah didn't like unanswered questions.

"…God told Donahue that the Ivory Nation has

served its purpose. It's fallen into the hands of evil, and he's been called to put an end to the corruption. That's where I come in," Brian was saying.

Hannah sat up. "What?"

"I agreed to help them, Hannah, in exchange for my immediate release and all charges against me being dropped."

"Help them how?"

"I'm going to be a pawn used to get Brown's full confession."

"No, you aren't. I—"

He took her hand again, silencing her with a look. "Hear me out, Hannah. Please."

For him, she'd listen. And then she'd find a way to put an end to this craziness. Holding his gaze, Hannah nodded.

"Donahue's meeting with Brown today. He's telling him that he's known for some time about the Save Resources for God's Babies project and that God has revealed to Bobby that Brown's a saint, a genius, for coming up with the plan. For being so in tune with their maker that he heard the voice when it whispered to him. God has told him that Brown was divinely led. Donahue's going to praise Brown for his attention to God, to faith, to messages. He's going to praise him for his loyalty to God's cause of making the world pure by whatever means. Brown's been brainwashed by Donahue's teachings for so many years that Donahue can now use those techniques to suck the man in."

"Which is how he's managed to run such a large group of criminals for so long."

"Exactly. You were right about one thing, Hannah. Ivory Nation brethren are everywhere. In all professions. After what I heard last night and today, I'm willing to believe that there isn't a company anywhere that doesn't have a supremacist implant. Anyway, Donahue is telling Brown that the cops are closing in, that my innocence is going to be proven and that the state has evidence that will implicate the Ivory Nation. That God has revealed to him that they must act quickly to save the Ivory Nation and that God has told him how to do it."

Hannah didn't like the sound of this at all.

"He's going to tell him that God led me to Donahue in jail. That I was a broken man, one who'd seen the light. That I swore allegiance to the Ivory Nation. That I wished I *had* killed those babies. That I've dedicated myself to the cause and that I'm willing to do whatever it takes to prove my loyalty. He's telling him that God has said they can trust me."

"That's bullshit, Brian!" Hannah pulled her hand away. She couldn't touch him and listen to this garbage at the same time. Not when it meant she was going to lose him. "These guys don't trust anyone."

"Actually, they do," Brian said. "They're as vulnerable as anyone else, Hannah. As human. They all need to feel that sense of belonging, just like the rest of us. As misplaced as their trust might be, they get their strength and courage from believing there is someone they *can* trust."

Hannah shivered. "You've certainly learned a lot

in the past twenty-four hours. What are you, some supremacist expert now?"

"I'm a man caught in someone else's web, choosing to take control of my life." Brian's delivery was calm. The lack of defensiveness in his tone confirmed to her that he meant to do this.

"I've had more than my share of lemons, Hannah," he said, his gaze open. "I'm making lemonade."

"If you partner with Bobby Donahue, you're committing suicide."

"I have to do this, Hannah."

"You aren't guilty," she said, her arms across her chest as she faced him across the table. "You didn't have to make this deal. We'd have gotten you out anyway."

"You don't know that." He sipped his coffee, laced with just a drop of whiskey. "These people are powerful. But it's more than that. It's about doing what's right. About making life matter. About using my life for the greater good, not just my personal good. The police need my cooperation if their plan to draw out the Ivory Nation is going to work."

"You help people in other ways," she said, arguing the case of her life. "You save lives, Brian. You help children grow up healthy and happy. You rid the world of sickness every day."

"Six of my patients are dead, Hannah! For God's sake, one of them is your son! You think I don't know what that does to you? I can't bring Carlos back, sweetie, but I can help bring his killer to justice."

Hannah's vision was so blurred with tears, she couldn't see him. And when she didn't speak, he continued on with the business at hand.

Hannah didn't blame him. There came a point when all you could do was go on. Because you weren't dead.

"Donahue's telling Brown that one of the brethren told the cops that the Ivory Nation—and not me—was behind the HGH baby deaths. And that the traitor didn't have a chance to say anything else."

"But if they have to have this great trust to feel safe, won't the knowledge that someone snitched destroy them?"

"They're being told that Miller was the snitch and that's why he died."

If she didn't know better, Hannah might've believed Bobby Donahue really was led by God. Everything seemed to fall into place for him. Everything, including a murder to save his ass, worked in his favor.

"And as long as Bobby's the one saying it, his followers will believe anything," Brian continued. "And amazingly, he's never taken a misstep as far as the brotherhood is concerned. It's almost eerie, like this guy really is perfect—just in his own world and living by beliefs that most of us can't accept. His real power comes not from the heinous acts or the fear, but from his faithful living, from his willingness to walk through the fire again and again, sacrificing over and over for the cause. There are very few members of the Ivory Nation brotherhood who haven't benefited from Donahue's personal dedication at least once. It keeps them faithful. If one of the brethren fell, then that brother is a traitor and will be dealt with accordingly. But as long as Donahue succeeds, they are strong and powerful."

Hannah's hands were shaking, her entire body trembling.

"Donahue's going to tell Brown that if they're going to hold off exposure, refute a dead cop's testimony, they're going to have to catch me red-handed so there won't be any doubt in the prosecutor's mind as to who killed those babies. There won't be any need for further investigation. Donahue's going to tell Brown that I've agreed to inject an infant with HGH. There will be a witness to the injection and the syringe will have my fingerprints."

There was a buzzing in Hannah's ears. "Who's going to be the witness?" she asked, dreading the answer.

"Steven Brown. He's being asked, as others of God's prophets have been, to sacrifice his infant daughter for the cause. He's being told he is the only one Bobby can trust to witness the injection. He's a doctor. He can give professional testimony in court. I'm to give him the syringe when I've completed the injection. He'll say he found it at the clinic."

Hannah tried to speak, and couldn't. A father was willing to sacrifice his own child? She stared at Brian, horrified. This was all too sick. Too...

"Why not just have you confess? Then there wouldn't need to be a trial. Or any of this."

"Right now, I'm charged with first-degree murder, but there are no capital charges. If I admit guilt, there would be no trial and the state would go straight for the death penalty. A sacrifice like that would make the brotherhood too nervous."

"Why should they care?"

"Because I'm only being asked to take the same risks as all of them. That's what bonds them so closely. They're all equally vulnerable, equally guilty, equally at risk. And they take those risks because they believe that Bobby—with God's help—can free them if they get caught. The last thing they want to see is a brother, especially a new recruit, who can't be saved."

It made a twisted sort of sense. The same twisted, sick thinking that marked everything Donahue.

"What if they find out that Donahue's betrayed them?"

"Then I'm of no use." Brian stood, warmed his coffee. And hers, adding a touch of whiskey. "And no threat, either. They'll already know that they've been found out. I'm only useful if I can help them stay out of jail."

"And you really think they'll fall for this stupid scheme? They really believe that you're willing to inject a baby girl with HGH, and leave the syringe where it can be found to clear the brotherhood, even though it means being found guilty of murders they committed? They believe you're willing to take the rap for them, to be arrested, because you know Bobby Donahue and God will protect you and get you out of jail?"

"Yes. They've all been asked to do similar things at one time or another. It's normal to them. This is how these guys work, Hannah. You have to go the distance, with no thought to self, only to the good of the brotherhood, in order to get in. That's how and why they trust each other as they do. They wouldn't trust a simpler plan. Sacrifice—self-sacrifice—is what breeds the adrenaline that keeps the Ivory Nation alive."

She just couldn't comprehend this. And at the same time, she could.

"And you honestly believe that this Steven Brown is so loyal that he'll sacrifice his own daughter just because Donahue tells him to? It's all so convoluted."

"Look at the Bible, Hannah. It's filled with convoluted tests of faith. It's another one of Donahue's techniques. He uses biblical examples, which instills loyalty.

"And yes, after sitting in a room with Bobby Donahue for much of the past twenty-four hours, I really think Brown will agree. He believes God is calling out to him, that he's being set apart as a prophet, and he's willing to sacrifice his firstborn to that end. Besides, the child is just a girl."

"What happens when the baby doesn't die? Obviously you aren't really going to inject the child with anything that will kill her."

Brian shrugged. "Of course not. And it doesn't matter. Brown will be there for the injection of pure saline. I get him to confess to the other murders, the wire I'll be wearing will pick it up and he'll be arrested on the spot."

"Or he somehow figures out that you're wired, pulls a gun and shoots you."

"I'll be wearing a bulletproof vest. Boyd and Donahue will be in the examination rooms on either side of us. Angelo is going to be in the cupboard under the examination table. I'll be fully protected."

If Brian's assurances were meant to ease her fears, they'd failed miserably. Hannah didn't trust Boyd—he'd been Miller's partner for years. She most certainly didn't trust Donahue. And now she had no faith in Angelo, either.

Or Susan. Or William. Her two other confidants, other than Brian. Who was clearly out of his mind.

She had no idea what to do. How to make him see sense. She didn't know where to turn. Who the hell did she talk to?

"As soon as we get Brown's confession, other arrests will be made within the hour," Brian said. "Once the key people from this project are in jail, Donahue is going to turn over years' worth of Ivory Nation paperwork documenting murders, tortures, robberies, vandalisms, drug deals, money laundering. Rape. And I'm sure a list of other things I don't want to know about."

"I don't believe that for a second."

"And he'll contact each of the remaining members of the core brotherhood privately, telling each one that God is calling that brother to confess everything he knows about Ivory Nation activities. He's going to make each of them think that he's the only one to be called. He's their prophet. They revere him, or at least have a total fear of his connection to God."

"They'll never do it."

"I believe they will."

"And if they don't?"

"It's a chance I'm willing to take."

He wasn't going to listen to her.

He believed them.

They had him.

"Donahue sends his apologies, by the way," Brian said. He'd changed over the past week. Become harder. Less innocent.

"What does Donahue have to apologize to me for?" If he hadn't known about any of this...

"For Callie. Your living room. The ring's disappearance. The photo on your desk. The scorpion."

"Callie?" She hadn't let the cat out? Her pet had been murdered? Same as her son had been? "The son of a bitch killed my family."

Cold to the bone, Hannah stared at her friend, who'd just been used to threaten her again. The Ivory Nation leader was in control even now, in the privacy of Brian's home. He was sending messages. Letting her know that nothing she loved was safe from him.

Including Brian.

She got the message loud and clear.

Donahue had Brian. And he'd have anything else Hannah ever cared about.

He was going to cut her heart out piece by piece. Because she'd dared to defy him. She'd dared to stand for justice.

"I don't want you to do this." Donahue had arranged to have a young boy break into her home—

and had had someone on the police force lie about it, saying it wasn't gang related.

Deputy Charles? Was he in, too?

"It's too late." Dressed in jeans and a long-sleeve maroon T-shirt, Brian looked more casual, more relaxed, than she'd seen him in ages. "I've already agreed. Things are in motion," he continued. "I couldn't stop them if I wanted to. If I don't do this, the Ivory Nation will continue to exist. And they'll just keep stalking us, Hannah—to take away anything we care about."

"So he wins. He's got us doing his bidding out of fear of retribution."

"Partly. Maybe. But in this case, his bidding is bringing about exactly what we want most. The end to all of this. Including the Ivory Nation."

"I don't believe that."

"I have to do this for Carlos, honey. And for the others, too."

"Nothing you do is going to bring Carlos back. I can't lose you too." She couldn't let this go. She knew something was amiss. That he was being played. Was going to get hurt. "You could leave town. We could take a cruise under assumed names." Donahue was behind the photo. The scorpion in her desk. Had he gotten to both Susan and William? Or just one of them?

And with his diabolical ability to inflict torture in whatever way he chose, to affect any aspect of life he chose to invade, could she blame either one of them for doing what they were told?

"Hannah." Brian sat forward, grabbed one of her hands again, held it between both of his. "It'll be okay. I'll be wearing a wire and a bulletproof vest, not that I'll need it, but they're being that careful. My part isn't dangerous at all. To the rest of the world, most particularly to the Ivory Nation brotherhood, I haven't been cleared yet. They'll know tomorrow after all of this goes down. For now, I'm out on bond."

"You don't believe that, do you? That no one but you and this…this Tucson detective, Daniel Boyd, and Bobby Donahue and Angelo and now me are the only ones who know? Get a grip, Brian." Hannah could hear her voice rising, but couldn't contain it.

The warmth of Brian's touch, his sure, steady hands, washed over her, promising her she wouldn't lose. Promising her the world wouldn't lose. Making promises she couldn't believe.

"Donahue wasn't involved in the baby killings. He stumbled on the IN connection by accident and was completely sickened. He's a twisted man, but he's got a code of ethics that doesn't budge," Brian said. "He came to the cops voluntarily. He was a free man. No one was onto him or the Ivory Nation. And even if they'd suspected the Ivory Nation eventually, there was absolutely nothing to implicate Bobby Donahue. Because he truly was unaware of what the brotherhood was doing."

"There's no way this ridiculous plan is a secret," Hannah continued despite knowing she'd lost. "The Ivory Nation is everywhere. They have contacts everywhere. In every level of the justice system from the courthouse to the jail cell. From cops to politicians. Lawyers, Even doctors. They aren't just thugs anymore."

"Yes, even doctors," Brian said, his hold on her hand tightening as he leaned closer. "And judges. They aren't going to leave you alone, Hannah, as long as the organization exists. Unless we cooperate here, unless we end this madness, they're going to be after you. The IN member you sentenced last year is the kid brother to one of the guys who tainted the formula. If we don't get him, you aren't safe."

"That kid was released on appeal. He barely served any time at all."

"Apparently it was long enough to get raped. And he hasn't been the same since," Brian said without emotion.

"They had it in for you, too," she reminded him quietly, though she knew now they'd already lost.

Carlos had been killed because of her. Because of choices she'd made at work. Many, many lives had been lost or irrevocably damaged over the years. The Ivory Nation *was* more powerful than God. She and Brian hadn't had a chance.

"You really think they're going to start thinking that this guy they were willing to hang by his balls is suddenly one of them?" she asked Brian. "Just like that? I'm telling you, Brian, this is just another Donahue scheme. There'll be HGH in the syringe. Or the vest will be faulty. Or Angelo will get caught in the cupboard and be unable to help you when

Brown attacks you. One way or another you're going to end up dead."

"I don't blame you for thinking so, Hannah, considering all you've been through. But you have to trust me on this. I've thought this through. In the first place, I was never as much of a target as I was a convenience. I had something Brown needed, but couldn't create—a motive. They had to be able to convince a jury that I had a good reason for killing babies. Avenging lost love is about the best reason there is. It's passionate, not logical. You just have to remind the jury of the power of passion and you've got them."

As a former prosecutor, Hannah knew that better than anyone.

"They had nothing to do with Cara's death. That was just their good luck. And yes, for a time, I was the worst kind of traitor. I was a supporter of the cause, because of the size of my donations to certain campaigns, yet I offered free health care to children of illegals. But that wrong is being avenged. I'm sacrificing myself for the cause—in the most dangerous way. That earns their respect. The large amounts I've contributed to support the campaign over the years will help to convince them that I've seen the error of my ways."

She hated every single part of this whole charade. She was going to lose him. "Don't do this, Brian. All charges are dropped. You don't owe anyone anything. We'll run away. Leave the country. We have savings…."

"I owe myself, Hannah." The pain in his eyes hit

her deeply. "Just like you couldn't recuse yourself from the tough cases, I can't stop now."

He was adamant. And foolish. And...

Hannah loved him.

Brian spent the afternoon attempting to reassure Hannah. She continued to argue with him. Eventually he got up to make them something to eat. A steak on the grill sounded good to him.

And a baked potato loaded with cheese and real bacon bits and sour cream. He hadn't had one in months. And in the interest of any future he might have, he'd forego the butter.

After a brief trip to the farmer's market with him, Hannah made the tossed salad.

"It's a setup," she said after dinner as she sat on one of the four patio chairs in the backyard with him, dirty plates in front of them. He'd done better than she had at clearing his, but they were both leaving food behind. "They'll get you in that office, then kill you. Nice and clean. When you're dead you have no rights. They can say whatever they want about you. You can't fight them. There's no testimony. That's how these people work."

"Hannah—"

"They've had a glitch in their hierarchy, Brian. A guy who thought he, not Donahue, was God. Brown set a series of events in motion, and now they've got the blood of six infant boys on their hands. They're in cleanup mode. And you're their mop. It's all in a day's work to them."

"I can see why you were the state's number-one prosecutor," he said, with a sip of the iced tea she'd made for them. He was seeing her best work. "And why you made it to next in command to the attorney general."

"Don't humor me."

"I'm not. You argue a good point."

Her face was no less lovely for her scowl. Her blond hair was like a halo, framing soft cheeks, those blue eyes so vivid. So sincere.

So Hannah.

He was used to seeing her in business attire. But she was no less intimidating in slacks and a sweater.

"And you still won't change your mind, will you?"

"No."

"There's nothing I can do or say to get you to see sense."

"I'm seeing sense, Hannah," he said, still calm, still confident as he thought of his decisions. "Just not the same sense as you. But it's equally clear. In fact, for the first time, I'm finally seeing what matters with complete clarity."

"Oh?" she challenged, as though she might get through to him if she could only find the secret passageway. "And what's so clear to you?"

Brian took a deep breath. The plan was in motion. He had no time to lose. Or room to misstep.

"The only things that really matter are love and the people you care about. Love, relationships, people, are the only things you can take with you when you die. They're all that's waiting on the other side."

Since Cara's death, he'd been aware that life didn't last forever. It was only recently, when he'd seen the possibility of his own life ending, that he'd faced the consequences—been driven by them.

Brian had no idea what Hannah's silence meant. Night was falling and dusk's fading light painted her expression with enough shadows to make her thoughts a mystery to him.

"I meant what I said Friday night," he murmured into the growing darkness. "I'm fairly confident that I'll live a long life, but, in case I only have tonight, I want you to know that I love you. That I'm in love with you. I want you to know that you have more of my heart than anyone has ever had."

He'd said the words aloud. And hadn't been struck down. Instead, he felt lighter. As though, if Cara was watching, she was pleased. Relieved.

Not hurt.

Toying with her fork, Hannah stared at the table. "Brian...I... It's complicated. I... There's William and..."

He let her hang there. He had to.

"I..." She glanced around the yard. At the sky. And then, finally, at him. When her eyes met his, and he saw the moisture glistening there, he took his first free breath in days.

She had to get out. Except that she didn't know where to go. While the citizens of Phoenix went about their daily lives, unsuspecting, unaware, another life was unfolding in their city.

Hannah knew. She was aware. She couldn't escape into the safety of anonymity.

With Bobby Donahue on the loose, the cops not trustworthy, with her son dead, at least in part, because of her and her associations, with her closest friend framed and her lover possibly doing her dirty, her job putting her life at risk and her heart…

She didn't have room for a heart. Not today. Not now.

She had to think safety. But she wasn't sure what she was keeping safe. Her body? That was safest at Brian's. Which was why they were there. While the brotherhood believed that he was working for Bobby Donahue he would be protected. And if she was with him, so would she.

Maybe.

Of course William or Susan was one of them. Or maybe they both were. Anybody could be IN. That was Donahue's way.

She was only safe as long as he decided to let her be.

So what was she protecting? Her heart?

They'd never have that.

Jason had. Carlos. Callie.

And William?

He'd had her affection. Her admiration. Her caring. He'd never had her heart.

Not in a man/woman way.

Jason had that.

And…

Looking at the man sitting next to her, watching her patiently as his last hours possibly ticked away, Hannah tried to run.

To hide.

"I love you, too." The words were loud. Shocking. She wanted to take them back.

And knew she couldn't.

"I'm in love with you," she said, and felt the stark truth as it hit her.

Life was about ultimates. Ultimate risk. Ultimate gain. There was no more waiting. No more staying safe. Tomorrow was a risk. Tomorrow he might die.

And tonight he risked his heart. Tonight was all he had.

Watching Hannah, Brian knew that he was fully alive for the first time since Cara's death. This was it. This was what living was all about. One moment. The current moment.

There were no guarantees. There was only listening. And having the courage to follow the dictates that came from within.

Brian stood and Hannah watched him wide-eyed, almost as though she were a young girl instead of the highly successful forty-year-old widow he knew her to be.

Holding out his hand, he waited, not certain what was to come, only knowing what he wanted. His heart skipped a beat when her fingers slowly slid into his, her gaze locked on his.

"I'm scared." Her voice was thick.

"We'll go slow."

"It means too much." Which made them more vulnerable than either of them could acknowledge.

"I won't hurt you." Just the thought of what he was saying, where they were heading, had the blood roaring through his veins.

He'd known Hannah Montgomery for twenty years and he'd never seen her naked.

That was about to change. He could see her hunger—a hunger that matched his own.

"We're going to make love," he said.

She nodded.

24

Hannah was no innocent. She'd been married when her peers were still in high school. And she'd had lovers since Jason. Circumspect, low-key partners, like William—men who she'd been dating exclusively and the length of the relationships was more of a factor in their going to bed together than any real passion.

And yet, as Brian undressed her, his hands caressing her body, Hannah shivered with a longing, with a need she didn't understand. Her entire being focused on his touch, responding with sensations she didn't recognize.

And couldn't stop.

She'd seen his bedroom only once, but paid no attention as he carried her inside and laid her on his bed.

Thoughts of the woman he'd shared that bed with only a week before surfaced, and then vanished. Cynthia, William, anything outside this moment was in another lifetime. A lost lifetime.

She and Brian were finally where they were meant to be.

"You're gorgeous." The words were torn from her as she watched him undress, revealing muscled thighs, hips that an artist couldn't have proportioned better, a flat stomach with a sprinkling of dark hair. Seeing his erect male nipples sent spirals of desire between her legs.

"I need to touch you," she whispered. With a boldness, a fervor driven by the knowledge that this might be her only night with Brian. That she might never have the chance to touch him again.

The images came fast and furious, ideas she'd never harbored before, things she needed to do to him, with him, that she hadn't even thought possible.

Brian seemed to occupy the same otherworld as her, knowing what she needed, where and when. They moved, sliding together, arms, legs, bodies connecting again and again.

There was no part of her unexplored. His hands touched everywhere. His lips tasted everything.

And when, finally, he entered her, Hannah knew this man had been made for her.

The night, the passion, was beyond incredible, as though they were making up for all the years they'd denied themselves. And making up for a future they might never have. As though they could escape—even for this moment—the deaths behind them and the danger in store.

Together they rode frantic waves until they both exploded; and together they made gentle love, holding each other close, and still reaching orgasm together.

Together they grieved. And together they comforted.

Then together, they lay sated, different than they'd been when they'd entered the room hours before. Stronger.

And when the world returned, the stakes were different, too.

"Please don't go tomorrow." Hannah knew she was begging. And did it anyway.

Brian's pause told her how much her wishes mattered to him, and it told her more than that. If she pushed hard enough, long enough, she could probably make him stay.

Her heart recognized the truth and settled.

"I have to do it, Hannah."

"There will always be an Ivory Nation," she said. "Yeah, we might get Bobby Donahue someday. We might get the guys that work for him. But there will be others like him waiting to take his place."

"Regardless of anything else, I have to do this for you. I love you. I have to do whatever I can to protect you."

"Getting yourself killed won't help me, Brian. To the contrary, it's going to devastate me. I can't lose you, too. I'd rather the Ivory Nation just kill me and be done with it."

His brows drew together, his lids lowered and Hannah knew she had him. He'd stay with her. Protect her…

"These people are after you," he said. "I couldn't protect Cara. Or Carlos. I *will* protect you. I'll do whatever it takes to destroy the Ivory Nation." She didn't recognize the hardness in Brian's voice.

"There might be others," he continued. "I'm certain there are others, but these are the guys who have targeted the woman I love. These are the ones I have to bring down."

Desperate now, Hannah laid a hand on his chest, prepared to do whatever it took, to use whatever emotional blackmail she could find. "Brian…"

"No, Hannah." He sat up, his gaze resolute. "If I don't go tomorrow, and you get hurt, I would never recover. I'd never be able to live with myself."

Looking into those eyes, Hannah knew she'd lost.

The plan was to have Brown bring his daughter in before regular office hours. Brian had insisted, as had Angelo and Boyd, that the office be otherwise empty during this particular rendezvous. He wouldn't risk innocent lives.

If anyone got hurt, he needed it to be him alone.

Kissing Hannah goodbye was the hardest part.

"I'll see you tonight," he whispered, wiping her tears as they stood by his front door. She had an hour yet before she had to leave for work and planned to go home to change and feed Taybee.

With trembling lips she nodded, saying nothing.

"I love you."

"I love you, too."

Brian turned away then. If he didn't, he might

not be able to. And that would be something he'd regret for the rest of his life.

Hannah went to work because that's what she did. Cases were scheduled weeks in advance. People depended on her. And it wasn't like she could call in a substitute.

She sat on the bench. She listened. She focused. And she waited.

"Hey, Brian." With his two-month-old daughter sleeping peacefully against him, Steven Brown held out his free hand as Brian opened his office door.

"Steven. It's an honor to work with you." Brian had been well coached long into Saturday night. The weight of the bulletproof vest he wore under his blue dress shirt and Piglet tie was a heavy burden—a reminder of what he was doing.

As was the wire taped to his chest.

Avoiding looking at the child in her father's arms, Brian led the way to examination room four. After today he'd planned to turn it into a play area for waiting kids. Brian was never going to be able to treat a child there again.

Steven Brown moved with purpose, his black hiking boots with their red shoelaces far different from the expensive dress shoes Brian was used to him wearing. In his supremacy garb, the man was a far cry from the professionally dressed doctor Brian knew from the clinic. He found himself staring at the shoelaces.

Black laces were for new recruits. Red laces for having shed blood for the cause. Other brothers wore white for showing loyalty. Today Brian was taking the accelerated membership course—moving past black and white and going straight for the red.

Because Bobby Donahue deemed it so and the brotherhood believed every word their prophet uttered.

"So, let's take a look at this little one." Brian trembled inside, fighting back nausea as he took the sleeping infant from her father.

Tiffany Ann Brown was dressed up for the occasion, in a pink, frilly dress, white tights and tiny black patent leather shoes.

"It's her mother's favorite dress," Steven said, his voice filled with emotion.

And for the first time, Brian thought of the child's mother. A faithful Ivory Nation wife.

"Does she know?" He had to ask.

"Of course. I would never do this without her."

Brian was going to be sick.

"We're very lucky," Steven said, intent, though shaking as he straightened the child's dress. "Our baby has been called by God. She's going to be an angel. What parents wouldn't want that?"

The man's gaze was almost pleading. And Brian faltered again.

Not because this baby would be harmed by anything other than a brief prick of a needle. Brian had triple checked. The injection he'd prepared for her was pure saline.

But the thought that her father believed differently, that he could stand there, handing over his still-sleeping daughter, so she could be put to death, was more than Brian could comprehend.

What kind of faith allowed a man to be so heinous?

Brian heard buzzing. The pretty pink dress took on shades of rose, then maroon.

"Just as God called those other babies." He found the words he'd been told to say at the last second. Pulling himself back. "The little boys who had to die this year."

Brown froze, staring. "No way, man. God didn't call those dirty devils. Satan did. God called me to rid the world of filth."

Nodding, Brian said, "I knew you were a saint. Not just because Bobby told me about you in jail, but because I felt it the instant I saw you at the clinic."

He was going to puke. Or choke on his vomit.

"I've known I was different since I was a kid," Brown said, startled out of his reverie when Tiffany whimpered in her sleep. Picking the baby up, he crooned to her, smiling when her eyes blinked briefly open, until she settled back to sleep.

"So tell me," Brian said, turning to get his stethoscope ostensibly to listen for a slowing heart rate. "What did it feel like, hearing God? What did He say?"

Tell me how you murdered six innocent baby boys, you bastard. Tell me how you broke Hannah's heart when you killed the baby she'd waited so long for.

*Tell me how she's ever going to live openly knowing
that her son died because she'd brought him to the
United States. Knowing that if she'd left Carlos in
Mexico, he would have had a chance to grow up. To
live.*

She'd talked about all of that and more during the
night and though he'd assured her that none of what
had happened was her fault, he'd felt completely in-
effective—powerless to help her.

He looked briefly at Brown. *Tell me how I'm
going to get through this without shoving a needle
into your heart and watching you die a slow, painful
death.*

The thought shocked Brian. Scared him.

What was happening to him? What was he becoming?

And then, as he listened to Tiffany's healthy heart
and lungs, counted her strong pulse, felt tiny organs
that were fleshy and perfectly proportioned, the
wiretap recorded the word of God as told to Steven
Brown.

"'Get that judge,'" Brown recited, his eyes closed
while Brian examined his daughter. The infant was
now awake, staring up at the lights above her. "'She's
hurting my work with her decisions. She doesn't
understand. Get her where she'll feel it most—and
rid the world of one of Satan's men at the same
time.'"

Opening his eyes, Brown looked at Brian. "He
told me everything," he said, his voice an awed
whisper. "How to strike right after a doctor's ap-

pointment, how to make it look like it was the vaccine, how to taint the formula. He even gave me the idea of delivering the sample in the mailbox…"

Ah, little Tiffany, all will be well shortly. You'll be in a loving home, with people who will cherish and protect you. The baby's extremities moved freely, her joints limber.

"I thought, at first, it was just the one, but then God came to me in a dream, he told me that we had a good plan, that there were more to dispose of. And a perfect fall man, if we ever got caught. The fact that you were not only the judge's baby doctor, but had also contributed to the cause shows you how God works. He has the perfect people for every perfect plan. It's all preordained. We simply have to be willing to listen to Him. And have the courage to live by His edicts."

Brian's hand slipped. And then he asked a question of his own.

"How'd you know which of my patients weren't pure?" he asked, amazement in his voice. "And how'd you know when I'd see them?"

"'Get help in the form of a woman,'" Brown said, his voice changing again to the voice of his God. "'The woman. Bobby's woman. She's desperate. She'll do anything to save her son. Promise her safe and free transport out of this life, out of this state, in exchange for one last job.'"

Amanda Blake?

"My Alliance partner said she jumped at the idea," Brown said.

"How'd she have access to my office? To my files and appointment book?"

"I never asked. That part was up to her. But she was well trained by God's prophet." Tiffany looked up at her father, blew bubbles, and Brown snuggled her to his chest. "Jesus walked on water," Brown said over his daughter's shoulder. "I'm sure Bobby's chosen had special abilities. It would be nothing for her to sneak in here at night, find the information I wanted and disappear without a trace."

And Brian had all he needed.

Except Brown out in the parking lot where he'd have his last taste of freedom.

First, Brian had to administer the injection.

"It's time," he said.

Brown nodded, closed his eyes. "God in heaven, if there be any way, let this cup pass from me."

Holding his daughter close, the man waited. One minute. Then two. "Let Thy will be done."

The words were a death sentence.

Opening his eyes, Brown didn't bother to hide his tears. He kissed his daughter on both cheeks. "I love you so much, little one. You've brought more joy to my life than I ever thought possible." He broke off on a sob. Took a deep breath. And handed the baby to Brian. "Go in peace, my sweet."

And then, holding her tiny fingers in his big ones, he watched as Brian injected the child.

25

Hannah got the news during her morning recess. Her deputy, Pete Shannon, came to her chambers after he took the inmates back to the holding cell where they would wait for their bus to the downtown jail.

"Steven Brown was arrested an hour ago," he said, as soon as he'd closed her inner office door behind him. Law enforcement officers were a close-knit group and Pete had been briefed to the plan because he was to protect Hannah if anything went wrong.

Hannah couldn't stop the tears that sprang to her eyes. "Thank God. What about Dr. Hampton? And the baby?"

"They're both fine. The baby's a bit bruised. I guess her father wouldn't let go of her when they arrested him. Said he was going to breathe every breath with her until she died. That it was his right. God had given it to him and they couldn't take it away."

Hannah felt faint. And wondered how Brian had

survived the morning. She had to talk to him. To see him.

And she had four more cases to hear that morning.

"Have you heard anything else?" she asked, because she had to know all she could. If the plan was going to work on a larger scale, instead of causing mass panic among the brotherhood and inciting riots in the city, the authorities had to move quickly.

Unless the authorities were Ivory Nation supporters.

"There've been almost twenty arrests in an hour," Pete said, sounding incredulous. "It's a record. And from what I heard, every available deputy, and even the sheriff himself, are taking depositions from Ivory Nation members who've been instructed by Donahue to confess. They've got safe rendezvous points set up all over the city so that each brother thinks he's the only one."

Pete sounded as though he wished he were out with his colleagues on the special duty rather than moving criminals around for her. She didn't blame him.

Donahue's plan was working. Just as Brian had said it would.

"If I didn't know better, I'd say this Donahue guy really does have power from God," Pete continued. "Hundreds of men and women across the state have been trying for years to get these guys and he manages to do it in a day. It's a true miracle."

I'll be damned, Hannah thought. Stunned.

Donahue's ability to manipulate was insidious. His intelligence dangerous.

And she wondered what he had up his sleeve.

Hannah didn't believe in the power of God.

His work was almost done. In his home office, Bobby Donahue clicked out of the program he'd been working in. All his documents, a lifetime of God's work, were in the hands of the police. All his e-mail folders, his sermons and even his private journal had been turned over to the authorities. They'd be coming for his computer soon, to dissect the hard drive.

Maybe they'd find pictures of the women who'd comforted him over the past two years. Maybe someone would call them. Keep them company for a while.

Closing his e-mail program, he shut down Jewel Quest and the media player—two programs that were always running. And then, leaning back in his chair, he turned off the computer, listening to the silence as the fan stopped.

He'd thought about visiting a woman himself. One more time. But God wanted him alone. It was just between them. Man and his God. His Maker.

God would see him home from here.

Undoing his fly, Bobby pulled out his penis, rubbing carefully as he said goodbye to the flesh, to the needs and pleasures of a body that had served him well.

He'd be seeing Amanda within the hour. The poor burned bastard in the hospital had told him everything. Stupid of Amanda to trust an Alliance man.

She was waiting in a deserted shack out on the Indian reservation just off the Beeline Highway. An Alliance brother was supposed to be there that afternoon with safe transport, money and new identities for her and Luke. She thought they were going to New York, to get lost in the crowds and start a new life.

Bobby rubbed harder.

The bitch thought she was taking Bobby's son to the seat of evil, where every other person was impure. The depot for nonwhites to invade God's land.

Up and down he stroked, straining his cock as far as he could.

And he heard God's words.

It's all good, son. You're my best boy. It will happen as it's meant to. I love you.

"I love you," Bobby said aloud, his hand gentling. "I love you." He moved his hips then, in a perfect rhythm, and when the milky juices came, spilling over his fingers, he rejoiced with God.

"Get up, you sick bastard."

His hand still on his cock, Bobby froze as he recognized the voice behind him. And waited for the voice from within.

"Leonard, I thought you'd left the country."

"You made one vital mistake, Donahue."

Bobby didn't make mistakes. He acted upon the word of God. "What's that?" he asked, standing to face the terrorist trainer he'd done business with a couple of years before. He stroked his penis one last time, a grateful goodbye, and then, wiping his hand on his shirt, buttoned and zipped his jeans.

"You didn't count on the power of a mother's love for her son."

Leonard Diamond was no fool. If anyone knew as much as Bobby about taking lives—and about self-defense—it was Leonard. But Bobby had divine protection and that won out every time.

"Amanda called you." He should have thought of that.

"She wants you gone," Leonard said, coming closer, his hands in the pockets of his nylon running pants. "Across the country isn't far enough away. She knows you'll find her. She'll never have peace."

Hearing the words, Bobby grew calm again. Perhaps this was God's way. Perhaps Diamond would be the one to take him home to his maker.

But not yet. Not without Luke. He had God's word on that.

"I'm surprised you let a twit like her interrupt your work." Diamond trained killers, excelling in survival technique, physical fitness and assassination.

"You underestimate me. All she did was prompt a few phone calls. You've turned on the brotherhood, Bobby."

Leonard came even closer and the voice in Bobby's head started to speak.

"I knew you'd squeal on our arrangement eventually," Diamond said, and Bobby leapt at him, shoving both palms up to Diamond's nose, pushing the bones back into his brain.

When Diamond fell, his shock still visible on his face, Bobby rid him of his various weapons, knowing exactly where to look for them, and, then rid him of his life. With one last look around the home that had served his earthly existence well, Bobby Donahue went to claim his son.

And meet his maker.

Shaking and slightly nauseous, Brian trailed down the hallway behind Boyd and Angelo, making his way to the private office in the back of the downtown Phoenix precinct. They were his personal body-guards until this was all over.

"All's going according to plan," Boyd said. Though Angelo was a Phoenix hot shot, the Tucson detective appeared to be running this show. "Another couple of hours and we'll be done. We've got con-fessions from three quarters of the brotherhood. As soon as we get the rest, Donahue's turning himself in. I've got men on him in the meantime. All the files he sent over have been verified. Guys are on their way to his house to pick up the computer now."

"What about Amanda Blake?" Angelo was like a dog gnawing a beef carcass. He wasn't going to let a single bone go unchewed.

"Once again she slipped the noose," Boyd said, sounding almost more impressed than frustrated. "By the time we got to where Donahue said she was, she was gone. The woman is a gifted escape artist— and with a child, no less. I just got off the phone with Simon Green. He's ex-FBI in Flagstaff. He and

Amanda had a special bond. If anyone can bring her in, he will."

"She's not much of a danger, is she?" Brian asked. "Am I wrong in thinking that all she's ever wanted is to raise her son in peace and safety?" Like someone else he knew. For the first time in days, he thought about Cynthia—his time with her seemed so long ago.

"She's an accessory to the deaths of six infants, Doctor," Angelo said. "Last year she fed a woman back to her rapist without batting an eye. You tell me if she's a danger to society or not. I'm sorry for what she's been through, but it's twisted her brain."

"So once you get her, bring in Donahue, this is all over, right?"

He had to talk to Hannah. She'd been kept informed. The call had come over Angelo's radio when Hannah's knowledge of the morning's events had been confirmed. But Brian had yet to speak to her personally.

And he badly needed to. Needed to reassure her. And himself as well. All he could think about was getting home. Getting her home.

And then he had to find a way to wipe the last hours from his mind, to forget who he'd been this day, what he'd heard and seen.

He had to forget....

And then, just like that, everything fell into place. He put two and two together.

Cynthia and Joseph. Amanda and Luke.

Woman and child on the run.

Cynthia in his office at night. Amanda in his office…

"Detective?"

The shack wasn't hard to find. No harder than it was to shake the cops Boyd had tailing him. Were they really that naive? They thought Bobby was going to give them Amanda when she was his? They thought he was going to spend another minute locked in a cage like an animal? Sharing air with the men who'd not only betrayed him, but God as well?

A jail full of Judases. If that wasn't hell on earth nothing was.

Bobby wasn't going back to hell. He had his Father's promise on that one.

Lying on the hard and occasionally sharp desert floor, Bobby moved like a snake, weaving in and out of desert brush, standing occasionally when a saguaro presented itself as an opportunity for stretching, finding ocotillo and prickly pear to hide behind as often as possible.

He slithered up to the dilapidated building, his body hugging the hot, splintery wood and crouched beneath the glassless window.

"That's great, Joseph!"

Amanda's voice!

But who was Joseph?

She's calling my son Joseph?

"Maybe you should add some color to that white building? What do you say we put a little blue there, like this…"

"No!" The squeal nearly tore Bobby apart. *Luke!* His son. God's son. It had been a long, grueling year.

As he waited there, tears pouring down his cheeks, Bobby didn't know how he'd had the strength to endure the past twelve months without his boy. How he'd endured a day without him.

"Daddy says white is pure and good and my house is always to stay white."

Daddy says. Bobby silently thanked God that his boy still remembered their lessons. He still knew what mattered most.

"Daddy's gone, Joseph. And he wasn't always right, you know…"

Blasphemy!

With the animal-like grace he'd been born with, Bobby was on his feet and through the window, an arm around Amanda's throat, ready to choke the life out of her, until he saw the terrified expression on his son's face.

He had to kill her away from the boy. No matter that he and Luke were leaving this earth within minutes. Their arrival at the pearly gates wasn't going to be tarnished with his son's fear.

Or pain.

This was a joyous occasion.

"Daddy?"

Amanda jerked against him as Luke said his name. "Bobby?" At least she had the sense to fear him.

"I like that, Mandy," he whispered, his nose to her ear. "I always liked it when you were just that little bit afraid. Turned me on, you know?"

And that was something God hadn't warned him about.

Being with Amanda again, holding the body he knew as well as he knew his own, the body God had given him all those years ago, Bobby hardened until the ache was more than he could bear.

God had asked for his celibacy in honor of his love for Amanda. He'd asked Bobby to bed no one but Amanda. And he hadn't.

But she was here now.

He had to fuck her.

And then they'd go. The three of them. A family. Two to heaven. One to hell.

And while he'd never let Luke see him hurt his mother, there was no harm in the boy watching a man love his woman.

That was a language all men, no matter what age, could understand.

"Take your clothes off, Mandy," he said, the small knife he'd carried with him at her back.

"No."

"Take them off or I'll cut them off," he said, his tone pleasant though he spoke through gritted teeth. "You owe me."

"I owe you nothing."

"Mama?" Luke's eyes were large, swimming with tears. "Daddy, don't hurt my mama."

Incensed at the favoritism, Bobby tightened his hold on his woman. "What have you done to him?" he growled.

And then, with a loving smile said, "Son, go on

outside for a couple of minutes. Your mother and I have a surprise for you and we need to wrap it first. And then the three of us are going to go away on a long trip to paradise."

"To Disneyland?"

"Yes, son, and beyond."

Luke stood his ground, staring at Bobby. "You promise?"

"Yes, son, I do."

With a last long, assessing stare, Luke nodded and, taking his paper and crayons, moved slowly outside.

One slice and Amanda's top was off. Another and her bra fell away from her breasts. Bobby was so hard he had to fight not to come.

"Take off those pants or I'll cut them off, and cut you in the process," he spat at her.

"Show me your dick first, Bobby. Show me how hard you are. Let me taste you. Remember what my tongue can do?"

When she licked her lips, Bobby knew he would oblige her. It had always been this way. They could fight until he believed there was nothing but hate, but as soon as they were together, their bodies spoke a language of love that only God could have given them.

Undoing his jeans, Bobby wrapped a hand in Amanda's hair, keeping a firm hold as he pushed her head down to his straining shaft.

"You bite and you die," he said, pricking the back of her neck with the blade he still held.

And then, unable to help himself, he thrust upward, into those sweet lips and out, squirting her face with his instant orgasm.

As the last of the liquid seeped out of him, Bobby's ecstasy didn't die. He was suffused with love greater than he'd ever known before.

He could see brightness. And hear singing.

And, too late, he saw the knife in Amanda's hand. He saw the blood.

His blood.

By the time Hannah left work Monday afternoon, it was all over. Bobby Donahue was in the morgue. Every known member of the Ivory Nation was behind bars, with many, many frightened associates tying up telephone lines with offers to testify against the brutal brotherhood. Dr. Brian Hampton was a hero.

Only Amanda Blake was still free, and while Angelo was adamant about finding her, getting her son away from her, and bringing her to justice, Hannah was happy to have the constant threat of death and destruction gone.

Amanda Blake was a murderer, no matter her motives. She had to pay. But she was no longer a threat.

William, having seen the news, called late that afternoon, asking her if they could meet for drinks. He had to see her, he said. Now that the Ivory Nation was off her back, he wanted to talk about their future.

Hannah agreed to meet him. But only to tell him

that they were through. William was a weak man. He didn't know the meaning of courage.

Brian had shown her that today.

And then she would go to Brian. To see if what they'd found the night before had been real.

To see if there would be life after death.

William had asked her to meet him at an out-of-the-way Mexican diner known for its Margaritas a couple of miles from the courthouse. Somewhere she wouldn't be recognized. Pete and a couple of his deputy buddies walked her out through the throng of press to her car and a police escort got her safely into traffic.

Taking an indirect route just to be sure there were no Ivory Nation laggers left, she made it only five minutes late. And took another two minutes to call Brian to tell him where she was and that she'd be stopping by her place to feed Taybee before coming to his house.

They had to talk, she told his voice mail.

Hannah put her cell phone meticulously back in her purse and hung the bag on her shoulder before unlocking the door of the Lexus. Though William wasn't the man for her, ending a relationship was still hard

"Oh!" Something hit her head. And then sliced her arm. Dizzy, nauseous, Hannah was only slightly aware that she was being put into the back of her car. And that, unbelievably, a child was there, too, a seat belt fastened around him.

"I…"

She tried to speak. To find her purse. But they were moving out of the parking lot and into the dusk that was falling around them.

She had no idea what time it was. Dark. Night. She was thirsty. And something was pounding her head from the inside out.

"She's awake, Mama."

Hannah recognized the voice. But that couldn't be. Joseph was long gone. Left Brian. Left with his mama.

Joseph was too young to kidnap anyone.

"Is she sick?"

Movement made it impossible for her to keep her eyes open long, but when she managed to get a peek, all she could see was darkness and a tiny hand on the seat beside her.

She was in a car. Her car. Still moving.

"No, baby, she's just sleepy."

Cynthia! Cynthia? "Cyn-cyn-cyn-thi-a?" She finally managed to force the word through the vibrations in her head.

"Don't try anything crazy and you won't get hurt." Cynthia sounded different. Harder.

Hannah tried to move. And realized that her hands were tied together in front of her. Her ankles were equally strapped.

"We're playing cops and robbers but you got tired." It was the longest sentence she'd ever heard Joseph say.

Hannah focused on that voice. And on the child sitting so innocently next to her. If she thought about Joseph she could stay awake.

"Why?" It took her at least five minutes to get the word out.

"You're my insurance policy until I get over the border. If they want to kill me, they'll have to kill you first. Besides, Joseph likes you."

"Why do you need insurance?"

"You think they were just going to let me go?"

She was missing something. If only she could think clearly.

"I…" Confused, Hannah shook her head, and then wretched. All over herself. The seat. The floor.

"She was sick, Mama."

"Okay, baby." Hannah heard the words as if from afar. "Here, do Mama a favor and pass these to her. And plug your nose so you don't get sick, too."

With one eye open, Hannah saw the packet of wet wipes the little hand held.

Ten minutes later, Hannah used the last cloth, as clean as she could get herself while tied up in the dark.

One question ran through her mind. Again and again. A clue, if only she could get her brain to focus.

Why did a woman have to cross the border because she left her lover?

"I…" And then, as though in a horrible nightmare, she realized something.

"Your name isn't Cynthia, is it?"

"No."

"Who are you?"

"Come on, Judge." The voice would've been almost cajoling, if not for the inhuman hardness lacing through it. "You're a smart woman, you figure it out."

And as fantastical as it seemed, when the truth dawned, Hannah felt no shock at all. She was being held hostage by a cold-blooded murderer.

"You're Amanda Blake."

The woman up front didn't respond. Hannah had to fight for rational thought through the pounding in her head.

"You used Brian," she said. "From the very beginning."

Still nothing.

"You never loved him. You were there to keep tabs on him. You had him watch your son while you fed his patient information to Steven Brown."

And then the rest came crashing in.

"And William. He's the one—"

"The poor sap," Amanda Blake finally said. "He was such an easy win. One threat to that son of his and he was whisking you off to Vegas."

William had taken her away, *made love to her,* so villains could break into her house?

And the scorpion. The photo. William had planted those, too.

"All he had to do was convince you to give up the case, but he wasn't man enough to pull that off," Amanda said as the car raced along a deserted highway into the night.

"My cat. The key to my house." Hannah's tongue was sticking to the roof of her mouth. "He gave that to you."

"Wrong." Amanda almost chuckled. "I don't work for the Ivory Nation. I work for me. And I keep myself informed. He let the cat out himself."

And then Amanda and her son went with Brian to choose a new one for her.

Inconceivable.

Hannah had to sleep. To escape. Give up.

Brian. Oh, my God. She couldn't let this happen. He'd never forgive himself. His lover killing his lover. He'd barely survived Cara's death. He'd never survive this.

Hannah sat quietly. Conserving her strength. Forcing herself to think. To figure out a plan.

Focusing on the child beside her kept her awake.

It was the longest night of his life.

Sitting next to Angelo in the unmarked car, Brian stared off into the darkness, his eyes stinging as he searched for the Lexus. Any sign of Hannah, or her clothing. Or of a young boy—Joseph.

He'd talked Angelo into letting him come along partially because of his rapport with the troubled boy. And because of his rapport with the boy's mother, as well. Because he was a doctor. And probably because the detective knew that if he didn't keep Brian next to him, Brian would be out there searching on his own.

According to the emergency GPS on Hannah's cell phone, until the phone had died or lost reception, they'd been heading south. In the desert. Where darkness was so thick any light at all blinded you. Where there was miles and miles of undeveloped, cactus-and-coyote-infested wild land in which to disappear. Hannah could be standing two feet from the side of the road and he wouldn't see her.

Which was why everyone was searching for the car. The chrome and metal would be easier to spot.

Cynthia…Amanda had to stop sometime. For gas if nothing else.

Mexico was not quite four hours from Mesa. Hannah had been gone two and a half.

"We'll catch them at the border," Brian said for the third time.

And for the third time, Angelo said, "I hope so, but we have to be prepared. Amanda Blake is an escape artist unlike any I've ever seen. She's not going to try to get through border patrol. She'll have a plan, but it won't be that."

The phone rang and Brian tensed. Daniel Boyd was a few miles ahead of them. Most of the Tucson police department, as well as officers and deputies from other parts of the state, were on the manhunt.

A superior court judge's life was at stake.

"Boyd's got the car in sight," Angelo reported, hanging up the phone. "It's about twenty minutes from Nogales."

A border town.

"How far are we from there?"

"Ten minutes."

"Turn on your lights, man." Brian didn't bother to keep his voice down. "Get there."

For once Angelo did as Brian wanted, worked for Brian instead of against him. When six marked cars caught up to the Lexus, Brian was there, too, ready to step in front of any bullet aimed at the love of his life.

Armed officers wearing bulletproof garments, accompanied by an equal number of men holding powerful flashlights, approached the car, calling out orders of surrender. They waited, briefly. Four of them opened the doors of the car, guns drawn, then lowered their weapons.

"It's empty."

Angelo flung out one arm but Brian didn't let that slow his progress toward the car. "Check the trunk," he said, reaching for the lever to pop the hatch. Officers were waiting, and a quick search turned up no bodies. Nothing seemingly out of place.

Seeing Hannah's car, touching it, both panicked and comforted him.

"Someone threw up," he said to no one in particular. Three or four officers, Angelo among them, swarmed around the car and the surrounding area. The others dispersed to comb the desert.

"There's blood back here," another man reported from just behind the driver's seat.

Brian was nearly sick himself.

Chances were that was Hannah's blood. Chances were Amanda wasn't the one who was hurt. And pray God it wasn't Joseph, either.

But if there was one thing he knew, it was that Cynthia…Amanda would protect her son at all costs.

She'd once told him she'd do anything for Joseph. He got that now.

She'd been warning him.

"No sign of them." Brian heard the shout and couldn't believe what was happening. An entire state of trained officers and one woman manages to get away with a hostage and small child in tow.

And then it dawned on him. Amanda Blake wasn't magic. She was just a very smart woman. Smart enough to know that the best way to escape was to stay right where she was. While the hunters looked in the distance, she was under their noses. In plain sight. At close range.

It was her standard MO. She'd done it every time. Living with one of Bobby's followers for an entire year, right under her hunter's nose. Living with Brian while she framed him for murder.

The ditch by the side of the road was deep. Officers had shined lights up and down it, but unless the beam touched exactly where the bodies lay hidden, they wouldn't have been seen. No one expected them to be there.

And there was a cactus bush that, if one was alert enough to move at the right moments, would easily hide two women and a child.

A child who'd been trained to keep silent. And a woman who, even injured and threatened, was strong enough, savvy enough, to stay alive.

They could be there, just a couple of feet from him, and be overlooked.

No one would expect a fleeing person to be so stupid as not to run.

He crept closer to the Lexus—coming in on an

angle to get a closer look at the ditch behind the bush, while the uniformed masses spread out through the desert on either side of the road. They were all so busy doing their jobs, no one seemed to notice him standing there. And he didn't dare alert them.

If Amanda knew she was trapped, she might do something crazy. Like shoot Hannah.

There was no movement in the ditch. No breath of air to touch a branch of the bush, and no insects. No one gave him any hints. But Brian knew they were there.

Turning his back, he gazed at the car, his ears tuning out the chase around him, focusing only on the space behind him. If he heard the slightest sound…

He could hardly see for the flashing bulbs from all the cop cars in the area. But he took a casual step backward. And then another.

His heart calm, frozen, he thought about getting Angelo's attention, warning someone, but knew he couldn't. Doing that would tip off his target, as well. Staring at the ground now, praying for night vision that would allow him to distinguish shadows, he almost stepped on Joseph's hand.

He stopped. Crossed his arms over his chest. Gazed out at the desert beside him. At the cars in front of him. For a full minute he didn't move. He couldn't give away that he'd found them.

Somehow he had to figure out which body behind him was Hannah's. He was only going to get one chance. Amanda would be moving soon, making them move, probably crawling through the ditch to places that had already been searched. And then away.

Hell, in this darkness, she could make a run for it, stopping whenever a spotlight came near, and still get away.

An hour's walk and they could be over the border.

He would have no second tries.

It took several minutes, but he finally saw shapes in his peripheral vision. So faint, he might have imagined it. But he knew he hadn't. There were three bodies. Hannah would be the one on the end. Next to the bigger body in the middle.

She was just to his left. About a foot, if he calculated correctly.

And he couldn't be wrong, or Hannah would very likely end up dead. Or with a gun to her head as Amanda used her hostage to force them to let her go.

That was why she'd taken Hannah to begin with.

William Horne had told them what little bit he knew as soon as he'd seen Amanda get in Hannah's car that afternoon—his sign that she was done with him. Brian wanted to sympathize with the guy, with the suffering he'd been through as he was forced to hurt the woman he loved in exchange for his son's life, but he couldn't.

The bastard made him sick.

Unfortunately it had taken half an hour for William to get through to Angelo. Amanda had warned him that if he made any calls, she'd kill Hannah on the spot. Thank God the man had finally decided *not* to listen.

And it had taken them another two minutes to get her cell phone number and track it.

Voices were growing closer. The officers were coming back.

His guess was, with Joseph's hand just to the right of him, and Hannah to the left of Joseph, Amanda was directly behind him, next to her son, but keeping her hostage with her as well.

Light beams from the officers in the desert were growing closer. They'd be calling to him soon. Bringing attention to where he stood. Causing Amanda to act.

He was out of time.

Unarmed, untrained, Brian did the only thing he could think of. Like the games of trust he'd played as a kid, he fell backward, stiff as a board, aiming at the body that was most likely armed.

If a bullet shot through him, so be it. That meant it didn't hit Hannah.

"Can I go home now?"

It was three o'clock in the morning and Brian opened his eyes when Hannah sat up among white sheets and beeping machines in the hospital emergency room. "I feel better. I want to go home."

"Lay down, or I'll lay you down," he grumbled from the chair beside her bed. The woman would be the death of him yet.

"It's true what they say, you know." Somehow amusement filtered through her exhaustion.

"What is?"

"Doctors make lousy patients."

"Yeah, well, we make pretty good bodyguards so I wouldn't complain if I were you."

The hospital staff had talked about admitting both of them for the night, but Brian intended to sleep in his own bed.

With Hannah.

Just as soon as the CAT scan came back and he could be certain there was no dangerous swelling in her brain.

They'd already put five stitches in the cut on the side of her head, compliments of Amanda's pistol.

His broken wrist was set. He'd be sore in the morning, having held Amanda down by sheer force of will until Angelo got to them, but there was nothing wrong with him that a shower, his bed and, mostly, the woman he loved couldn't cure.

With that thought, the pain medication they'd slipped in Brian's IV took effect and he fell asleep.

"Let's go, cowboy."

Dizzy, leaning against the back of the bed in which she sat, Hannah still managed a smile as she watched Susan help the nurse get a very sleepy Brian out of the hospital lounger and into the wheelchair that would take him out to her JA's car.

"You sure I can't talk you two into staying here tonight?" Dr. Anita Lansing, their emergency room physician, asked from the door.

"Uh-uh," Hannah croaked. "As you've said, there's nothing wrong with either of us that a good rest won't cure, and trust me, Doctor, we'll sleep much better at home than we would here."

It was the longest sentence she'd managed all night.

"And besides," Susan said, coming over to gently help Hannah into the chair that had been waiting for her. "I'd hate to be you if Dr. Hampton woke up and found himself here after giving such express orders to be removed from the premises at once."

It was only one of the things that Brian had said in the past hour as the medication he'd been given kicked in. The nicest thing.

And while Hannah knew that narcotics had powerful effects on people, she also knew that Brian was suffering, as she was, from burnout. The fight to survive had been exhausting.

The past weeks had changed them both.

They had a lot of healing to do.

But she also knew that they'd be doing it together. Forever.

From that point forward she and Brian would walk side by side, for the rest of their lives.

"Ready, Judge?"

"Ready," Hannah said, and then put her foot down to stop the chair from moving.

"I…Susan, I…" She and Brian weren't the only ones who had healing to do. She had a very dear and loyal employee, a friend, whom she'd hurt badly.

Perhaps irreparably?

"Shh, Judge. Don't. I understand."

"I…"

"Please, don't say anything. You were in an impossible situation. Scared out of your wits. Forced to choose between your boyfriend and an employee…"

"You were never just an employee."

Susan knelt by the chair, looking Hannah straight in the eye. "I'd have made the same choice, Judge."

Hannah had never been at such a loss for words and felt tears of frustration, grief and sorrow fill her eyes.

"Stop," Susan said, wiping away the tears before they trailed down her face. "You called me tonight," she said softly. "You have other judge friends, lawyer friends, and you called me to come get you. That's all I needed."

Nodding, Hannah smiled and squeezed her assistant's hand.

"Oh, and one other thing," Susan added, an achingly familiar sparkle in her eye.

"What's that?"

"My job?"

"That's a given," Hannah told the young woman, looking for the first time to the immediate future beyond Brian's bed.

But she thought about the future as Susan wheeled her out into the predawn light and helped her into the car. She thought about it as her assistant walked behind her and Brian as they entered his house, as Susan saw them settled in Brian's bedroom.

She thought about it as Susan insisted she'd spend the night on the couch.

And after her best friend who'd somehow become

the man of her dreams pulled her into his arms and fell asleep kissing her good-night, she thought some more.

The world was always going to carry some darkness.

But the world also held love. And hope. Kindness. Susans.

And Lilas. The nurse had called Brian's cell phone the night before, after seeing the news. She was as eager to get back to work as Brian was to have her.

And for Hannah, there was Brian.

Would they marry? Or continue as best friends, supporting each other, but never quite joining completely?

Would she ever have another child?

Would she ever know the magnitude of love she'd seen shining in Amanda's eyes as she lay dying of Boyd's gunshot wound on the side of the road, using her last breath to tell her son that he was a good boy and she loved him very much?

Hannah didn't know.

But she hoped so.

Epilogue

The room held a hundred people, and every chair was filled. Arizona's governor was there. As was the attorney general. And the immediate past attorney general. And the one before her, too. Every senator in the state had arrived, including George Moss, who was rumored to be retiring after his term ended next year. Representatives from neighboring states were there. Judges filled in the peripheral seats. Among them was William Horne, there at Hannah's invitation. She would never forgive him for Callie's death, but she could partially sympathize with the motivation behind his hideous act.

A parent would do anything to save his child.

Just when the buzzing of the crowd seemed deafening, Supreme Court Justice Adam Sammon stood at the dais at the front of the room.

"Ladies and gentlemen, we're glad you could all be here today for this very unusual but happy occasion. We debated over the order of today's program, but decided, since judge swearing-in ceremonies are boring to the young, and to the young at heart…" he paused while laughter erupted "…to get that over with first."

He read. Others read. A couple of people spoke. And then Hannah Montgomery was asked to join the Supreme Court Justice on the dais.

He asked her to raise her right hand. And to take the oaths he administered. And then, finally, Brian heard the words he'd been waiting for, mostly because he knew how badly Hannah needed to hear them.

"Ladies and gentlemen, by the power vested in me by this great state of Arizona, I present to you our newest Supreme Court Justice, Hannah Montgomery Hampton."

Hannah stepped up to the microphone, but Brian couldn't hear a word she said over the thundering applause. He didn't need to. She was looking straight at him, and the promise, the determination, the love in her eyes told him all he needed to know.

This new job came with risks. She'd be in the limelight now. There could be more threats.

But life was risky. A car accident could take her from him tomorrow. Or him from her.

What life would never take from either of them was the love they felt for each other.

That was going to see them into eternity.

"And now, on to the second part of today's program," Justice Sammon said and called Brian up to join his wife at the front of the room. Looking to his left, the judge motioned to someone off to the side. A door opened. And Susan came in, holding Joseph's hand.

Hannah's lips trembled as she watched the nearly five-year-old boy, dressed in the tux he'd chosen for this most special occasion, march with his head held high to join her and Brian.

And a few minutes later, she didn't even notice the tears of joy that streamed down her face as Justice Sammon changed Joseph's last name to Hampton and made her and Brian the proud parents of the most amazing little boy.

The *Sun News* caught it all, picture after picture, word for word. And ran a special story later that week. A tribute to the good people in the world. To love.

And to happy endings.